The counterfeit killers

A multimillion-pound counterfeit manufacturing operation with money-making international connections had moved into the Scottish crime scene and had prospered as it spread. Then a rival group who called themselves The Cutters arrived with brutal plans to take over. The Cutters ruled by fear.

Detective Superintendent Colin Thane of the élite Scottish Crime Squad was given the task of smashing The Cutters. At first, he found it hard to accept as a genuine priority – he already had his own worries, from a mislaid bank-raid witness and a top-brass demand that he improve his hated paperwork to new problems caused by promotions within his team of detectives. Even the arrival of his old second-in-command, Detective Inspector Phil Moss, drafted in to help, still left him uneasy.

Then Thane discovered how wrong he'd been. Two men shot execution-style, with bullets through the back of the head, were found in side-by-side shallow graves beside a moorland loch. A woman who dared to talk about The Cutters had her face slashed and almost bled to death. Thane himself walked into a petrol-bomb ambush.

The Cutters had to be stopped. Joined by Gypsy Adams, a bear-like undercover Trading Standards expert, Thane plunged into a search which led to places as far apart as Glasgow tenements, rich suburbia, and an out-of-town industrial estate. He was shown a strange half-world where people made and traded in counterfeit goods of every kind from named designer clothing to fake perfumes and the latest in copied video games.

Thane's first real breakthrough came when he and his wife were invited to a glittering rag-trade fashion show for charity. Then a combination of some help from a trade union official and a lead from a forensic scientist at last led him to the final truth.

The Crime Squad itself was to be hard hit before the all-important answers came together. They led to a final horror at an innocent-looking one-time farm in the shadow of the Scottish Highlands.

Books by Bill Knox

The Thane and Moss police series:
Deadline for a Dream (1957)
Death Department (1959)
Leave it to the Hangman (1960)
Little drops of Blood (1962)
Sanctuary Isle (1962)
The Man in the Bottle (1963)
The Taste of Proof (1965)
The Deep Fall (1966)
Justice on the Rocks (1967)
The Tallyman (1969)
Children of the Mist (1970)
To Kill a Witch (1971)
Draw Batons (1973)
Rally to Kill (1975)
Pilot Error (1977)
Live Bait (1978)
A Killing in Antiques (1981)
The Hanging Tree (1983)
The Crossfire Killings (1986)
The Interface Man (1989)

The Webb Carrick fishery
protection series:
The Scavengers (1964)
Devilweed (1966)
Blacklight (1967)
The Klondyker (1968)
Blueback (1969)
Seafire (1970)
Stormtide (1972)
Whitewater (1974)
Hellspout (1976)
Witchrock (1977)
Bombship (1980)
Bloodtide (1982)
Wavecrest (1985)
Dead Man's Mooring (1987)
The Drowning Nets (1991)

Other crime fiction as Bill Knox:
The Cockatoo Crime (1958)
Death Calls the Shots (1961)
Die for Big Betsy (1961)

With Edward Boyd:
The view from Daniel Pike (1974)

Non-fiction
Court of Murder. Famous trials at
Glasgow High Court (1968)
Tales of Crime (1982)

Written as Robert Macleod
Talos Cord investigator series:
The Drum of Power (1964)
Cave of Bats (1964)
Lake of Fury (1966)
Isle of Dragons (1967)
Place of Mists (1969)
Path of Ghosts (1971)
Nest of Vultures (1973)

Jonathan Gaunt 'Remembrancer'
series:
A Property in Cyprus (1970)
A Killing in Malta (1972)
A Burial in Portugal (1973)
A Witchdance in Bavaria (1975)
A Pay-off in Switzerland (1977)
An Incident in Iceland (1979)
A Problem in Prague (1981)
A legacy from Tenerife (1984)
A Cut In Diamonds (1985)
The Money Mountain (1987)
The Spanish Maze Game (1990)

Andrew Laird marine insurance
series:
All Other Perils (1974)
Dragonship (1976)
Salvage Job (1978)
Cargo Risk (1980)
Mayday From Malaga (1983)
Witchline (1988)

THE COUNTERFEIT KILLERS

Bill Knox

Constable · London

First published in Great Britain 1996 by Constable & Company Ltd
3 The Lanchesters, 162 Fulham Palace Road, London W6 9ER
Copyright © 1996 by Bill Knox
The right of Bill Knox to be identified as the author
of this work has been asserted by him in accordance with
the Copyright, Designs and Patents Act 1988
ISBN 0 09 475640
Set in Linotron Palatino 10pt by CentraCet Ltd, Cambridge
Printed and bound in Great Britain by Hartnolls Ltd, Bodmin

A CIP catalogue record for this book
is available from the British Library

For Kyle

The story varies in some aspects of procedural detail from the real-life Scottish Crime Squad's operational methods. They prefer it that way. I have been told why.

B.K., Glasgow

PRELUDE

May in Scotland is when the days are long and sweet, a tourist's
happy time of purple heather and yellow gorse on the hills, of
velvet green fairways on golf courses. Even in the towns, people
get back into the habit of smiling again.

Les Harrow had his own, separate reasons for smiling as he
drove his elderly Ford station-wagon home towards Glasgow at
the end of a long but successful day's business mileage. He had
worked his way round a string of clothes and sportswear bou-
tiques in almost a dozen small towns and villages north of the
Clyde. He had sold all the stock he had been carrying, always for
cash. At his prices, he had been offered orders for at least as much
again – Les Harrow offered massive discounts at the same time as
he made it clear that he didn't believe in tax invoices or any
paperwork nonsense.

He didn't mention that few customers were ever likely to see
him again.

The Ford's radio was tuned to one of his favourite country and
western nightly programmes. Tammy Wynette's voice singing
'Stand By Your Man' could soothe anyone's troubles – not that he
really had many for the moment. Not so long ago, things had been
bleak. Then, unexpectedly, his luck had turned. Now, in fact,
there was only one situation where there was a risk of real trouble.

But you had to take chances to get anywhere, didn't you?

The day was heading towards dusk. The sun was already
touching down on the distant Argyll hills, turning them into black
silhouettes, dying rays glinting on the buildings of the city just
visible on the horizon ahead. The Ford was travelling close to the
broad expanse of the Firth of Clyde, which had become the colour
of burning gold.

On the radio, Tammy Wynette gave way to Faron Young
declaring that he'd 'Got Five Dollars And It's Saturday Night'.

Les Harrow chuckled. It might only be Wednesday. But he was doing fine.

The evening was still warm, and he wiped a bead of sweat from his forehead with the back of one hand. He was the kind of man who sweated a lot, fat, past forty, medium height, and with short, mousy hair. As it had been a business day, he was wearing a slightly crumpled grey suit with a white, now open-necked shirt. His feet were in grey slip-on moccasins. The gold-plated watch on his left wrist was a Rolex replica. His discarded tie, red with polka dots, lay on the passenger seat. Beside it, in a brown paper grocery sack, was the bottle of Chardonnay wine he'd bought at his last stop.

He had already eaten at a roadside pull-in. Since his wife had left him a couple of years before, he usually ate out – which didn't worry him. When he got home, he would do some real relaxing, maybe watch an old movie on TV.

Another twenty minutes brought the Ford into the north side of the city. Dusk was shading into darkness and the street lights were coming on as Harrow took a right turn out of the main-road traffic at the start of the Hyndland district and steered the station wagon into a small network of faded, tending towards shabby, residential streets. He slotted it into a lucky space among the parked vehicles lining both sides of one of the streets.

Les Harrow collected his tie and the bottle of wine, got out, locked the Ford, and walked the short distance to his house, one of a row of identical doors and windows in a single-storey brick-built block fronted by a narrow strip of bare ground that had been intended as a garden. He used his key, went into the darkness of the small lobby, put on the lobby light, closed the outside door behind him, and went through into the kitchen carrying the wine bottle.

He switched on the kitchen light, then froze with a sudden, stomach-tightening fear. Two men were already there, bland-faced, waiting on him. Two men he knew, both in their twenties, well dressed in business suits and ties. One, tall and thin and scarred, was perched upon the edge of the kitchen sink unit with his legs gently swinging. The other, smaller, thick-set, sat saddle-style on a chair, his arms leaning on its back.

'You're late on the road, Les,' murmured the tall, thin figure. 'Had a good day?'

'Not bad.' He swallowed and licked his lips, then carefully set down the wine bottle on the kitchen table. He knew why they had been sent. There was only room for fear in his mind.

'Seems you've been stupid, Les,' said the same man. 'You've upset our people. They set you up, they give you credit for what they call Venture Capital, right? But you don't pay back the way you agreed.'

'I know. Things – well, things happened.' Les Harrow's whole mouth felt dry. He knew he'd got behind, but there had been situations to square and none of them that could wait. Somehow, he'd been optimist enough to think it would still work out. 'I – look, tell them I'm sorry. But they'll get it – soon. Very soon.'

'Not good enough,' said the man in the chair. Despite his size, he had a soft, piping voice. 'You've been earning, right?'

'Yes.' Harrow knew he was starting to shake. Nodding eagerly, he reached into his jacket pockets and dragged out two thick wads of banknotes, each secured by a thick elastic band. 'There's – there's this. It could be on account. A good couple of thousand – '

'On account, right.' The man in the chair grinned. 'Toss them over.'

Carefully, Harrow obeyed. The man caught both wads and tucked them away. Then he glanced at the tall, thin man and gave a slight, sardonic grin.

'It helps,' said his companion. Dropping down from the sink unit, he took a couple of steps nearer Harrow. 'Trouble is, Les, our people are really worried about you. They think you need a lesson.' He smiled almost sadly and for a moment his hand crossed over and seemed to finger the top, handkerchief pocket of his well-cut jacket.

'Wait – ' began Harrow desperately.

'Sorry, Les,' said the tall, thin man. A flicker of movement brought a strange, thin, razor-sharp little knife from his top pocket. It glinted under the light for an instant then the man's hand swung in an almost lazy arc. Pain sliced down Les Harrow's face from just above his left ear almost to the left-hand corner of his mouth. At the same time as the sudden agony of the slash wound began, there was the sudden warm salt taste of blood in his mouth.

He whimpered. Cowering back, he brought up an arm to protect his face from the next slash.

'Like I said, nothing personal, Les.' The thin man smiled and balanced the strange little knife in his hand for a moment. It was made from two small hobby-knife blades, finely honed top quality steel, separated by a narrow strip of wood and taped together into a black plastic handle. The twin blades, a 90s update on the old cut-throat razor, carved deep, parallel slices only millimetres apart like a miniature, blooded railway track. He tucked the knife back in his top pocket. 'Just a job to do, right?'

His companion rose from the kitchen chair, took a dish towel which was lying beside the sink, and handed it to their shocked, moaning victim.

'So get yourself to a doctor,' he suggested with a chill solicitude. 'We'll close up here. Just forget how it happened.'

'Then take a rest,' suggested the thin man, still smiling.

'Once you've healed up, they'll give you another chance at it, no tricks this time. Right?'

The towel pressed to his face, blood soaking through and down his shirt front, Les Harrow stumbled out of the kitchen. He caught a glimpse of himself in the lobby mirror and almost fainted at what he saw. But he stumbled on, collected a fresh towel in the bathroom, then staggered out of the house.

Somehow he reached his Ford station-wagon, got into it, and set the elderly vehicle moving while more blood seeped through the fresh towel against his face. He could still think clearly enough to resist the temptation to stop at the nearest big casualty hospital, the Western Infirmary, and kept going. His face was a throbbing agony, the towel was soaked with red, but sheer animal instinct had taken over.

On the other side of the city centre he reached his goal, the massive blend of Victorian stonework and modern concrete of the giant Royal Infirmary. He left the Ford in a side-street, then staggered and weaved his way across to the entrance to the Royal's casualty department. The Royal was far enough away from home, he knew he had to keep what had happened his secret. Once inside, still clutching the blood-soaked towel to his face, he sank down on a bench beside others on the nightly battlefield list of walking wounded.

When his turn came, Les Harrow gave the desk orderly a false name and a false address. At the Royal, it hardly mattered. Their priorities were different. A young staff nurse winced as she gently cleaned his slashed face while Les Harrow stuck to his story that he'd been on his way to meet a friend for a drink when he'd been attacked in the street by two wandering muggers. As she finished, the duty casualty surgeon took over.

'This I could have done without,' said the casualty surgeon softly as he examined the long twin-track slash, so deep at one point that the cheekbone showed through. He grimaced wearily at the staff nurse. 'So I know – it's too late to start embroidery classes.'

Then he began the long, slow and delicate job of trying to stitch Les Harrow's face together again.

Les Harrow fainted half-way through the eighty-two stitches he needed. He came round again on a recovery stretcher with his face bandaged, the job done. He saw two uniformed police were in the next cubicle, talking to someone they'd brought in.

He had a feeling his turn would be next. His shirt had gone, but his blood stained jacket lay at the foot of the stretcher. Slipping on his jacket, light-headed but desperate, he took his chance and slipped out past the police without being spotted. He made it out of the hospital, somehow got back to his car, then drove home.

When he got there, the front door lay open. The men had gone, but every room had been turned over and anything valuable taken. Still, they'd left the bottle of wine and they'd missed the emergency fund of five hundred pounds in cash and a few gold krugerrands he kept hidden in a plastic bag under the ice cubes in the freezer compartment of his refrigerator.

Les Harrow took the bag, drank most of the wine, then collapsed on his bed and tried to rest for a couple of hours. His face began hurting again, and he took some of the pills the Royal staff nurse had given him.

At last he gave up, got up, packed some clothes into a suitcase, added one or two small possessions that mattered, then left. For good. He wanted out. He was too scared to risk anything else. The suitcase went into the back of his Ford and he started driving. By dawn, he was a long way south of Glasgow. By afternoon he was in London where he sold the Ford to the first used car dealer he spotted. From there, he travelled into the city by Underground then got a room in a cheap hotel.

Next morning, he found a doctor who didn't ask too many questions and who took cash for replacing the bandaging round his face with a less conspicuous strip of adhesive dressing. For the next couple of days, he mostly stayed in his room and watched television.

But he was bored by the third evening and decided to go out. He headed for the bright lights around Piccadilly Circus, where he had a meal and a couple of drinks.

11

Les Harrow felt good when he left. Good enough to be careless. Crossing the street, he was knocked down and killed outright by a double-decker bus. The pathologist who carried out an autopsy noted the hospital-stitched twin-track slash wound. Somebody, somewhere, had done a neat job.

Nobody at the hotel worried when he didn't come back to it. In London, that happened all the time and he had paid for the week. At the end of the week a maid cleaned out the room. She found most of Les Harrow's emergency fund hidden in a drawer. She kept it.

Why not?

1

It was well into June and the start of what looked like being another warm and pleasant day for Glasgow. The morning sun glinted on the brightwork of the vehicles parked outside the Scottish Crime Squad headquarters building.

Single-storey and with a flat roof, totally functional in design, headquarters was located in a stretch of green parkland hidden behind trees only a couple of miles away from the centre of Glasgow and its high-rise skyline. It was 10 a.m. and a shirt-sleeved squad of mounted officers were putting their perfectly groomed charges through the intricacies of a carefully choreographed exercise. They were riding with drawn batons at the ready while a small sergeant on a large horse screamed orders.

At his office window, Detective Superintendent Colin Thane watched, then shrugged as the riot control exercise ended in a thundering charge which vanished into the trees. The Strathclyde force's mounted branch had their depot just beyond the trees, beside the dog branch. The mounties always disappeared at the gallop when it was tea-break time.

He turned away from the window, a tall, grey-eyed man in his early forties with thick dark hair, regular features, and a muscular build. He was wearing a lightweight heather-blue suit of Donegal tweed, a grey shirt, and a loosened dark-blue tie. His feet were in soft brown leather moccasins.

Colin Thane was joint deputy head of the Scottish Crime Squad. He was in a sour mood because so far he had not had a good day. He reckoned it could only get worse.

It had started at home, with a sudden fall-out with his wife at breakfast – although he still wasn't sure what had started it. Then he had arrived at his office at Crime Squad headquarters to a new overnight report that after a full week of hard trying there was still no trace of a vital woman witness who had simply done a voluntary runner and had disappeared, quitting her job at less than a day's notice without explanation, not telling friends or family why.

If she wasn't found, if her evidence was lost, then the already scheduled trial of an armed robbery team would fall flat on its face. They had hijacked a bank security van. When it had been recovered, it had been minus half a million pounds in used banknotes. What had happened to them was an unsolved mystery.

Suddenly, the telephone began ringing.

He winced, knowing it had to be trouble. Every cop learned early in life that troubles always came packaged in threes; he was already two down. Lifting the receiver, he was prepared for the worst.

'Thane.'

'Come through, Colin.' The voice of the Squad's commander, Jack Hart, rasped in his ear. 'Whatever you're doing, forget it.'

Leaving it at that, Hart hung up. But there had been an unmistakable urgency in his words – and as Thane left his office and started towards Hart's room he heard other telephones ringing and passed other hurrying figures. Whatever was going on, it was spreading like an alarm call. Then Maggie Fyffe, who was Hart's always smartly dressed middle-aged secretary, was coming towards him with a quick clicking of high heels on the terrazzo floor. She didn't slow.

'Go on in,' she called over her shoulder as they passed. Then she had gone, heading for the front office reception area.

Hart's door lay open and the green 'enter' light was lit. Thane went into the large office, which had a thick green carpet, a collection of police memorabilia on the walls, and a large window which didn't get the sun until afternoon. Jack Hart, a sad-eyed man in his fifties with a lined, leathery face and thinning grey hair, was at his big dark oak desk. It was a desk he had bought at an auction after he had seen the previous owner, a knight of the realm, jailed for embezzlement. Finishing a telephone call, Hart put down the receiver and grimaced at Thane.

'HMCI, damn him,' he said without preliminaries. 'Five minute warning that he's on his way to visit.' A sudden thought sent Hart grabbing for the telephone again and he tapped an extension number then sucked his teeth impatiently until it was answered seconds later. 'Main gate? Commander Hart. You'll have a white 4.2 litre Jaguar arriving any time.' He cut short the querulous voice at the other end. 'No. You ask for full ID, and don't rush anything. Do your job, show we're on our toes.' Grimly, he slammed the receiver down again.

'Surprise, surprise?' asked Thane drily.

'And a last-minute tip-off. Somebody who owed me one.' Hart dumped the papers on his desk into a drawer. He banged the drawer shut. 'Do the rounds, Colin. If there's anything nasty, hide it.'

'Like blood on the walls?'

'There's maybe worse.' Hart wasn't amused.

Thane knew why he was wound up tight. Like everyone else, Jack Hart had been seconded to the Scottish Crime Squad. In the outside world, he ranked as a detective chief superintendent, next step up he'd be an assistant chief constable. But HMCI – Her Majesty's Chief Inspector of Constabulary for Scotland – held his commission directly from the Queen and answered only to God on all matters concerning Scottish police. Usually it was claimed HMCI insisted that God first made an appointment.

Patrick Ronaldson, the current HMCI, had been a distinguished chief constable. Earlier, he had carried a lot of the load in the aftermath to the Lockerbie terrorist bombing. Equally significant, he was a professional who knew every conniving trick a cop might use to cover up a problem. He had probably invented some of the tricks. His first action after appointment was an announcement that had made him as popular as the plague among his former colleagues. He would make surprise no-warning visits to every Scottish force, carry out rigorous spot inspections, then publish his criticisms.

'Damn it, Colin, move, will you?' Hart made it a plea. 'Anything he shouldn't see, bury it. That includes Felix Electricals and any other damned enterprises we're breeding.'

'They'll vanish,' promised Thane.

'Then stay handy,' added Hart before he could leave. 'I may need you to take over a meeting with someone.'

Thane nodded. Tom Maxwell, the Squad's other detective superintendent and the other half of his 'joint deputy' job, was down at Stranraer in the south-west with an operations group which was a dozen strong. Stranraer was the main ferry port for the crossing to Northern Ireland, and Special Branch always kept an eye on that. But some local fishing boats were suspected in a new spate of gun-running traffic to both sides in the fragile truce across the water. The Scottish Crime Squad didn't like the spooks of Special Branch, Special Branch didn't like the Scottish Crime Squad's head-on style, but they could work together when it mattered.

But that left Thane as Hart's only backstop.

'I've seen the update about your witness,' said Jack Hart almost as an afterthought. 'But let's sort this out first, talk later. All right?'

'I'm on my way,' promised Thane.

It was a full ten minutes before the white Jaguar 4.2 with a registration plate every officer in every Scottish force was expected to know by heart finally swept up the driveway towards the headquarters building.

Ten minutes was long enough for Thane to make a tour round the duty rooms, the offices, the facility areas and even the locker rooms. Everywhere he met sheepish grins and signs of frantic clearing away. Even Joe Felix, a middle-aged detective constable who was part of Thane's private team, had anticipated Jack Hart's possible wrath.

Felix, one of the Squad's electronics and surveillance experts, ran a sideline enterprise repairing electric kettles and radios, the occasional hair-drier, and any other small domestic appliance brought in by other officers. Now his desk, normally piled like a junk shop, was clean. Felix was smugly content, certain that even HMCI was unlikely to raid the cubicles in the women's washroom.

From the outer office with its flickering VDU terminals and telex machines to the desks and maps and telephones of the main duty room, where any of the day shift still around usually gathered, the sweep was complete. An official issue line-up photograph of government ministers, used as a dart board, had gone. The badly punctured section of wall exposed had been covered over by pinning up a Scottish Office chart on crime statistics. Notice-boards had been cleaned of the worst graffiti.

That left only the Squad's members. Whether pecking at type-writers or word processors or using telephones, few looked like police officers. They were, at best, casually dressed. Some could have been candidates for a street-level line-up parade. A petite blonde with a tight sweater, short skirt and very high heels was frowning over a court report. A plump man with a wispy ginger beard and work overalls didn't like something in it and didn't care who heard. They stopped long enough to greet Thane as he passed. The blonde had an honours law degree; the bearded man had two commendations for bravery.

Like all the total of ninety officers in the Scottish Crime Squad, they had been hand-picked for the job. Drawn from every police force in the country, every man and woman selected served a maximum of three years, then returned to his or her home force.

Central government funded, free of ties to any individual force, the Squad's role was unique. They prowled anywhere their commander decided and into any situation he felt they should. Sometimes that meant ignoring police protocol. Sometimes they bent rules without breaking them. Their discipline might seem elastic at the edges. But every officer knew the penalty for transgressing the invisible limits. Next day, they would report back to their home force for reassignment.

Thane reached the far end of the duty room, paused, and looked around. Everything looked reasonable.

'Ready and waiting, sir,' reported the thin figure in a black leather jerkin who ambled over to join him.

'It'll do.' Thane nodded drily. 'Makes a change, Francey.'

'All done by raw fear.' Francey Dunbar, his personal sergeant, still in his twenties, had a mop of jet-black hair and a thin straggle of a bandit moustache. Detective Sergeant Francis Dunbar had the reputation for being an awkward troublemaker – but he was a good cop as well as the Squad's elected Police Federation delegate. 'How soon do we get rid of His Holiness, sir?'

'You don't get rid of an HMCI,' said Thane wearily. 'He gets rid of you. If he as much as blinks, then you come to attention. Right?'

'I'll try,' promised Dunbar solemnly.

Thane moved on.

He caught up with Jack Hart in the sunlight just outside the front door at almost the same moment that the official white Jaguar swept into sight. Hart raised an eyebrow in an unspoken question, Thane nodded, and the Squad commander gave a satisfied grunt.

'We'll wait for him,' said Hart drily. 'Why pretend?'

Dogs were barking over beyond the trees. Strathclyde's dog branch were their noisiest neighbours, but still helped the Squad maintain a low profile in the background.

Not that the ousider saw much. Even their few visitors tended to feel disappointed. Austere in appearance, the headquarters building could have been a school annexe or a low-cost warehouse unit. There were no cells. Prisoners, wherever they might be collected, were lodged in whatever local force divisional office was nearest.

'Here we go,' murmured Hart as the Jaguar came nearer and drew to a halt.

A uniformed sergeant-driver, smart enough for the Brigade of Guards, sprang out to open a passenger door and a tall, dark-suited figure emerged. At the same moment, Thane saw a sudden movement not far distant in the general parking area, then winced as a lanky figure in khaki overalls and rubber boots emerged from a grubby, battered Land-Rover. Jock Dawson, one of his missing team members, climbed out followed by a massive tan and black German Shepherd dog. Dawson, the Squad's dog-handler, grinned apologetically towards Thane. Then the German Shepherd lifted a leg against one of the Land-Rover's wheels and relieved itself as if it would never stop. The two men from the Jaguar stared.

The dog's name was Rajah. When he at last lowered his leg he vanished back into the Land-Rover followed by Dawson.

'It makes a different kind of welcome, commander. Maybe – ah – more personal?' Patrick Ronaldson, Her Majesty's Chief Inspector of Constabulary for Scotland, allowed himself the luxury of a thin smile. He didn't wait for an answer. 'Looks like you expected me.'

'Jungle drums,' agreed Jack Hart solemnly. His lined face didn't alter. 'You always advocate staying in touch, sir.'

'And you were always a crafty bastard, Jack,' said Ronaldson, equally deadpan.

They shook hands. Then it was Thane's turn for a formal handshake and a brief murmur before Ronaldson turned back to Hart again.

'Forget the formal inspection – that's for another time,' he said crisply. 'This is interim, showing the flag. A general tour around, Jack – and there are a few things we need to talk about, alone. Call it a couple of hours. Then I've invited myself for lunch with Strathclyde's Chief Constable.' He paused. 'Any problem with that?'

Hart shook his head in a way that held a touch of relief that the visit wouldn't be longer. Then they set off together, with Thane trailing a couple paces behind.

Meeting people, officers or the few civilian staff alike, HMCI

18

went around smiling and sometimes joking, on the surface doing a skilled public relations job – except that Thane suddenly realized that the man's easy-going informality was gathering up more information about what went on in the Squad than any number of formal question-and-answer sessions could have achieved.

Patrick Ronaldson on the loose could be dangerous.

Sitting on the edge of a desk in the main duty room, he chortled and coaxed while a large, hairy detective mainly known as The Animal told how a foul-up over identity had resulted in a man and wife being wrongly arrested in a drugs raid. The Squad team had raided the wrong house, and even though they'd accidentally found the loot from several housebreakings, who could they charge with what after that kind of mess? It was just a freak chance that two men with the same name and the same date of birth, both active criminals, lived in the same street.

The story wasn't new. But The Animal gave details that hadn't been in any report while Jack Hart, ready to kill, glanced at his wrist-watch.

'That meeting.' He eased next to Thane, his voice a hoarse whisper. 'You'll need to take it for me. The man's name is Bill Peerman. He's reliable, and there's a file – Maggie knows you'll probably need it.' Pausing, Hart glared in The Animal's direction while the man talked on. 'Damn the idiot – look, whatever it takes, try and keep Peerman happy. Say I'll get back to him.'

Thane was glad to escape. No one seemed to notice as he slipped out of the duty room and headed back along the corridor. Half-way along to Maggie Fyffe's location, he slowed as he saw her coming his way with a thin blue file envelope in one hand.

'Mind-reading?' he asked.

'It goes with the job.' She handed him the file and smiled. 'How's the Grand Tour?'

'Like to guess?' Thane shook his head.

'My horoscope said it could be one of those days.' Maggie Fyffe, a cop's widow, wasn't scared of anything in trousers. 'Will I send Peerman your way when he arrives?'

'Do that.' Thane nodded his thanks. 'Who is he, Maggie?'

'Local authority, a deputy director in Trading Standards. Been to see the commander before. He seemed civilized.' She turned away and headed back towards her own territory.

Thane took the file along to his office, now bright with sunlight and warm. He closed the door, removed his jacket, hung it on a hook, then sat behind his desk and took a first, skimming glance through the scanty contents of the file.

Then, totally puzzled, he started again.

The file was from Hart's personal registry collection with the label 'T.S.'. Partly it was an odd mix of brief notes and fragments from squad intelligence reports. But there were telexes from different police forces including some in England and Wales. There were fax messages from Trading Standards officials, including a couple signed 'William Peerman, deputy director, Strathclyde Region'.

But how much did they really mean? They offered a scatter of fact and rumour. There was an occasional name, including a few known, mildly middle-weight criminals. Even seeing some of the surprising cash amounts being quoted, since when did a collection of counterfeit copy products involving items as varied as sports clothing and training shoes, fashion sweaters and fake perfumes, rip-off watches and phoney computer softwear add up to serious enough crime to land on the Squad's high-powered plate?

There was a knock at his door.

'Come,' he called, looking up.

The young, uniformed orderly who entered had someone with him.

'Mr Peerman, sir.' He grinned hopefully. 'I was told you expected him.'

'Right.' Thane rose as his visitor was ushered in. They shook hands while the orderly closed the door again and left.

'What happened to Commander Hart?' asked the stranger. Bill Peerman was grey-haired, probably in his fifties, and wore a dark business suit. He was carrying a leather briefcase. 'He was supposed to see me – '

'Something urgent turned up,' said Thane. 'He sends his apologies and me instead.'

'Did Commander Hart explain what this was about, superintendent?'

'There wasn't time.' Thane shook his head. 'There's a file. But – '

'But you're not very sure why the hell I'm here?' Peerman finished for him. The Trading Standards man opened his briefcase, brought out a white envelope and a thin package wrapped in a plastic shopping bag, and laid both on the desk. 'Suppose I explain a little, enough to get by on?'

'It might help,' agreed Thane wryly.

'Then put it this way. Mainly through Commander Hart, the police and my people have been sharing mutual aid. You've heard of counterfeit manufacturing, counterfeit selling?'

'A little.'

'But not a lot?' Peerman shrugged. 'It's crime, superintendent. Small-time at street level – but not for the people behind it. They live in big houses, they drive big cars, they run their scams as full-scale business operations. They make a great deal of money. Follow me so far?'

'Links.' Suddenly some of the items in the file he'd been reading came to life for Thane. 'Known criminals and your counterfeit operators?'

'Links, connections, anything you want to call it,' said Peerman softly. His fingers tapped the white envelope lying between them. 'But we're talking serious money, maybe drugs-connected, maybe not.'

'Laundering it?'

'Part laundering, part investing – anyone new buying into the counterfeiting business needs a lot of capital. But the profits can be mega-style. So now we get to why I'm here.' Peerman paused, puzzled by a strange, growing, rhythmic noise coming from somewhere outside. 'What's happening?'

'Our neighbours,' said Thane wryly.

Another moment passed, then suddenly the whole squad of police horses went past at a gallop, riders crouched low in the saddle.

'Not exactly mice,' mused Peerman as the noise faded. He became serious again. 'We run our own intelligence-gathering people. We call them the CATS team – for Consumer and Trading Standards. For the past few months, we've had steady hints of a new group moving into the counterfeit clothing scene. People who had the money to set up an independent operation and who keep totally on top of every fashion trend.' The man grimaced. 'They've become aggressively nasty.'

'Any names?'

'Not the way you mean.' Peerman shook his head. 'But around the back streets they've acquired their own name – The Cutters.' He saw it hadn't registered. 'Think Tailor and Cutter, superintendent.'

'Thanks,' said Thane drily. Street-style nicknames often told their own story. 'The Cutters – what do they cut, Mr Peerman?'

21

'Like people?' Peerman shrugged. 'We've heard whispers of violence when some of the competition has been squeezed out. Commander Hart has picked up the same vibrations.' He pushed the white envelope across the desk to Thane. 'These are statements from two of my people who were attacked last night – when and where and some vague descriptions.'

'Badly hurt?' Thane lifted the envelope.

'They'll mend.' Peerman was stolid. 'They'd been following someone who could have been a lead back to The Cutters.'

'And this – ' Thane tapped the envelope.' Was it reported anywhere?'

'A waste of time.' Peerman grimaced. 'Our punter got away, we haven't even got a name for him – only a description.' He paused, opened the shopping bag, and took out a red and white designer sweatshirt still in its sales display plastic. 'But he delivered the best part of a van load of these to different locations around town. Looks good doesn't it?'

'Yes.' Thane picked up the garment, feeling out of his depth. But the sweatshirt seemed well made, the label seemed authentic. 'It does.'

'It looks like a Reebok design, quality merchandise. The label says Reebok. It's still a fake – wash it twice, and I'll guarantee it would be a disaster. Anyone buying that is being ripped off.'

'Made where?' Thane frowned, fingering it again. 'The Far East?'

'No way. Probably in Britain, probably somewhere Scottish and local. Low overheads, just as cheap to make here.' Peerman grimly wrapped the sweatshirt again and put it back into its shopping bag. 'It cost maybe a couple of pounds to make, it would probably be offered as a sale bargain at around thirty pounds – that way, the buyer isn't going to get far with a complaint. You'd pay between sixty and ninety for the genuine article.'

Thane drew a deep breath, knowing he could have been fooled as much as anyone.

'I'll leave this for Jack Hart.' Peerman indicated the shopping bag. 'I'd appreciate it if you'd tell him everything is hardening the way we expected.' He rose and smiled. 'Nice meeting you, superintendent. But I'll have to go. I've a desk that needs me.'

'Thanks for coming over.' Thane rose. 'I'm an outsider. Can I ask a stupid question?'

'Try me.'

22

'In money terms, how big an operation are we talking?'

'In clothing alone?' Peerman rubbed his chin. 'It's a computer-generated guess, based on the Greater Glasgow area. Given the usual plus and minus error factors, and we think maybe thirty million pounds sterling a year.'

Thane stared at him, open-mouthed.

'That's total manufacturing and trading, then allowing for exports and imports,' murmured Peerman. 'The way you'd expect.'

'What else?' said Thane gravely.

He escorted Peerman through the corridors to the front door, where they parted. Peerman had a large red Nissan waiting in the parking lot. As he drove off, a white Volkswagen belonging to the Crime Squad vehicle pool arrived. It stopped and the woman driver, slim and red-haired, got out and walked towards the building.

'And where the hell have you been?' asked Thane as she arrived.

'With one of my girls, sir.' Detective Constable Sandra Craig, in her late twenties and with a recent pass in her force's sergeant's examination, was in one of her usual working outfits of denim trousers teamed with a short black jacket, black Cuban-heeled boots, and a grey silk blouse. She had ice-green eyes and a husky charm school voice. Her 'girls' were drawn from Glasgow's night people. 'I'd been trying to get to her for a couple of days.' Sensing an atmosphere, Sandra looked around. 'Is something happening?'

'We've HM Chief Inspector on a raid. He's turning us over.' Thane considered her with a scowl. 'How was your meet?'

'I'm not sure, sir.' From the red-haired detective constable, that was unusual. 'Her name is Liz Hill. She lives over in Flannan Street. And out of the blue she says she knows a man who had a walk-on part in our security van job.'

'And now she's suddenly eager to tell us?' Thane wasn't impressed. Their missing witness was still a close secret. But right from the start of the hijack raid a trickle of stories and names had come in, each a try for a share of the offered bank reward for information. 'Why?'

'With Liz, who knows?' Sandra Craig shrugged. 'But sometimes she has it right.'

'Then run some checks, see where they take us.' Thane kept some of his scowl in place. 'And next time you decide to disappear, remember to tell someone first.'

'I will.' She gave a mildly penitent nod. 'Just let me find a sandwich first, then I'll start checking, sir.'

She headed off. Sandra Craig's existence seemed to depend on a constant intake of sandwiches and junk food. Yet no matter what she ate, nor how often, it didn't affect her weight or her figure.

Thane followed her in. The uniformed men on duty at the reception desk gave him an update on HMCI's progress through the building. He had last been seen disappearing into the armoury area.

So far, there was no report of blood being spilled. Relieved, Thane went back to his office.

Jack Hart's personal registry 'T.S.' file was still on the desk where he'd left it. He started to reach for it, then changed his mind. There was something more important needing to be done.

He lifted the telephone receiver, started to dial his home number, then tried another. It was one of the mornings when Mary Thane worked job-share as a practice manager at their local health centre.

'Sorry, Mary's at a meeting.' The health centre receptionist who took the call recognized his voice. 'Can I give her a message?'

'Just tell her I called,' said Thane wryly. 'I'll maybe try again.'

He hung up and shook his head at the sunlit world outside his window. Try every way he could, he still couldn't remember what had sparked off that breakfast-time war. He knew it hadn't helped that he had forgotten yet again to make an appointment to take their dog to the vet for his annual shots. Maybe it had all really begun the evening before, when he hadn't noticed soon enough that she had drastically changed the way her hair was cut and styled?

Whatever it was, they'd been married long enough to have two teenage children, happily enough for any kind of war to be unusual. When they had first met all those years back, he had been a new young Glasgow beat cop in one of the toughest divisions in the city and she had been a hospital nurse. He caught himself grinning. Mary had looked good in that new hair-style. Abject surrender was a justifiable tactic on his domestic agenda.

He turned back fo the T.S. file, a lot of things in it making more sense now. Then, at almost noon, his telephone rang. Maggie Fyffe was at the other end.

'He's still with the commander,' she said briskly. 'They want you to join them.'

Thane rose, checked his tie, collected the Trading Standards file and the additions that Bill Peerman had brought, then went through. When he knocked on Hart's door, the green 'enter' light spat an immediate answer and he went in.

Hart and Ronaldson were seated beside a small table where various files and computer print-outs lapped the edges of a tray with used coffee cups and saucers. Maggie Fyffe had even provided a plateful of doughnuts, and HMCI apparently liked doughnuts. Sugar and a few crumbs showed down the front of Ronaldson's dark jacket.

'Sit down, Colin,' invited Hart, indicating a third chair. 'You saw our Trading Standards man?'

'We talked.' Thane sat down.

'Superintendent, can you recall a previous time we met?' asked Her Majesty's Chief Inspector suddenly. The thin, high-cheek-boned face gave a half-smile. 'You were a divisional detective chief inspector in one of the Glasgow divisions. It was – ah – '

'Millside,' said Thane. 'And I remember, sir.' He had been hoping since Ronaldson arrived that it had been forgotten.

'As I recall, you came rampaging out of your territory in some alleged hot pursuit, and I was the Chief Constable who had to kick you back home again.' mused Ronaldson. 'And now you're here.' He brought his fingertips together in a thoughtful steeple. 'Well, for all practical purposes you'll shortly become deputy commander – forget the "joint"part. When Detective Superintendent Maxwell retires in a few months, he won't be replaced. On that basis, you should know what I've been telling Commander Hart.' He glanced towards Hart. 'Jack?'

'This is an interim inspection, nothing more. On it, the Squad gets a moderately clean bill of health,' said Hart cautiously. He used a pencil to doodle on one of the computer print-outs in front of him. 'Operationally, we've no real problems.'

'Anyone can lose a witness,' said Her Majesty's Chief Inspector. He sniffed. 'But then I asked to see the background documentation and paperwork on the case, Thane.' His voice took on a caustic edge. 'I wasn't impressed. If you went to court, even with that witness, a competent defence lawyer would have a good chance of sinking you without trace.'

Hart sucked his lips, saying nothing. But his eyes warned Thane to keep his mouth shut. Listening cost nothing.

'Police stock in trade today is more about computerized records than barbed wire in the handcuffs, more about tape and video statements than writing fairy stories in a police notebook.' Ronaldson slapped an open hand hard on the table. The grim set of his mouth illustrated why he had been chosed for his job. 'Remember this, Thane. Not everybody likes the police service. Arrest anyone today, and you've got to keep one eye on who you're grabbing and the other eye on whether the law says you're doing it right.'

'I understand, sir,' said Thane woodenly.

'Do you?' growled Ronaldson. 'Maybe – maybe not. But I've told Commander Hart this Squad has to try harder in terms of everything to do with paperwork. And I'll be back to make sure it does.' He shrugged. 'I'll also see if I can get you some outside help – a little, not a lot.' He paused. The lecture was apparently over, and he glanced at Hart. 'Commander, let's get back to policing – and your counterfeit scam.'

Hart nodded thankfully. 'What have we got that's new, Colin?'

'Two Trading Standards people beaten up, more suggestions that a new team is moving in.' Thane gave a grimace, part apology, part relief. He felt as if his tail feathers had just been severely singed. 'I'm still trying to understand the background.'

'My fault,' said Hart. 'Go on.'

Thane laid the file and Bill Peerman's envelope in front of Hart and placed the counterfeit sweatshirt beside them. Then he told what Peerman had said, his audience listening in silence. The silence continued for a moment when he'd finished, but he saw Hart and Her Majesty's Chief Inspector exchange a glance and a satisfied nod.

'I'd say it's on, Jack,' said Ronaldson softly. He turned his attention to Thane. 'Surprised at some of it, superintendent?'

'If it's all true,' said Thane cautiously.

'Believe it,' said Hart in a grim voice.

He took Peerman's report from its envelope and skimmed through it. While he did, Her Majesty's Chief Inspector took the counterfeit sweatshirt from its wrappings and considered it carefully. Ouside, a low-flying passenger jet on its final approach to Glasgow Airport passed overhead in a way that made Hart's office window rattle. A telephone rang somewhere and kept ringing.

'This mentions a CATS team supervisor named Gypsy Adams.' Hart kept Peerman's report between his fingertips. 'I've met Adams. He's an oddball. But if he says something, rely on it. I'm dropping this one in your lap, Colin.'

'What about the security van job?'

'It can tick over for a few days, lower key. Then we'll talk details again. Agreed?'

'Sir.' Reluctantly, Thane nodded. It was the usual story. The Squad was short-handed, having to stretch resources.

'This is no down-market target, Colin,' said Hart softly. 'We're not lowering our sights. Counterfeit manufacturing is surfacing just about world-wide. Interpol has begun circulating crime trend analysis reports which show that more and more criminal bank-rolls are moving into the counterfeit game – not so much to launder their cash but as a side-by-side investment way to make money.' From Hart, it was almost a speech. 'Well, we're going to hit some of them – and I want it to be hard.'

'This is purely Jack Hart's decision, Thane. But I back it.' Her Majesty's Chief Inspector joined in again, tossing the sweatshirt aside. 'Who buys this cheap tatt? Ordinary people on razor-edge budgets, families trying to stretch their damned pennies any bargain way they can!'

'Maybe it's not high profile, because this kind of crime doesn't hit the rich,' said Hart grimly. 'But it's fraud, Colin. Fraud on people who already have all the problems they need in life. There are links into alleged intimidation and violence – and more.'

'And I hope you get some of the bastards, Thane,' said Ronaldson in a surprisingly harsh voice. 'That's not for quoting. But I want to be kept informed on progress.' He glanced at his watch in a way that had its own meaning. 'Thank you, Superintendent Thane. Now – ah – what else have we left, Jack?'

Thane left them. Once outside, the door closed behind him, he swore under his breath. He had been landed with a target which was not just the Crime Squad commander's pet project, but something which for some reason seemed to have the more than sympathetic interest of the most powerful cop in the kingdom.

Maggie Fyffe was in the outer office, tapping at a keyboard. More reports in the making. The old adage had it right, troubles always came packaged in threes.

'Dear God,' he muttered aloud.

'You called?' asked Maggie Fyffe, grinning up. Then, having considered him, she wrinkled her nose. 'That bad?'

'That bad,' he agreed.

'When it's that bad, there's a form you complete in triplicate.' There was a twinkle in her eyes. 'And if you got chewed about your case recordings, remember I warned you.' She eased back in her chair, stretching her shoulders, enjoying the break. 'Mary phoned while you were in there. She said you'd tried to call her. I've to say sorry, she has to go out now – whatever it is, leave it until evening.'

'Thanks,' said Thane stonily.

'Anything wrong?' Maggie Fyffe knew them well. 'She sounded – you know.'

'No, nothing,' he lied.

She shrugged, turned away, and her fingers started on the keyboard again. He walked along to the duty room, now almost empty of people, and saw Francey Dunbar with Sandra Craig, both sitting on the edge of a desk and in earnest discussion. Joe Felix was in another corner of the room, making coffee. Only Jock Dawson, the dog-handler member of his personal team, was absent.

'Sir.' Dunbar saw him first as he came over. 'Any word?'

'About what?' asked Thane.

'About the counterfeit scam,' said his sergeant blandly. 'We've got it, haven't we? Just like there's a stop on the security van job?'

Thane nodded. Whatever could be said about the Squad's criminal intelligence gathering, it couldn't match the jungle-drums efficiency of its internal grapevine.

'I bought a skirt like that once,' mused Sandra Craig. 'It looked good, it had a Calvin Klein label that made the price a bargain.' She scowled. 'Second time I wore it, there was rain. The skirt shrank a full size, the colour ran down my legs. If it comes to a hanging, I'll help.'

Thane looked at them, the two parts of another problem, but one he wasn't going to do anything about until pushed. He was glad as Joe Felix came over and offered him a mug of coffee. It was Felix-style coffee – very black and very sweet – and he sipped it gratefully.

'Here's how it stands for now,' he told them. 'Sandra, you and Joe wind down the whole security van job – mothball it, like anything else we've got waiting.' He saw Sandra Craig's frown of protest. 'All right, nibble if you've spare time. But nothing more. Not till we're told otherwise. We're concentrating on counterfeit goods – making and selling. Forget the rest.'

Joe Felix grumbled a little. 'Can we use Jock Dawson?'

'Jock, his dogs, any other help we need,' said Thane wearily. 'But get the damned paperwork done along with it.' He saw the grin on Francey Dunbar's face. 'Amused, sergeant?'

'Not specially, sir.' Dunbar was expert enough at reading signs not to push his luck.

'Then earn your keep the same way – and stay handy. I may need you.' He made it a growl.

Leaving them, taking his borrowed coffee mug, feeling marginally better for having blasted Dunbar, Thane went back to his own office. He found that while he'd been harassing the troops the Trading Standards items he'd left in Hart's room had landed back on his desk again.

This time he studied them carefully, ending with the counterfeit sweatshirt. The woven motif across front and back said it was made by Reebok. Only a couple of months before he'd bought the real things for his two teenagers.

Yet the fake example looked convincing. Maybe the cloth was thinner, maybe the stitching was erratic in places – but if he hadn't known, if the price had seemed a bargain, he might have bought. Then been wiser later.

Another fifteen minutes passed, then Commander Hart threw open the door and marched into the room. Hart seemed mildly pleased with himself.

'He's gone?' asked Thane.

'Gone. Saying he'd try and squeeze some paper-push help for us.' Hart went over to the window, looked out at the grassland view, then turned with his hands clasped behind his back. 'I phoned Gypsy Adams. I said you'd be over in about half an hour.'

'Over where?' asked Thane.

'He's selling oranges from a barrow in Candleriggs.' Hart smiled just a little. 'He sends apologies.'

Thane nodded. 'About HMCI – did you expect the kind of support you got?'

'No. But he told me why,' said Hart unemotionally. 'He has a nephew who smashed his pelvis in a car crash two years ago. The kid was a do-it-yourself mechanic, he had fitted new brake pads to his car, a bargain lot. The labels said they were German – they

29

were el cheapo lookalikes from Communist China. They broke up like so much cork tiling the first time he tried them at over 60 m.p.h.'

Thane winced. 'How is he?'

'Crippled,' shrugged Hart. 'If you want more horror stories, talk to Adams. He could write a book.'

He went out. Thane sighed, glanced at his watch, then lifted the telephone and dialled his home number just in case Mary might have got back early. The number rang unanswered for a full minute.

Then he gave up for oranges in Candleriggs.

The black 2 litre Ford Mondeo was one of the latest acquisitions to join the Squad's vehicle pool. It was brand new, with a sixteen-valve twin o.h.c. Zeta engine aboard, and Thane had managed to grab it as his own by unashamedly calling in a couple of favours that the all-powerful vehicle pool sergeant owed him.

But he agreed with the pool sergeant in one respect. Detective Sergeant Francey Dunbar stayed in the passenger seat as Thane drove away from the headquarters building. Francey Dunbar's driving style owed too much to his favourite private love, a big, somewhat battered 650 cc BMW motor cycle, for Thane to let him get near the Mondeo's wheel in any situation short of an emergency.

'What do we do with this Trading Standards character, sir?' asked Dunbar, slouched back in his seat. 'Hold his hand or something?'

'If that's what it takes. So get used to it,' said Thane. 'We're supposed to be on the same side.'

'We're Crime Squad, yet we're into some rag-trade rip-off!' Dunbar shook his dark, unruly hair. His thin droop of a bandit moustache curled indignantly. 'What's for next week? Handing out parking tickets?'

They reached the end of the parkland, passed the scatter of buildings that housed Strathclyde's horses and dogs, and exited on to the main road beside where a large sign said "Police Training Area'. The uniformed constable at the exit swung a barrier pole clear and gave a fractional salute. Thane took the Ford out into the traffic flow towards the city, and caught another glimpse of what his sergeant was doing.

'Francey.' He made it a warning snarl. 'Get your damned hoof off my dashboard! Now!'

'Sorry.' Dunbar had sense enough to lower the offending foot. But he was still indignant. 'Anyway, what about our security van? That's what we should be at – right back from the beginning again if that's what it takes. Somebody, somewhere – '

'We keep it on the back burner,' said Thane patiently. 'When we've any time to spare we can still give it a stir.'

Their runaway, Hazel Wells, was a twenty-five-year-old brunette, the receptionist at a motor-inn-style hotel near Dumfries, about eighty miles south of Glasgow. Her evidence placed three men together at the motor inn on the night before the security van hijack – and also placed them back there a few hours after it had happened. The three she had described and then identified were Finn Thomas, who was a Scot, and two others from the north of England, Gonzo Patrick and Sweep Lannan.

Thomas, Patrick and Lannan were all long-established villains but it was the first time they were known to have worked as a team. Until Hazel Wells had been found, six weeks after the event, none of the three had been on any kind of short list.

They were in custody awaiting trial. But without Hazel Wells' evidence, including the damning fact that she'd accidentally barged into Gonzo Patrick's room where she had found the three men counting wads of banknotes on the bed, the case against them hadn't much hope.

'So why the hell did she take off like that?' he muttered to himself.

'Women,' declared Francey Dunbar sadly. 'No telling with women. Any reason or none. You know how it goes.'

Thane shrugged but didn't answer. Hazel Wells had simply and cheerfully told her hotel boss that she was leaving, had packed a suitcase, and had gone. No forwarding address, no anything. Just a vague promise they'd hear from her soon.

'Damned women.' This time, Dunbar sounded almost aggrieved. He scowled out of the car window to the alarm of an elderly woman they were passing. 'They're trouble. Always.'

31

2

Candleriggs was part of the rejuvenated Merchant City heart of Glasgow, which meant blending old with new and charging rents to match. The vast wholesale fruit market that had once filled most of its length had moved, taking with it the tangles of delivery trucks, the smells, the colour and the bustle and noise. New, mostly faceless businesses had moved in and there was even a multi-storey car-park.

The only lingering trace of what had once been were the few fruit and flower stalls still clinging here and there along the pavement's edge because the owners didn't want to leave. Thane drove down past them, found a vacant parking slot in a side street, left Dunbar in the passenger seat, and walked back. There was no puzzle about where to go.

'Finest from Spain, none better anywhere!' bellowed a large, barrel-shaped man positioned behind a street barrow piled high with nothing but oranges. A hand-painted sign hung above it said 'Adams Oranges. None better. None cheaper.'

Thane went over. The barrel-shaped man was swarthy and balding, and his heavy, cheerful face needed a shave. Frayed black-and-yellow plaid trousers were secured around his substantial middle by a brass-studded leather belt, his feet were in grubby white trainers and he was wearing a khaki army surplus shirt from which a matt of dark chest hair was trying to escape at the neck.

'For you, boss? Hold on a minute.' The man's grin switched to his other customer, an elderly woman with a shopping bag. 'Half a dozen, lady? No problem!'

Six oranges cascaded over a weighing scale, into a paper sack, then into the woman's shopping bag. She paid, and as she turned away the barrel-shaped man ambled a step nearer Thane.

'Thane?' he asked softly, all coarseness gone.

'Yes.' Thane pretended to look at the oranges.

'Gypsy Adams.' The man's voice stayed a murmur. 'Have you got wheels?'

'Next street down,' said Thane.

'Good.' Adams glanced past him, as if expecting someone. 'Give me five minutes.' He raised his voice as a young couple came over. 'Just two for you, boss?' Two oranges were dropped into another paper sack and handed over. 'Last of the big-time spenders, are you?'

The young couple grinned. Thane dragged out some change, paid for the oranges, and turned away. Behind him, the bellow rang out again.

'Finest from Spain, folks. None better, none cheaper!'

Thane crossed the road, moved along a little to a doorway, then watched. Adams had a few more customers, then one who was different from the others came along. He was thin and middle-aged, he wore a coat over what looked like an hotel porter's uniform, and he looked around nervously before he talked with Adams. When he left, he took a small bag of oranges with him. But Thane had seen the package that Adams had pocketed in the process.

As soon as the man had gone, Adams beckoned and a thin woman wearing denims appeared to take his place. As Adams cheerfully smacked her rump she took over and where Adams had bellowed, she used a shrill screech of a sales pitch. Thane went back to the parked Ford.

'Any luck?' asked Francey Dunbar laconically as he got aboard.

'He's on his way.' Thane dumped the bag with the two oranges in Dunbar's lap.

Figures showed approaching in Thane's mirror. Then the rear passenger doors opened and Gypsy Adams and another younger man, tall and bean-pole thin, got aboard.

'Can we drive around?' asked Adams in a surprisingly quiet, educated voice. 'I wouldn't like too many people to see me in bad company.'

'Ruin your reputation,' agreed Thane. He started the car. 'Heading where?'

'Queen's Dock direction, superintendent.' Adams now wore a lightweight fawn short-length coat. He indicated his companion. 'This is one of my people, Harry Bain.'

Thane gave a quick glance round at the bean-pole figure, who wore a knitted wool roll-neck sweater with denims and black trainers, and who had a livid weal of a bruise down one side of his face. He nodded. 'I read your name on a report.'

'About last night,' confirmed Gypsy Adams. 'One of our two who were attacked. Harry ran fastest.'

'It's a gift I have,' said Bain, unperturbed at the libel.

Caught by traffic lights, the Ford stopped in a queue of revving vehicles and exhaust fumes. Thane took the chance to introduce Francey Dunbar and exchange handshakes with the two Trading Standards men.

'How often do you use the fruit barrow?' As the lights changed, he set the Ford moving again.

'On and off, when we need it.'

'Like a letter drop?' asked Thane. 'Your hotel porter?'

'He's being paid off at the end of the week, he's getting a little of his own back.' Gypsy Adams's unshaven face shaped a grin. 'That was a sample of casserole steak from their kitchen – they're buying in cheap condemned meat that was meant for dog food. We'll run a couple of laboratory tests, then we'll close them down.'

'Dog food.' Francey Dunbar gave an uneasy wince. 'Uh – which hotel?'

'An expensive one, sergeant. Do you eat in town often?' asked Adams maliciously, then turned back to Thane. 'A lot of what we do starts off as an anonymous tip-off – not everybody likes to be seen knocking at Trading Standards' door. So they phone us, a CATS team checks, maybe we arrange a meet.' He gave a small gesture with his hands. 'Last night began that way.'

Then the younger Trading Standards man gave a scowl. 'If you want the real truth about last night, we blew it.'

'How?' Francey Dunbar turned round to face him. 'What went wrong?'

'We weren't careful enough,' shrugged Bain. 'It started when we had a squeak that someone was scheduled to deliver a load of counterfeit Reebok sweatshirts to traders out on the north side. That's all we had, except that he'd have a grey van, and a couple of the shops he'd visit. At that stage we got lucky, we spotted him – dark hair, thirtyish, medium height, medium build.'

'A few of them around,' muttered Gypsy Adams acidly.

'He was on his own, and the van an old grey Fiat.' Bain ignored the interruption, obviously used to them. 'I was with Jonny Taylor – we usually team together.'

They heard the rest while the Ford nosed on through heavy traffic on the route towards dockland. The two CATS team men had followed their quarry around several calls. At each halt, the Fiat would stop a short distance away from the shop or discount store then their man would unload a large suitcase from his vehicle and go the rest of the way on foot.

They had followed him as close as they could. At one store, Bain had boldly marched in afterwards and had charmed a sales assistant into selling him two of the newly delivered sweatshirts.

The delivery man had still been on his rounds into the early evening. Then the two Trading Standards men had suddenly been ambushed as they followed him on foot down a lane near Duke Street.

'Neds,' said Bain simply. 'Four of them.'

Around Glasgow, 'ned' was the label used to describe any rank and file hoodlum. Neds were crime's unskilled labour, cheap to hire, always bad news. One of the four had come in swinging an iron bar. Another had a knife, but didn't use it. The remaining two used their boots.

While it lasted, it had been nasty. Taylor, the second Trading Standards man, suffered two cracked ribs, a broken arm, and bruising. Harry Bain, beaten and bruised, with some minor cuts, had managed to get them both clear when an approaching car interrupted things for their attackers.

'But that doesn't mean anybody knew they were Trading Standards.' Gypsy Adams scowled. 'The thought could have been that they were from another counterfeiting team, nosing in where they weren't welcome.'

'Did you try a check on the van?' asked Thane, still threading through traffic.

'False plates. We got them run through the PNC computer,' said Adams. 'We've been round some of the discount stores – the usual story. A stranger came offering bargains, they were tempted, they bought – honest, they'll never do it again.'

'Till next time,' said Thane drily.

'But that's how it goes,' said Gypsy Adams. Then he leaned forward as they reached the start of the Queen's Dock area. 'Take the next left, then the second right – we're almost there.'

'Being where?' Thane began following the directions, which took them out of the traffic flow.

'Seaway Street.' Adams chuckled. 'I'm taking you to meet a

friend of mine, Stewart Rae. He's a main agent for Reebok and some other sportswear makes. His only fault is he thinks God is on the side of the Scotland football squad.'

'A professional martyr?' suggested Thane.

'Something like that,' agreed Adams sadly.

Two minutes more of a drive past old tenements and corner shops brought them to Seaway Street. It was a short stub of roadway, one side mainly occupied by an old, rundown building which had once been a marine engineering yard. The waste ground on the other side still showed traces of the buildings which had been demolished.

There were many streets like Seaway Street along the riverside. Shipbuilding and marine engineering had slipped away from the Clyde. Its new future was being created out of silicon chips and New Age skills. But the memories remained, thought Thane as he parked. He knew old men who still remembered when the Clyde had been wall-to-wall shipping.

He was last to leave the Ford and Gypsy Adams was waiting like a slightly impatient bear, Dunbar and Bain beside him.

'Lead on,' invited Thane.

Adams did. The old building had been subdivided into units, most of the windows bricked up for extra security. The ground-level doors looked as if they were likely to be backed by steel plating.

'Like so many forts,' said Adams, as if reading his mind. 'Around here, the neds don't break in – they make frontal attacks out of the sun.'

One door, its steel plating totally undisguised, bore the name Rae Agencies in small lettering. Beside the lettering was a buzzer button and a recessed speaker grille. Adams pressed the button and there was the soft buzz of a circuit being activated.

'Me, Gypsy,' said Adams into the grille.

A loud click, a soft hiss of hydraulics, and the door swung open. They went into a small, brightly lit but totally empty lobby area and a moment later the door shut again behind them. As it did, Thane saw that the whole lobby area was covered by a TV surveillance camera mounted above another door which faced them.

'Come on in,' said a metallic voice from a concealed speaker. Another click, and the second door sighed open.

This time, Gypsy Adams let the other three go first and they entered a large, thickly carpeted and softly lit showroom area which was another world away from what was outside the building. It was a place with quiet colour schemes, where small, individual keylights picked on the racked displays of sportswear and sports shoes. Seated at a reception desk, an attractive, fair-haired young woman wearing a blue track suit with 'Play Raeway' embroidered across the front smiled up at them.

'He says to go right through, Mr Adams.'

They went further into the showroom area, passing another girl in a blue track suit who was showing customers samples from a range of running shoes. Thane noticed two other track-suited staff, both equally good-looking, restocking shelves – and also noted the way that every inch of the showroom was covered by infra-red anti-intruder beams.

'What's this? A deputation?' asked a man who appeared from behind another of the display stands. His voice was unmistakably the same they'd heard through the speaker, cheerfully confident. 'Should I panic?'

'Any time you want,' agreed Adams.

Stewart Rae, the head of Rae Agencies, was a neat, well-built man in his forties with well-groomed greying hair and a small dark moustache. Alert blue eyes went with a tanned, rugged face. He wore a brass-buttoned single-breasted blue blazer and dark blue trousers with a white roll-neck shirt and expensive soft black leather casual shoes.

'I've got business company,' said Rae. 'Mind your manners, Gypsy.'

He led them through into his office area, a clear space in the middle of another group of stands and racks. It held a large desk and a semicircle of chairs around a glass table. A woman rose from one of the chairs as they entered, picking up a briefcase.

'Maybe we picked a bad time,' said Adams, openly curious.

'No problem. We're almost finished.' Stewart Rae smiled at the woman. She was tall and in her thirties with short, tightly drawn-back honey-blonde hair. She had an attractive face despite a strong Roman nose, with a wide but narrow-lipped mouth; her voice was husky. 'Gypsy, this is Emma Raleigh, one of my better-class customers.' As she laughed, showing strong white teeth, the man went on with the introduction. 'Emma, this stubble-faced vision is Gypsy Adams, from Trading Standards.'

'Counterfeit lines again – Stewart just told me.' The woman

nodded at Adams and gave a mildly curious glance at his companions when Adams didn't extend his side of the introductions. 'Good luck with it.'

'It's early days,' said Adams vaguely. He eyed her with unconcealed interest. Emma Raleigh wore an expensively light-weight tweed suit with a white lace blouse, and a gold ring set with diamonds showed on her wedding finger as her only jewellery. 'Are you in the sportswear business?'

'Only as a sideline.'

'But she pays her bills on time,' said Rae.

'I try.' Emma Raleigh frowned at them. 'I went through the counterfeit mill in a way that cost money. So good luck.' She turned back to Rae. 'Stewart, the order will be confirmed by tomorrow. Don't forget to pray for your team for Saturday.'

Another smile, sweeping them all, and she left.

'I like,' said Gypsy Adams appreciatively. 'Stewart, what prayer?'

'Her regular joke,' shrugged Rae. 'I took her along to a home game last year. We lost, she laughed. End of story.' He sucked his teeth. 'But Emma certainly knows about counterfeiting. She took a lot of hurt a while back when two of her best designer label tennis styles were trashed that way. It was traced back to an Italian scam.'

Adams frowned as if a vague memory had stirred, then his thoughts moved on. He thumbed towards Bain. 'This one you know. The other two are police. Housetrained.'

They completed the introductions, shook hands, and settled into chairs. Stewart Rae buzzed his receptionist and told her to bring coffee. Then he opened a desk drawer and produced another of the fake Reebok sweatshirts.

'Now?' he asked Adams.

Adams nodded and turned to Thane. 'I phoned Stewart first thing this morning. Then I had a messenger drop off one of the sweatshirts we got. Stewart knows the background.'

'But Stewart can't always perform miracles,' warned the sportswear agent. He glared at the sweatshirt. 'For me, this is today's bad news.'

'How bad?' frowned Adams.

'This happens to be a copy of one of Reebok's latest designer stylings. Now coming into production at our main French factory.' Rae prodded the sweatshirt and shook his head. 'So far, I've only seen this one in a catalogue. I'm not due my first sample delivery until next month.'

'So it won't make anybody happy,' murmured Francey Dunbar.

'Reebok are going to be totally gut-sick,' agreed Rae gloomily.

'How good a counterfeit?' asked Gypsy Adams.

'Middling, in looks.' Rae shoved his hands into his blazer pockets and shrugged at Thane. 'Superintendent, the real thing is a moderately expensive top-of-the-range item. You buy quality, you pay quality. This sweatshirt, whatever it looks like, is a cheap nasty. They've copied the Reebok design doing a low-cost knit-up job and cutting every corner they could. Any sales tags are colour photocopy jobs. The only genuine thing in the whole damned garment is the Reebok label inside the neckband.'

'You've lost me,' said Thane, puzzled.

'About fifty thousand of these labels were stolen last month from one of our English factories,' said the agent patiently. 'This has to be one of them. They're machine-embroidered, difficult to duplicate.'

Francey Dunbar whistled softly. 'The authentic touch.'

Harry Bain nodded agreement. 'Better tell them how much that number of labels could be worth to a faker, Stewart.'

'He'd maybe pay thirty thousand pounds, clean money.' Rae grimaced at the thought. 'Well worth it. Punters can be indecently suspicious when they see a bargain. People like us tell them it's always clever to check labels before they buy. If the label seems right, they reckon they're safe.'

Rae's receptionist appeared with a tray of coffee cups and a spare saucer stacked high with biscuits.

'These beat damned oranges, believe me!' Gypsy Adams demolished two of the biscuits sandwich-style, then got back to business. 'Stewart, you're our expert. What else about the sweatshirt? Same story as last time?'

'That's near enough positive.' Stewart Rae nodded. 'The stitching tells most of it. New equipment, good equipment, skilled machine operators. The work these people turn out is its own signature. They're the same who turned out those fake Levi jeans last month and the phoney Nick Faldo sweaters before that.'

'Should I forget?' Gypsy Adams swore at the reminders and shrugged at Thane. 'All right, it's The Cutters again. All we really know is a steady whisper that they have a factory base somewhere north of Glasgow – but not too far away. We first identified their stuff when some Jaeger-style women's jackets began to surface a few months back. They started small, but they've grown fast.'

'And don't get in their way?' suggested Francey Dunbar, sucking an edge of his straggle of moustache.

'That's the other part of the whisper, sergeant,' agreed Harry Bain. The junior Trading Standards officer took a swallow of coffee. 'When you work for them, the word is you do what The Cutters tell you and when they tell you. Otherwise, you get a heavy kicking.'

'But do it right and the profits are good?' asked Thane.

'Bars of gold,' agreed Stewart Rae sourly.

'Don't look so doubtful, superintendent.' Gypsy Adams scratched his substantial middle. 'Look, are you married?'

'Yes.'

'Family?'

Thane nodded.

'Most people like their kids to be upsides with other kids,' said Rae. 'That means Flavour of the Month T-shirts and the rest. A kid who doesn't have the right brand of trainers is a social outcast.'

'So I've heard,' said Thane drily.

'Then take an example,' said Rae bitterly. 'Imagine you're unemployed or low income and every damned penny counts. Along comes Cheerful Charlie Counterfeit with his bargain bag of fake designer goodies. What do you do?'

'Shout hooray?'

'Loudly,' grunted Gypsy Adams. 'If the stuff looks good and is cheap, you don't ask questions. You go for it.'

'Exactly.' Stewart Rae gave a grunt. 'Except that once you wash your "bargain" a couple of times you're left with a low-grade dishrag. I'll give you a tip for your friends, superintendent. Any time they're tempted that way with what looks like a designer bargain, check down the inside seams. That's where most of the real thing has a wash care instruction label. It would be an extra overhead on a counterfeit, so they don't usually have one.'

For a moment, no one said anything. But Gypsy Adams studied the agent's face carefully, then broke the silence.

'Damn you, Stewart,' he said softly. 'You've got something, haven't you?'

'Maybe.' Rae gave a shrug. 'No guarantees.'

'None asked.'

'All right. You wanted help, I started spreading the word first thing this morning.' Rae wouldn't be hurried. 'Nothing happened, until about 10 a.m. Then I had an anonymous call – a woman. She says last night's counterfeit Reeboks were being sold by a bit of rough named Terry Anson. Anson runs a grey Fiat van. He lives in Blenheim Rise, over in Yoker. Know it?'

Thane nodded. Blenheim Rise was a development of high-rise low-rental housing. Most cops in Glasgow got to know Blenheim Rise.

'Did she say anything else?' he asked.

'No.' Rae shook his head. 'I asked her name, and she didn't answer. I asked how she knew to call me, and she just repeated Anson's name again, then hung up.'

'Her voice?' asked Francey Dunbar.

'Ordinary, Glasgow accent, sounded tense.' Rae shrugged. 'Sorry – that's it. What do you think, superintendent?'

Thane glanced towards Gypsy Adams. 'Anson?'

Adams shook his head. 'Don't know him. But that doesn't mean a lot.'

'It's still worth a trip out to Blenheim Rise,' said Thane. He murmured his thanks to Stewart Rae and rose, Francey Dunbar doing the same.

'Mind if I come along?' asked Gypsy Adams mildly. 'Just to keep the Trading Standards flag flying?' He beamed when Thane nodded, then he frowned at his Trading Standards junior. 'Harry, not you. You're still walking wounded.'

Bain gave a grateful grunt and didn't argue.

Yoker is a part of Glasgow lying along the north bank of the River Clyde, a long drab straggle of old sandstone tenements and unattractive factory buildings. During World War Two, some fierce bombing raids overshot the intended targets of docks and shipyards and instead flattened houses. It gave Yoker the double benefit of being where modern high-rise housing could move in.

Yoker's blitzkrieg was the first time in almost nine hundred years in history that anything which happened there had really mattered. The other time had been back in the year 1164, a sad day for anyone in the world named MacDonald – and there are at

41

least a couple of million of them. Somerled MacDonald, first Lord of the Isles, thrashed an army of Norsemen who had invaded his territory, then decided that he wanted to be king of Scotland.

Somerled's fleet of oared galleys stormed their way down the west coast of Scotland, then turned left when they reached the Clyde. He came ashore with his army at a little cluster of fishing huts called Renfrew. The reigning King Malcolm the Fourth, who had no intention of giving up his job, had his own army gathered just across the water at another cluster of huts called Yoker.

When the two armies met in a particularly bloody hand-to-hand battle, the invincible Somerled was up front, carving away with his two-handed sword. It was his hard luck that the legend that he couldn't be beaten had not percolated down to at least one of King Malcolm's basic grade foot-soldiers. When Somerled came at him, swinging that sword, the foot-soldier ran him straight through the middle with a twelve-foot-long spear of bog oak, tipped with fifteen inches of needle-sharp steel.

History being that way inclined, nobody knows what happened to the foot-soldier. But in Yoker now, not too may people have heard of Somerled. Unless they are MacDonalds.

People had enough problems. Yoker was APT territory. Area of Priority Treatment labels were for deprived, under-privileged locations anywhere in Britain. Places where there was high unemployment and a threadbare social fabric. Where drugs, vandalism and petty crime helped break the monotony for a growing minority who otherwise lived on welfare benefits.

Colin Thane drove into Yoker along the long straight of Dumbarton Road, then turned left for Blenheim Rise, a concrete square of four drab fourteen-storey housing blocks. They had an address for Terry Anson. Terence Anson was listed at 3/10 Block C – meaning he had apartment number three on the tenth floor in the third block.

Some grey cloud had drifted in and there was a slight drizzle of rain as he parked the car in a broken area of rubbish and litter-strewn tarmac outside the building. The only other vehicles were a blue and fawn Social Work Department van delivering meals on wheels to some pensioner in the block and the burned-out wreck of what had been an old Toyota coupé.

'Stay,' he told Francey Dunbar. 'Watch our wheels.' Around Blenheim Rise, unguarded cars were often stripped of their wheels by young children. The older gangs simply took the cars and

42

dismantled them, starting with the engine. 'If you want us, use the horn.'

He beckoned to Gypsy Adams and they left the Ford in Dunbar's charge while the Social Work Department van suddenly came to life. As it drove off, passing them, a trio of dispassionate teenagers watched nearby and drank beer from cans.

Inside Block C's main swing doors the world was a place of damp smells and worse, with graffiti on the walls and the elevator doors, and various Housing Department edicts pinned on the communal notice-board. Two middle-aged women emerged from one of the elevators, saw Thane and Adams, and hurried out of the building without a word.

But at Blenheim Rise an elevator that worked was more important than social niceties. They got aboard, Adams winked, pressed the button for the eleventh floor, and once the doors closed the dilapidated cage began to struggle up.

'If he's there, who's running our show?' asked Gypsy Adams.

'We each get a share of him,' suggested Thane. 'Fair?'

'Fair.' Adams grinned. 'Which half do I get?'

They left it at that. Someone was buzzing from the sixth floor, but the elevator ignored it and groaned on until its doors opened at the eleventh. Going up one floor too many was good, practical, grab-them-where-it-hurts tactics in a multi-storey situation, where the sound of an opening elevator could mean unwelcome visitors.

Together, moving quietly, they went down the concrete stairway to the tenth floor. On the half-landing, a broken window meant the fine rain was sheeting in, and Thane caught a glimpse of the Crime Squad car far below. Then, at the tenth floor, he grabbed Gypsy Adams' arm. Number three, Terry Anson's apartment, was almost opposite the stairwell. The door lay open, the lock smashed. There were noises coming from inside.

Thane signalled, Adams nodded his understanding, and they went forward on tiptoe. The noises stopped, they heard a laugh and an answering voice, then as they entered the apartment a teenager in denim trousers and a faded red sweater emerged unsuspectingly from one of the rooms. He froze, stared, then recovered.

'Freddy! Help!'

A crash came from somewhere inside as something heavy was dropped. Then, at the same instant, the teenager made a dive to get past Gypsy Adams. Adams grabbed, threw him bodily against

43

a wall, and the intruder crashed down. But he rolled even as he hit the floor then scrambled up desperately and hurtled off along the landing to disappear.

Thane and Adams suddenly had other priorities. Two more teenagers in denim trousers had come bursting out from one of the apartment rooms. One had short, fair, spiky hair and gripped a black metal tomahawk in one hand. The other figure, smaller, a girl with long dark hair, came close behind waving a wine bottle like a club.

'Get the pigs!' urged the boy. Backing his words, he swung the tomahawk in a black arc at Thane's head.

Whatever his age, he wasn't very clever at it. Thane's reflexes took him out from under the blow and left him placed to grab the tomahawk arm as it came up again. Spinning his opponent round, making him yelp with pain, Thane neatly chopped the flat edge of his hand hard down on the younger man's inner elbow.

This time there was a scream and the tomahawk fell with a clatter on the floor.

Spiky-hair had had enough. Face twisted in desperation, he tried to run – except that Gypsy Adams was there blocking the way. He collided hard with Adams' bulk, and this time the Trading Standards man wasn't making any mistakes. His stubbled face smiling mildly, he brought a knee up hard into Spiky-hair's crotch. There was an explosive gasp of agony from the teenager. He slumped back against the wall and slid down until he was on his knees, his head almost touching the floor.

Which left the girl, uncertain but still defiant, still gripping the wine bottle, ready to use it.

'Jean Franchi, what in God's name are you doin'?' yelled a woman's voice. She had come into the apartment from the outside landing. She was small, she was plump, she was elderly, she wore a faded wrap-round housework apron over her dress. Her feet were in old, faded carpet slippers. Face flushed red with anger, concentrated rage in her voice, she glared at the bottle. 'You daft wee bitch, put that thing down. Your mother will kill you when she hears about this – an' you know it!'

The girl swallowed hard, hesitated, licked her lips, then reluctantly let the bottle fall to the floor and hurled a new string of curses at Thane and Adams.

'Know her, do you?' Thane asked the elderly woman mildly as the tirade went on.

'I do.' She moved purposefully nearer and slapped the girl hard across the face, the sound loud enough to make Thane wince. 'Jean, cut the language. Understand?' The cursing stopped abruptly, and gave way to something close to tears. The woman turned back to Thane. 'Breaking in, were they?'

He nodded.

'She wouldn't, not on her own. I knew her in her pram, her mother and me are still in the same Church Guild.' Her attention switched to the moaning youth, still on his knees and in no hurry to get up. 'This one's different – Freddy Peters, pure badness. He's the one you want.'

'Are you a neighbour, missus?' asked Gypsy Adams.

'I'm Mrs Harvey at 7/10.' She gestured at the girl. 'The Franchis are in Block A. Nice people. Even her, most of the time.'

Thane took over. 'Do you know Terry Anson?'

'With his smart talk an' his wee grey van?' She pursed her lips. 'Who doesn't?'

Leaving Gypsy Adams and the elderly woman to watch over their two captives, Thane made a brief check through Anson's apartment. It had three rooms. Each had been ruthlessly turned over, drawers hauled out, contents emptied. Bedding had been dragged free then tossed aside. A mattress lay slashed open.

Thane went back out to join the others again.

'Did you hear them breaking in?' he asked Mrs Harvey.

'Not me, son.' She shook her head. 'I had the TV on. The first I heard was when you pair started on them.' Her eyes glinted with delight. 'If that's police brutality, we need a bit more o' it! Most folk on this landing are pensioners. We get enough hassle from teenagers an' the only thing some of them understand is a good thumping!'

'How would they know Anson wasn't at home?'

'Jean?' The grey-haired woman glared at the girl for an answer.

'We knew he was away,' she said sullenly. 'Freddy told us.'

'Did he?' Thane stooped, grabbed a handful of spiky fair hair, and brought Freddy Peters' face looking up towards him. 'Tell me how, Freddy.'

'I just knew, right?' Peters scowled. 'An' it was goons who trashed his place, not us. Right?'

'Sonny, don't mess us about,' said Gypsy Adams in a rumble. He brought his swarthy, stubbled face to within inches of a suddenly wide-eyed youth. 'When we leave here, it's a long way down in that elevator.' Turning away a little, he gave Thane a covert wink. 'Try again.'

The teenager swallowed hard. 'Two goons took him away around midnight last night.' Having started, Freddy Peters didn't need further encouragement. 'I saw them go. They had wheels of their own an' a mate waiting outside. They took his van with them when they left.'

'Do you know anything about it?' Thane asked Mrs Harvey.

She shook her head. 'Just that he keeps his van in one o' the lock-ups behind the block.'

'Back row, fourth from the left,' volunteered the girl uneasily.

But like Peters, she stayed stubbornly silent when they tried for a name for the youth who had escaped. Glancing at his watch, thinking of Francey Dunbar outside, Thane gave up.

'Can you cope with her for now?' he asked Mrs Harvey. 'We'll get someone round to decide what to do about her. They can get the apartment made secure while they're at it.'

'I'll get her mother over,' said the woman grimly. 'She'll bounce her off a few walls while we're waiting. Uh – what's your name, mister?'

'Thane.'

'Detective Superintendent Thane,' amplified Gypsy Adams casually.

'A superintendent?' The woman blinked, impressed. 'For a wee break-in?'

'They're short of real police,' explained Adams tongue in cheek. 'If things get any worse, it could be the Chief Constable next.'

'That'll be right.' She laughed derisively. 'An' what about you, then?'

'I just work for the council,' said Adams modestly.

'Like a rent collector?' Any friendliness faded.

They left her. They took Peters, handcuffed and submissive, down in the elevator, then out of the building and through the light drizzle over to where the Crime Squad's black Ford waited. Francey Dunbar climbed out as they approached.

'No Anson. Some of his pals collected him last night, did his place over,' Thane told him. He turned to Gypsy Adams. 'Like to oblige us, keep an eye on our little friend for a few minutes? I'm taking Francey with me to check round the lock-ups.'

'You've made my day,' said Gypsy Adams drily. He dropped a large hand on their spiky-haired prisoner's head and kept it there while he shoved him into the Ford's rear seat. Adams followed him in, flopping down in a way that made the Ford's suspension sway, closed the door, and waved them on their way through the glass.

Thane and Dunbar walked together through the light, damping rain and down the garbage-strewn service road which led around the side of C Block. The grey prison-like bulk of the fourteen-storey high-rise threw its own shadow across them.

They reached the rear of C Block and two facing lines of flat-roofed brick lock-up garages stretched in front of them. As they got nearer, Thane began counting doors, then cursed softly. It was the way he'd expected. Back row, fourth from the left, had its up-and-over door open and was obviously empty.

'Goodbye, grey van?' asked Dunbar, chewing sadly on an edge of his thin straggle of moustache.

Thane didn't answer. He had a feeling that something else was wrong, something he couldn't label. He looked around in the drizzle of rain. Nothing moved, there wasn't a child, wasn't a dog, wasn't a sound. C Block's windows were conspicuously empty of life.

They were another few yards along, walking between the two lines of lock-up garages, nearly at the one which Anson had rented, when a high-pitched, gleeful whoop came from behind them. Instantly, it was answered by another whoop from ahead.

The first petrol bombs came hurtling in behind them a moment later, each a smash of glass, a dull whoosh as the fuel inside ignited, then a savage orange-hearted explosion of flame and heat. They were being thrown by a masked group of yelling, taunting teenage neds. Another, larger group had appeared at the far end of the lock-ups and were marching forward, already throwing petrol bombs as they came, closing the gap.

It was a total ambush, both sets of bombers obviously expecting them, obviously having being hiding behind the garage blocks. Petrol bombs would be no problem. Neds of all ages kept a constant stock hidden ready for use as needed.

'Jesus, look out!' Dunbar yelled a warning as one bottle, thrown further than the rest, burst in a yellow fury which almost enveloped them. He looked around. 'What the hell are they doing?'

'Herding us,' snarled Thane. 'To where they want us.'

Towards the open door of that empty lock-up, the bombers at the far end in no hurry for the moment, the group behind forcing

Thane and Dunbar along. Then if the two Crime Squad men were forced inside the lock-up, a final salvo of petrol bombs would finish the job.

Already, almost without realizing it, they had retreated almost a third of the distance towards the lock-up trap.

'Sir – ' Francey Dunbar, white-faced, suddenly looking very young, made it a plea.

Thane couldn't remember when he had last drawn his short-length detective issue baton. He just thanked God that he had it along with him for once, dragged the baton out, and saw Dunbar do the same. But he wished bitterly that they had two of the .38 calibre Colt automatics locked away in the armoury room back at headquarters.

'Wait for it, Francey,' he said harshly, and they fell back another few paces while the nearest group of neds advanced. As they halted, a new cluster of petrol bombs curved over and exploded on the tarmac.

There was a new wave of heat and flames and smoke. Then there was the moment when the flames flickered back.

'Now!' shouted Thane. 'Stay close!'

He charged forward, striding through the wavering flames, rushing straight for the startled, unprepared tormentors on the other side. Dunbar was pounding beside him and he heard angry yells from the other group of neds at the far end of the lock-up rows. A brief glance back showed that they were rushing to join in, still senselessly throwing petrol bombs as they came.

Then he had reached his targets. He used his baton flat across the head of one leather-clad figure, slammed the stick's blunt point hard into the stomach of another screaming, long-haired shape who was brandishing a knife. He saw Dunbar was equally busy, then had two more shapes coming at him. One had a bicycle chain, the other waved a metal tube.

Then, chaotically, the shouts suddenly changed and the figures were scattering. The petrol bombs had stopped exploding and the neds rushing from the other end of the lock-ups went past and kept going without slowing.

Because police sirens were yowling, blue lights were flashing, and vehicles were skidding to a halt almost beside him. More than that, two snarling, angry, white-fanged dogs – one a giant of a tan and black German Shepherd named Rajah, the other a lightning-fast young yellow Labrador bitch named Goldie – were in there

48

snapping and biting their way through the wild scatter of fleeing bodies.

Even crazier, two of his own people were right behind them – Sandra Craig swinging at any ned who came her way with what looked like a cut-down baseball bat, the massive figure of Jock Dawson, the Squad's dog-handler, equally busy with his fists and boots. The dog-van Land-Rover was abandoned nearby. Some Strathclyde patrol cars had also arrived. Their uniformed crews were in there batoning away, happily getting rid of some of the frustration that went with being young, being fit, and spending too many hours handing out speeding tickets to disgruntled drivers.

Other sirens were on the way. Other lights were flashing. Whatever had happened?

Then, very quickly, it was all over. Half a dozen neds, mostly teenagers, had been rounded up in various stages of bruised and bleeding distress. About the same number lay dazed and groaning among the broken glass and smouldering asphalt. The rest had scattered. Gypsy Adams was putting in a late appearance, openly chagrined at arriving too late.

'Are you all right, sir?' asked Sandra Craig, trotting over.

'Yes.' Thane drew a deep breath. Francey Dunbar was also intact, although the fire-bombs had scorched their clothing and the smell of burning still hung in the air. 'Sandra, what the hell are you doing here and where did the troops come from?'

'Call it chance, sir,' said Detective Constable Craig. 'We didn't expect a war.'

'Chance?' Thane scowled his bewilderment and pointedly ignored the baseball bat still swinging in the redhead's hand. 'What kind of chance?'

'The possible new lead in the security van job.' Sandra was patient. 'The one I told you about.'

'I remember.' Thane watched another scowling, handcuffed figure being brought in. Already he had a wincing premonition. 'What about it?'

'I made those check calls, like you wanted.' Suddenly, as if the same possibility was dawning, she was a little more wary. 'I got lucky with a name and an address – '

'Terry Anson, C Block, Blenheim Rise?' asked Thane stonily.

'Yes, sir. He's on file for theft and assault.' She watched him carefully. 'Jock said he'd come out with me – '

'So you decide to charge in,' completed Thane grimly. 'You don't think to check with me first.' He drew a deep breath. 'It happens that Anson is why I'm here. For another reason. And I don't read minds.'

He saw her flush, and knew he was due at least part of the blame – except he wasn't going to admit it. He was equally guilty of charging in without telling headquarters.

'I'm sorry,' said Sandra Craig sadly.

'This once, I'm not.' Thane watched Jock Dawson bringing his dogs back to the Land-Rover while the patrol car crews continued to sort out prisoners. 'So – where did the cavalry come from?'

Sandra indicated the towering high-rise block. 'A woman telephoned in a 999 call and reported fighting on the tenth floor. She made it sound like a battle. The divisional cars answering got here about the same time that we did.' Her grin broke through again. 'Things looked – uh – busy.'

'They were.' Thane indicated Gypsy Adams, hovering in the background. 'He's with Trading Standards. It looks like Anson was working in the counterfeit business. But he was put into someone's bag last night.' He drew a deep breath. We'd better get the rest of this tidied before anyone else complains.'

She nodded. 'I'll get things started.'

'Sandra.' He stopped her. 'Tell Jock he can charge four bones on his expense sheet.'

'Four, sir?' She blinked.

'Two for the dogs, one for himself, another for you,' he said, wooden-faced. 'Your teeth need sharpening.'

'Thank you for the thought, sir,' she said stonily.

Sorting things out took well into late afternoon, including a diplomatic session with the local division's chief superintendent, who came out all leather gloves and dry-cleaned uniform to find out what the hell Crime Squad officers meant by having a private, unannounced war in his territory. The prisoners were ferried away, two going by ambulance. A Strathclyde police helicopter, nothing better to do, also took a pass over to see what was going on.

Thane left Dunbar with Sandra and Dawson to mop up statements from C Block about the way Terry Anson had vanished. He dumped the spiky-haired Freddy Peters on the divisional men, then he used the chief superintendent's washroom to clean himself up as best he could. Feelling reasonably civilized again, he gave Gypsy Adams a lift back in towards the city.

When they got there, the last trace of the drizzle of rain had ended and the sun was shining again. He dropped the CATS supervisor off close to the oranges stall in Candleriggs, and noticed a flower seller further along the street.

He walked over, winced at the price of red roses, but still bought a full dozen. Taking them back to the car, he laid them on the passenger seat, then checked his watch. It was 4 p.m. For once, the rest could wait. He had his own priority. Setting the Ford moving again, Thane headed for home. Home was in a south-side suburb of Glasgow, a small bungalow in a short avenue of almost identical houses with tiny, almost identical gardens. But he owned it now. Paying off what was left of the mortgage was one of the first things he'd done with the pay increase that went with being promoted to detective superintendent. He frowned. There was a jammed upstairs window that needed to be repaired. It was something he'd promised to fix for more than a couple of weeks. Maybe that had had something to do with Mary's mood that morning.

The street near their avenue was busy with youngsters still straggling home from school. One of them signalled furiously and Thane pulled in, opening the passenger door. A large pimple-faced adolescent swung himself aboard, then thudded down into the passenger seat.

'Thanks, Dad,' said Tommy Thane. He saw Thane's horrified stare. 'Uh – something wrong?' Then carefully, his dark-haired son eased up from the seat, reached under, and brought out the squashed, flattened remnants of the one dozen red roses. Several had been broken from their stems. 'Sorry. Did they matter?'

'Yes,' said Thane bleakly. 'They did. They also cost a fortune.'

'Pity you left them there,' said his son blithely and tossed the ruined bouquet into the back seat. He sniffed hard at the air. 'There's a funny smell in this car, like burning. Is it you?'

'Don't push your luck,' growled Thane.

He parked the Ford outside their home, left the squashed roses lying on the back seat, and followed Tommy indoors.

Mary was in the kitchen, already changed into corduroy trousers and a white shirt, studiously ignoring his arrival, going on preparing a meal for the large, lazy-looking Boxer dog, Clyde

51

by name, that loafed at her feet. Thane looked at the slim, dark-haired woman.

'Busy day?' he asked.

'Yes.' She said it frostily, letting his lips just brush her cheek. She sniffed. 'Been near a fire?'

'Something like that.' He nodded at the dog's meal. 'Want me to do that?'

'No.' She busied herself opening a tin.

'About this morning – ' he began.

Mary raised a silent eyebrow, waiting.

Then they were interrupted. Kate, their daughter, was a couple of years younger than Tommy, had her mother's colouring, and was going to have her looks. A couple of wary-eyed boyfriends had already begun sniffing around.

'Hi!' She burst into the kitchen with a cheerful grin. 'Dad, you left these in the car.' She dumped the battered roses on the table beside the dog food. 'Been raiding a cemetery again?'

'Tommy sat on them,' said Thane sadly.

He heard a strange sound coming from Mary. Then she was giggling, shaking her head. And he was grinning like a fool.

'Help with the dog's dinner if you want,' she suggested. 'Make some extra. That's about all you damned well deserve!'

They salvaged about half of the roses and put them in a vase for the front room window. Peace formally declared, the rest of the evening went by.

Then much later, in bed that night, the moon shining in through the curtains of their room, Thane got round at last to asking.

'This morning – what started it?'

Mary thought. She snuggled closer. She frowned. 'Does it matter?'

Then it didn't.

3

When he wakened next morning, bright sunlight was filtering through the closed curtains of their bedroom. Mary was already up and from the barking coming from downstairs she was rescuing the morning mail from Clyde's attentions. When that ended, other noises told him that Tommy and Kate were also up.

He showered, shaved and dressed, then went down to the kitchen, where Tommy and Kate had almost finished breakfast to their usual required TV background. Mary was with them, still in her dressing-gown. He kissed her; she gave him a small grin, then poured him coffee. Since his last force medical, when he'd been told he should lose some weight, she had trimmed his breakfast back to coffee, orange juice and toast.

'My turn.' Thane salvaged the morning paper from his daughter, who had been reading the horoscope column. His own horoscope wasn't upbeat, so he tried the news pages. What he found there told him that the world was going to hell on a bicycle.

'Can I have the paper again, Dad?' asked Kate hopefully.

'I can tell you why,' jeered Tommy. 'She's checking on Monkey Brushworth's stars.'

'Who says?' Her glare blistered.

'Monkey who?' asked Thane, lost.

'Tall, spots and metal-frame specs,' said Mary with clinical precision. 'The one who called you Sir.'

'He's nice,' declared Kate defensively.

'He's a crooked, cheating rat,' said Tommy flatly. 'So crooked he has to screw on his socks.'

Verdict delivered, he left to get ready for school. Still in a fury, Kate followed him out.

'Monkey?' Thane raised an eyebrow.

'Flavour of the week,' said Mary resignedly. 'Slightly odd. His father is a lawyer.'

'That figures.' Thane poured the last of the coffee in the pot, got up, and took his coffee across to the telephone. Once he'd checked the directory listings, he dialled Yoker sub-division. When he got through to the duty sergeant, he asked about the prisoners brought in from Blenheim Rise. All would appear at the district court sitting that morning, except for two still in hospital and the spiky-haired Peters. He was going straight to a Sheriff Court remand.

As far as the sergeant knew, nothing else had changed overnight.

Thane thanked him, hung up, and took a quick glance at the morning mail. It amounted to a credit card statement, two charit appeals and three circulars from firms he didn't know who offered to lend him money by return. He checked his pockets for money and keys, then was ready to leave. Mary went with him to the front door.

'We've a problem,' he warned. 'I could be late.'

'Today's surprise?' She chuckled. 'Colin, I might just manage to survive.'

Neither Tommy nor Kate was around as he went out to the Ford Mondeo, got aboard, and set it moving. The sunlight was causing enough of a glare on the glass to have him reach for his sun-glasses. It was going to be yet another warm day – maybe even very warm by Glasgow's northern standards.

The rush hour traffic was already heavy as he drove in towards the city, but at least it was moving. He resigned himself to its pace, using the chance to think his way through his mental list of loose ends that needed sorting. Some were going to depend on what the Squad night shift team had turned up. Others, like the strange possibility of a link between their missing Counterfeit Charlie salesman and the earlier security van hijack, would set their own priorities.

Thane gave a lop-sided grin to himself. He had been thinking of how Sandra Craig's arrival on the scene, impulsive or not, had been as welcome as the cavalry coming over the hill in saving Dunbar and himself from the prospect of being barbecued. They owed her one.

Although it might not help to admit it too much.

Thane reached the Scottish Crime Squad headquarters building a few minutes after 9 a.m. and won his usual parking space by a short head as a visiting Fife Constabulary car tried to pull in.

Pleased at the small victory, he left his sun-glasses on the Ford's dashboard shelf and walked briskly into the building.

'Morning.' He smiled at the woman officer hobbling her way around behind the reception counter. Her left leg was in plaster, broken when she was thrown down a flight of stairs by a drugs dealer who was now starting five years in Perth Prison. She could still have been on sick leave; but she'd come back early because she was bored. 'All quiet?'

'Don't ask me, sir,' she said drily. 'I think I'm on mushroom duty. Everyone keeps me in the dark and tries to feed me manure.' She scratched her leg just above the cast. 'Am I allowed to go mad?'

'Make an appointment,' he suggested.

Thane went on through the wakening building towards his office, then slowed, puzzled, as he neared his room. The door was lying half open, which was unusual. He could hear someone moving around inside.

Suddenly, the relative quiet of the building was broken by a massive explosion of a belch – long enough and loud enough to vibrate its way down the corridor towards him. He blinked, grinned, then went straight in. He only knew one individual who could produce that kind of noise.

'So what the hell brings you here?' he asked.

'And good morning to you, sir,' grinned the small, mousy-haired, scrawny-built figure who was sitting on the edge of his desk. 'Do you usually get to work this late?'

'Go to hell,' said Thane amiably. Detective Inspector Phil Moss had spent years as his second-in-command and partner when he ran Glasgow Millside Division's CID. Not much about Moss had changed. He still looked one stage short of being a welfare case, with all the appearance of having slept in his clothes and being short of money for a shave and a haircut. 'Been waiting long, Phil?'

'About half an hour.' Moss gestured with the opened folder in his hands. Thane recognized Jack Hart's T.S. counterfeit file. The cabinet where it should have been locked was lying open. 'Gave me time to catch up.'

'Meaning?' Thane frowned, puzzled.

'Nobody told you?' Moss gave a dry grunt. 'Typical. Colin, I've been drafted. Think of me as a damn lifeboat. God help me, I'm transferred – Her Majesty's Chief Inspector leaned on someone at lunch yesterday and said the Crime Squad needed help with their report. Urgent. Like before they all sink without trace.'

'We get you?' Thane stared at him. 'For real?'

Phil Moss nodded. "Kicking and screaming, Colin.'

The grinned at each other. At Millside Division, they had been a legendary team – Moss, the abrasive, acid-tongued bachelor with a methodical, complaining approach to life, Thane the younger though senior, more ready to back a hunch, take a risk, and sweat out the result. But when Thane had been promoted and moved, things had also changed for Moss. After a decade of fighting off threatened surgery for a rampant duodenal ulcer he had surrendered to what his surgeon cheerfully described as a 'cut and weld' bypass shunt.

When he recovered, Moss had been bounced into a loathed liaison desk job at Strathclyde headquarters. Pushing paper. Keeping the wheels turning for a collection of assistant chief constables who had somehow escaped from nursery school – or so it sometimes seemed.

'When do you start?' asked Thane.

'An hour ago.' Moss grimaced at the T.S. file. 'And if this is the kind of thing – '

'They come worse,' cut in a new, grim voice from behind Thane. Jack Hart had silently arrived. 'Colin, I've told Moss what's needed – and that doesn't include active thief-catching.' He raised an eyebrow towards Moss. 'Settling in all right so far?'

'Sir.' Moss gave a nod.

'Good.' Hart glanced at Thane. 'Come through in a minute.'

He turned to leave. As he did, Moss gave a small, low-key belch. Hart stopped, then seemed to change his mind and kept going.

'As bosses go, he's all right,' said Thane.

'That's what I heard.' Moss put the T.S. folder down, fished in his shirt pocket, and brought out a couple of large and grubby pills which had once been white. He flicked one into his mouth, swallowed it with a grimace, and returned the other to the pocket. 'I get along with most people.'

'Some of the time.' Thane was more interested in the pill-swallowing performance. 'Stomach acting up?'

'Some.' Moss grimaced. 'But no more hospitals. They carved me up enough.'

'Back to pills again?'

'What else?' Moss patted his shirt pocket. 'These are new – garlic and charcoal compound. I met a herbalist who swears by them.'

'Do they help?'

'Not a lot, so far.' Moss gave a shrug. 'It's no big deal.'

'You know best.' Thane left it there. 'All right, let's get started. Say hello to my regular team, then have them in the duty room ten minutes from now.'

Moss nodded. Ambling out of Thane's office, he headed along the corridor and moments later, a loud thunder filled the air.

'Dear God,' said Thane. He grinned. Being handed Phil Moss, even on loan, amounted to a bonus. One he needed. Then he turned to checking the overnight reports on his desk.

There was still no news of Hazel Wells, his missing hijack witness. The equally missing Terry Anson and his grey van were still outstanding, but the night shift had managed to locate a wife and child abandoned three years earlier. They lived in Castlemilk, that great sprawl of local authority housing estate on the south side. Anson's wife claimed she hadn't seen him for over a year and said she didn't give a damn if he never turned up.

Thane checked through the other reports, marked some for more attention, dumped the results in his out-tray, then went through to Jack Hart's office. The Squad commander was sorting the morning's mail with Maggie Fyffe, but she nodded and left.

'Who chose Moss?' demanded Thane as soon as he was alone with Hart.

'Someone with a sense of humour,' grunted Hart, then relented. 'It was HMCI. Any objection?'

Thane shook his head. 'None.'

'He's not your personal property,' warned Hart. 'But he can start with your lot.' He considered Thane for a moment with a degree of malicious intent. 'I read the report on what happened at Blenheim Rise. Nearly got your feathers scorched, didn't you?'

Wryly, Thane nodded.

'So finding Terry Anson is a priority.' Hart beat a gentle two-finger rhythm on his desk top. 'What else?'

'Another talk with Trading Standards.'

'Meaning Gypsy Adams?' Hart chuckled a little. 'Sounds sensible. Widen it out.' He paused and sucked his teeth. 'There's something else, while you're here. Moss arriving could be helpful in another way. There's a situation shaping in your personal team. Promotions.'

'Sandra?' Sandra Craig had passed her sergeant's examination with top marks. She had earned them.

'Sandra.' Hart nodded. 'Like to keep her?'

'Yes.' Except he already had Francey Dunbar, and two sergeants would be one too many on his personal team. Yet Francey had also earned his place.

'Francey Dunbar, right?' The Squad commander enjoyed reading Thane's mind. 'No problem. Francey's promotion to inspector is overdue – his own damned fault, the way he keeps stirring trouble. But I think he's ready for it now, so do other people.' He paused, pleased at Thane's surprise. 'Sometimes we send people back to their home forces on promotion. But I'm keeping these two. I'm moving Sandra up with immediate effect to acting detective sergeant, Francey gets an acting detective inspector slot, both promotions permanent by the end of the month. The bad news is you'll have to lose him. I need a replacement DI in one of the drugs teams.'

'Inspector Dunbar.' Thane chuckled at the thought. 'That'll shock a few around here.'

Maggie Fyffe had brought in a single cup of coffee, which she placed in front of Hart. With it came a bundle of fax and telex messages, which she also laid on the desk. It was time for Thane to leave.

'Send Sandra and Francey along,' said Hart briskly, sampling a first sip of coffee. 'Let me do the telling. I think I'll enjoy it.'

The main duty room was bustling and noisy when Thane reached it, filled to almost overflowing with Crime Squad personnel and other officers, many total strangers, some in uniform. He spotted his team and Phil Moss isolated in a far corner, outsiders in what was happening.

'Set to go, everyone?' A slim and tanned woman in a flared cream linen skirt and dark shirt clapped her hands loudly above her head. Tina Redder, who had short, jet-black hair, was a Crime Squad detective chief inspector. She also possessed what were arguably the best-looking legs in the Squad and as always was wearing high heels to help display them. She looked around and was satisfied. 'Then let's move and do it!'

Thane watched her follow the last of the tide out. Tina Redder was wrapping up an extortion investigation which had taken nearly two months, the target an eight-strong highly professional gang who backed blackmail threats with dynamite bombs. Their latest intended victims had had the courage to talk, the bombers had been under observation for over thirty hours, and it was sweeping-up time.

He heard muttering among his own group as he went to join them.

'All our Tina needs is a flag and a drum-and-bugle band,' declared Sandra Craig in a stage whisper.

'I go for the suntan,' mused Francey Dunbar.

'Sunbed time,' sniffed Sandra. She finished demolishing a chocolate bar.

'Could be.' The placidly plump Joe Felix sighed a little. 'I like suntanned women.'

'Forget it, Joe.' Sandra Craig chuckled. 'At your age, you wouldn't know what to do with one.'

A silent scowl from Moss ended the banter as Thane arrived. Jock Dawson was again missing, but he remembered that he had loaned Dawson and his dogs to DCI Redder for her raid.

'You know why Inspector Moss is here?' asked Thane without preliminaries. He accepted their silence. 'He'll start by being your report officer on what we're going into. Joe – ' He glanced at Joe Felix. 'You start by checking over what the night shift dug up on Terry Anson. That includes having another try at his wife. She may still know something. Use your natural charm – that should worry her enough.'

The moon-faced Felix grinned.

'Francey – ' He switched to Dunbar. 'The commander wants to see you and Sandra. In his office, now.'

'Why?' demanded Dunbar suspiciously.

'Because he says so,' said Thane stonily. 'Move. Both of you.'

The pair exchanged a puzzled shrug, then left. Thane waited until Joe Felix had gone off on an errand of his own, then told Moss what Jack Hart had in store for Dunbar and Sandra Craig.

'Nice to know.' A brief grin creased Moss's face. When he'd shaved that morning, the razor had missed a patch of beard on his left cheek. Maybe that was why some shaving cream had dried on his shirt front. 'I like what I've seen of them.'

'But we won't let it go to their heads,' mused Thane.

'Nail their feet back on the ground, right.' Moss approved the idea. He eyed Thane sardonically. 'Never does anyone any harm. Anyone – does it?'

'No.' Thane said it bleakly.

Fifteen minutes passed before Francey Dunbar and Sandra Craig returned, both looking dazed. As Squad commander, Jack Hart had seen them separately and formally, had given each of them their promotion news, then followed it with a handshake and the brief, standard lecture about increased responsibilities, before sending them on their way.

'You both earned it,' Thane congratulated them. Phil Moss was near, and he beckoned him over. 'Phil. What's the first golden rule on CID promotions?'

'First chance they get, they put up drinks all round.' Moss gave an authoritative low-key belch. 'But there's another golden rule. They get their existing paperwork sorted out, so they don't leave too many problems behind for the next arrival.' He gave a bland glance towards Thane. 'Agreed, sir?'

'Agreed,' said Thane woodenly, and glanced at this watch. 'Sandra, let's go see your woman.'

They used Sandra Craig's current pool car, a white Volkswagen coupé, and Thane was happy enough to settle in the passenger seat. His new sergeant, dressed in faded but crisply laundered denim designer jeans teamed with an equally crisp white blouse and a short denim waistcoat, handled the VW with a deceptively casual skill.

She had been trained that way. Her service record included a merit pass in the pursuit driving class at Tulliallan, the Scottish police college all officers had to go through. At Tulliallan, success at anything didn't come easily.

They travelled east from the Crime Squad headquarters. That meant passing through the modern housing development that had taken over from the old sewer-pit Gorbals tenement slums. The new Gorbals now contained everything from trees and greenery to a new Muslim mosque, a theatre complex and a modern college building. But somewhere along the way the planners had lost the genuine warm humanity that had always survived in the old Gorbals. New was not always better in every way. Even when you were a cop.

Now and again a service message came from the VW's radio, locked on the dedicated low-band Crime Squad frequency. But Sandra Craig also had a personal portable clipped to the car's dashboard, and it was tuned to a station that had a taste in music which included Dizzie Gillespie jazz.

'Sir.' Her eyes still on the road, his driver suddenly broke a lengthy silence. 'When we get to Liz, can we start things off my way? Just at first?'

'She's yours,' agreed Thane.

It was what he'd been planning. Although mainly what he'd been doing had been just watching in a detached fashion the way the sunlight coming into the car turned the red hair to the colour of glinting gold. In the denim outfit she looked young enough to be a college student, something which had been useful more than once. 'She's one of your regular people?'

'Now and again.' She dabbed at her brakes to avoid a kamikaze motor cyclist. 'She often hears things. She telephoned a couple of days ago, wanting to see me. But like I said, I was too busy until yesterday.'

'At what time?'

'Towards midday, sir.'

They had begun travelling past supermarkets and shopping streets and into an area of grey, time-worn tenements – part of the old Glasgow.

'Tell me about her,' said Thane.

She pursed her lips. 'Liz Hill won't see forty again. She's blonde – when she remembers to do her roots. Used to be married, but they split up years ago – he's doing heavy time now in Peterhead Prison for attempted murder. She lives on her own, she drinks a lot, sometimes she whores a little – but she's fussy with it.'

'How did she come your way?'

'You know how it goes, sir.' Sandra Craig shrugged. 'I gave her some help with something.'

Which could mean anything when you were a cop. Thane didn't press it.

'And Anson?'

'They'd been drinking together, he'd boasted.' Sandra Craig was less than happy. 'I rushed the rest of it. I'm sorry.'

61

'It happens.' Thane nodded. 'What does she do for a living?'

'Through the week, she works part-time as an office cleaner.' Sandra Craig allowed the Volkswagen to slow and flicked the indicator for a right turn. 'At weekends, she sells ice-cream from a van.'

'There's good money in selling ice-cream,' murmured Thane. It also meant a possibility, part of something that had been missing. He looked around as the Volkswagen first turned off the main road, then, after cruising on a short distance, drifted to a halt at the kerb. They were outside one of the grey stone tenements. 'Here?'

'Number thirty-four, top floor, her name on the door.' Sandra Craig opened her door.

'Top floor.' Resignedly, Thane got out of the car, looked at the entry to the tenement close and stairway, and drew a deep breath. When anything happened in a tenement, anything that needed a cop, it always seemed to be the top floor. It was seldom anything happened lower down.

Maybe undertakers felt the same way.

'You know what I'm after?' he asked.

'I think so.' She left it at that.

The entry close had the usual litter of discarded fast food wrappings and other trash on the stone floor. The air smelled of cats and worse and as they started up the long stairway Thane noticed that some empty solvent aerosols had been dumped on the first landing. No drugs needles. That would come next.

They started climbing the worn concrete steps. At the second floor, a house door opened and a child began to emerge. Then they were seen. A man's arm appeared, the child was hauled back inside, and the door slammed.

'And greetings to you,' muttered Thane, plodding on, trying to keep up with his red-haired young sergeant's effortless pace.

He could hear an argument going on inside one door they passed, a TV set blaring behind another. Then they reached a top-floor door which boasted several locks and which showed all the signs of having been kicked in more than once. It had a cheap plastic nameplate which read 'L. Hill'. Ignoring a bellpush, Sandra Craig thumped on the door with her fist.

'Liz is always home this side of noon,' she told Thane.

They waited. Another neighbour opened her door, peered out,

then the door quietly closed again. Grimacing, Sandra bent down and pushed open Liz Hill's letter flap.

'Stir yourself, Liz. Move it!'

After another few moments locks clicked and a chain rattled. Slowly the door opened, then a woman looked out.

'You again?' The woman managed a weak attempt at a smile at Sandra, then it faded as she saw Thane. 'Who's this?'

'My boss,' said Sandra. 'We want to talk, Liz.'

Liz Hill shrugged and stood back to let them enter, then slammed the door shut again once they ere inside. A tall woman, thin and raw-boned, yawning, her feet bare, she was in a rumpled cotton nightdress. Leading the way past an open door which gave a glimpse of a bedroom and a bed where the blankets had obviously just been thrown back, she took her two visitors into a small living-room.

'Talk about what?' The woman took a cigarette from a pack on a table, lit it with a kitchen match, drew hard on the smoke, then let it out slowly. Her eyes were wary as she considered her visitors again. 'Well?'

'Terry Anson,' said Sandra.

'What about him?' Liz Hill took another draw on the cigarette then sank down into a chair.

'He was collected the hard way. Then his place at Blenheim Rise was turned over.' Sandra Craig got no response. 'We need some answers, Liz.'

'We could be here until we get them,' said Thane.

As he spoke, he settled uninvited into another of the chairs and looked around. It was a shabby room, the furnishings marked and worn, the table's surface patterned with overlapping rings left by glasses. A bird cage on a stand was placed near the window, but was empty. There were few ornaments, but two framed family group photographs on top of a large TV set preserved old memories. When he looked at Liz Hill, she quickly glanced away and flicked ash from her cigarette on to the carpet. Her dyed blonde hair, short and unkempt, framed a face which showed all the signs of a lot of hard living over the years. But if he was right, if he had accurately spotted her in one of the family photographs when her hair had been long and dark, she had once been a good-looking teenager.

'Terry Anson,' persisted Sandra. 'How well do you know him, Liz?'

'Just good friends?' suggested Thane sardonically. 'Come on, Liz.'

She glared at him. 'Who the hell are you, anyway?'

'Sandra's boss, like she said.' Thane's whole mood hardened. 'You say Terry Anson had a walk-on part in the security hijack. Doing what?'

'He was a mile from where it happened, with a stolen truck. He used the truck to block the road as soon as the getaway car went past. Then he just walked away.'

Thane was silent. It had happened that way. But it had never been in any media coverage. Slowly, he got up again and stood over her.

'When did he tell you?' he asked grimly.

'The day I called Sandra.' She moistened her lips.

'You're lying, Liz,' said Thane unemotionally. 'You're putting Anson in the frame for the hijack. But you also made the call that he was the Counterfeit Charlie unloading fake Reebok sweatshirts, didn't you?'

'Not me.' Liz Hill swallowed hard. 'No way.'

'You,' grated Thane. 'And smoking's bad for your health, Liz – like the company you've been keeping.' He leaned forward, plucked the smouldering cigarette from her fingers, and mashed it out in a brimful ashtray on the table. 'Anson. Try again.'

Ashen-faced, Liz Hill sat silent.

'Then I'll tell it,' said Thane brutally. 'You've known for a long time that Anson carried a short spear in the hijack. But it is only when you've some kind of grudge to pay off that you decide to shop him to Sandra here. Except when you call her, she doesn't show up fast enough.'

'Sir!' Sandra Craig made it a protest.

'Later,' snapped Thane.

'Sir.' An angry glint in her ice-green eyes, the redhead made a tight-lipped retreat across the room towards the bird cage.

'You decide not to wait, Liz,' said Thane. 'You decide to launch your double-whammy – and Stewart Rae the Reebok man gets your telephone tip-off only about an hour before Sergeant Craig – ' He saw the woman's eyes flicker. 'Yes, I said Sergeant. Before Sergeant Craig shows up.'

'Go to hell, mister.' The woman started to rise.

'Sit down,' snarled Thane. 'I'll tell you when we're finished.'

The woman slumped down again, starting to tremble, leaving

Thane mentally hating what he was doing. But it was no time to allow her to stop.

'You wanted him stuck between a rock and a hard place, Liz. Do you know who grabbed him from Blenheim Rise?'

'No.' The answer came hoarsely.

'What did you quarrel about, Liz?' he persisted. 'Was the ice-cream run part of it?'

'Yes.' Her resistance suddenly collapsed. 'Do you know what happened when I said no?' Carefully, she brought one sleeve of the nightdress down, fully exposing her left shoulder. It was a single livid bruise which crossed into the curve of her breast. 'I was trying to stop him. He threw me across the room.'

'Stop him?' Thane was puzzled.

'Dear God,' said Sandra Craig softly, still beside the empty bird cage. 'Liz, where's Ringo?' She glanced at Thane. 'Her parrot, sir.'

'He broke its neck.' Liz Hill shook her head in helpless despair. 'Everyone knew I loved that wee bird!' She raised her head defiantly. 'Whatever happens to the swine, I won't weep.'

Wordlessly, Sandra Craig came over, ignored Thane, adjusted the older woman's nightdress so that the agony of a bruise was hidden again. She gave the woman a cigarette and lit it with a match.

'When did he do it, Liz?' asked Thane quietly.

'The end of last week.' Liz Hill drew on the cigarette a couple of times before she looked up. Then she did. 'It was the ice-cream van. You were right. He wanted to use me that way, selling his fake Reeboks.'

Thane nodded. It happened. Ice-cream vans working round the housing schemes could end up selling everything and anything to their customers. For a cowboy minority of salesmen, offering stolen goods from cigarettes to car radios, from hijacked liquor to pornographic videos, was just as much part of the day's trading as the ice-cream and fizzy drink trade.

'Terry Anson got me to do it a couple of times before.' The woman ignored the smoke drifting from the cigarette. 'I'll tell you his idea of a deal – cash on the nail or sex as a deposit. God, the man smells in bed – I'd had enough. So this time, I said no.' She glanced again at the empty cage. 'Then he killed Ringo, so I shopped him.'

'When did you see him last?' asked Sandra grimly.

'Two nights back.' Her eyes hardened at the memory. 'I was

65

having a drink in the Falklander Bar across the road when in he came, ignoring me but telling the world that he'd escaped getting caught by a couple o' Trading Standards snoops.'

'Did he say how he got out of it?' asked Thane.

Liz Hill snorted. 'He went into a Big Man act about letting some friends know, then they put the snoops out o' the frame.'

'What time was it?'

'Maybe nine, nine thirty – he had a couple of drinks an' then left. It was like he hoped to meet someone who didn't show up.'

'Liz, why contact Stewart Rae? Who told you about him?'

'Terry did,' she said wearily. 'Terry Bloody Anson. It was a big joke. He was selling fake Reebok stuff, he'd met this agent who sold the real stuff.'

'Where?' asked Sandra. 'Did he tell you?'

The woman shook her head. 'Just that.'

Something heavy drove along the street outside, making the top-floor tenement windows rattle as it passed. Silently, Thane handed Liz Hill a new cigarette and struck a match for it, waiting while she lit up and drew hungrily on the smoke.

'You knew Anson was working for The Cutters?'

'I knew he was scared o' them. Who isn't?' She smoked on.

'What do you know about them?'

'Not a lot, an' I'm glad of it.' Her hard-bitten face grimaced. 'But I heard what happened to another man who worked for them. His name was Les Harrow. He made some kind o' mistake about money.'

'Which wasn't clever?' suggested Thane.

'He had his face carved up,' said the woman unemotionally. 'Then people say he got out for London. Terry Anson took over some o' his patch.'

'What else, Liz?' encouraged Sandra Craig. 'It won't get back to you – that's a promise.'

'Should I shout hooray?' The woman made it almost a sneer. Letting the smouldering cigarette dangle between her lips, she slipped a hand under the neck of her nightdress and nursed her bruise. 'Why risk more trouble?'

'He hurt you.' Sandra made a small gesture towards the empty cage. 'He killed Ringo.'

'Then threw him in my lap.' Liz Hill's eyes were moist again, her face seemed to crumple. She turned to Thane. 'I'd watch and

66

cheer if Anson fried in hell, mister. Ringo was my best friend. Can you understand that?'

'Yes,' said Thane patiently. 'So try, Liz. We haven't all day.'

That drew him another scowl from Sandra Craig. But he split the further questioning of the woman with her for the next few minutes.

In some ways, Liz Hill knew little. But in others, she knew more than they'd expected. Terry Anson occasionally drove something much bigger than his van for The Cutters. He sometimes was a relief co-driver on some of the large, anonymous trucks which every week or so took a load of counterfeit stock south from Glasgow down into England. The return trip wasn't wasted. Usually, almost on a barter basis, the trucks brought back crates of other counterfeit products from England. Usually, too, there were two trucks on each run, the drivers under orders to watch each other.

But it was only when Thane and Sandra started to leave that Liz Hill remembered something else.

'About those delivery runs.' She snapped her fingers, pleased. 'There's someone called The Crusher who organizes things. He's in charge, and that's it. Even your Terry Bloody Anson is scared of him.' She paused, a new thought striking her. 'Anson could be dead already, couldn't he?'

Thane didn't answer. But the way things were shaping, a Terry Anson who turned up at a hospital only needing his face stitched back in place might still be lucky.

They told the woman someone would be back to talk with her again and went. When they left the building, two small delinquents – neither of them into their teens – quickly moved away from the Volkswagen. One had had a stick of chalk and a couple of ill-spelled obscenities had been written on the vehicle's dusty bodywork.

Sandra swore. But the two young perpetrators weren't worth chasing. She opened up the car, rubbed away the obscenities with a rag, then got in beside Thane.

'No education,' said Thane sadly. He sat back. 'You know her, sergeant. Do you believe her?'

The redhead hesitated, then nodded.

'You could be right,' mused Thane. He considered the car's radio, then shook his head. 'Find a telephone. I've a call to make.'

67

There was a public pay-phone just round the next corner. They parked beside it, Thane went in, and the telephone hadn't been vandalized or had its coinbox stolen. He fed in change, dialled the Crime Squad number, and a few seconds later he was talking to Phil Moss.

'Saves me hunting you down,' said Moss laconically. 'You've a problem.'

'What now?' asked Thane resignedly.

'The lawyer for one of your bodies for the security job arrived. Martin Hilson, representing – '

'Gonzo Patrick,' Thane finished for him. 'What did he want?'

'Our Mr Hilson heard that we've mislaid a witness.' Moss gave a grunt which condemned all lawyers to the eternal fires. Or longer. 'He wanted to suggest that friend Gonzo should be released out into the big wide world.'

Thane swore. Sooner or later, it had had to happen.

'I told him to get lost,' said Moss mildly. 'You go along with that?'

'Like I'd said it myself.' Thane noticed a pencilled piece of graffiti on the wall. Big Jean, it declared was so ugly that Peeping Toms reached in to pull down the blinds. There were other pieces of mostly obscene advice it. 'Phil, run a check on a Les Harrow – another counterfeit salesman, now maybe in London. Then try the modus operandi computer on whether the name Crusher means anything. He's an enforcer.'

'Harrow and Crusher.' Moss gave a grunt over the line. 'Will do. We've a few other things moving. Joe Felix has gone out to Castlemilk to talk with Anson's wife and the brand new Inspector Dunbar has gone knocking on doors, like you wanted.' He gave an acid snort. 'Dunbar was making noises about it like he had better things to do.'

'You discussed that?' asked Thane drily.

'We had a small discussion, he's doing it,' said Moss flatly. 'He called back with one item he thought might interest you. At a couple of stores where Anson dropped off his fake Reeboks he said to expect him back soon – next time with a range of new-season women's fashions. Top-grade replica stuff, bargain prices.' Moss paused, then his voice took on an edge. 'If you want to talk with Gypsy Adams about it, he says he'll be stuck in his office for most of the day.'

'I'll go there next,' Thane told him. 'Sandra can give me a lift over, then I'll send her on to have another prowl around Blenheim Rise. I'll stay in touch.'

When he got back to the car, Sandra was nibbling her way through another chocolate bar. As Thane got aboard she tossed what was left of the chocolate into the Volkswagen's glove box, then they were moving again.

Gypsy Adams and his undercover CATS team were based in a grimy former warehouse and office located off Saltmarket, on the east side of the city centre and one of the oldest surviving sections of Glasgow. In more ways than one, the dilapidated three-storey building suited the Trading Standards supervisor and his people.

Anyone who asked was told that they were a vermin control facility.

While the Volkswagen drove away, Colin Thane walked into the shabby brick building, noticing that the apparently unguarded lobby with concrete floor and old tiled walls was guarded by twin infra-red sensor units, then a side office door opened. A young, fair-haired woman with black boots and a black leather skirt and black sweater looked out.

'Hello.' She flicked a ponytail and raised a quizzical eyebrow. 'Looking for someone?'

'I'm expected.' Thane showed his warrant card.

'You are, superintendent.' Her whole attitude changed. She smiled. 'Down the corridor, last door. He's in there.'

Thane walked along the concrete, passed a stairway with broad wood steps and long disused gas-light brackets, then opened the door at the far end. He stepped through into a brightly lit garage area which had its outer doors closed. Two delivery trucks were being unloaded by a group of men. Gypsy Adams was one of them. The CATS team supervisor was heaving bulging plastic bags out of the rear of one vehicle and tossing them down into a trio of supermarket shopping trolleys.

'Almost through, superintendent!' Adams heaved another two bags down towards the trolleys, then turned to the men below. 'Harry, finish it off for me.'

Harry Bain heaved himself up on the tailgate of the vehicle. The young CATS man's bruises looked as fierce as ever, but he grinned a welcome in Thane's direction, then took a tallysheet which Adams handed him.

'Thirty bags so far, Harry. Watch the count,' instructed Adams. Dropping down from the truck, he came over to Thane with a beam of welcome on his face. Indicating the bulging plastic bags, he gave a happy boom. 'From a regular client we jumped this morning – we call him Mega Mickey. Want to see what we got?'

He didn't wait for an answer. Lifting one of the plastic bags from the nearest of the trolleys, he ripped the top open and held it out for Thane's inspection. It was filled with a jumble of computer game discs, some in boxes, some wrapped, some just glinting under the light.

'How many?' asked Thane.

'About six thousand – all pirate copies. Another two thousand or so blank discs.' Adams thumbed towards the second truck. 'We're confiscating his computers and copying gear. Nice, sweet operater, Mega Mickey. He had pirate copies on sale, yes. But he was offering a While You Wait service for anyone with a disc they wanted copied.'

'Ideal Rotary Club material,' suggested Thane.

Gypsy Adams took the opened plastic bag across to a bench and emptied out the contents in a chaos of titles and systems. Some were discs Thane recognized, Commodore and Amiga systems, including a World Wrestling Federation title and a Lethal Weapon game which had both been part of his son's last birthday list.

He looked up at Adams. 'How much in money?'

'Punter style?' Adams shrugged. 'My boys will work it out later. Say around a hundred thousand sterling, maybe more.' Pausing, he chuckled. 'This is the third time we've nailed Mega Mickey – with his luck, he should give up. We heard he was operating out of an old funeral parlour in Partick, so we went in this morning while he was still having his cornflakes. Like to see more?'

Colin Thane found himself taken on a guided tour of the CATS warren. It was like a down-market Aladdin's Cave and began in an area behind high brick walls and barbed wire at the rear of the one-time public health facility. Most of the space was occupied by three giant metal container wagons, their wheels removed. Trading Standards needed them as overflow accommodation.

The first held a completed consignment of Far East electrical goods, seized as they were unloaded from a cargo ship on the Clyde. A basic wiring fault meant they were potentially lethal. Yet every one bore a fake British Standards safety approved sticker. Next was a container filled with several thousand pairs of shoes, all labelled as expensive Italian brands, all produced in a remote corner of Eastern Europe. Container number three was a mix of audio equipment and sports gear, counterfeit whatever their labels, most of them seized in raids on two agricultural showgrounds.

Beckoning, Gypsy Adams led the way back into the building and down a short flight of steps into the basement.

There, pride of place belonged to a massive and almost new industrial photocopier unit seized in a raid while it was still copying labels for perfume bottles.

Wire mesh cages housed the cartons of fake perfume in what looked like regular packaging. The names included Chanel and Opium, Ysatis and Givenchy. They had been produced for a travelling trader who sold them for a 'bargain' twenty-five pounds a bottle and who made sure he was far away that same nightfall. Beside them were the glinting yellow metal faked Rolex and Gucci watches, crates of counterfeit Scotch whisky brewed in North Africa and a collection of fake medicines and prescription drugs.

Above that, on the ground floor, any spare space available was occupied by piled cardboard boxes filled with pirated video and studio tapes. In one grubby corner, two women Trading Standards staff were cataloguing their way through a collection of counterfeit violins. All made in Poland, all carefully aged and scarred with labels which said they were by Stradivari.

'One of our new lines,' said Adams proudly. 'They were coming in at the airport. The crates said vodka.'

The next floor up was half filled with seized counterfeit clothing, from naf tops and sweaters to padded Adidas anoraks. The remaining area could have been mistaken for a miniature department store with baled underwear side by side with ten thousand alleged woollen sweaters which had never known a sheep.

Along the way, the Trading Standards man kept up a steady flow of his own kind of street lore.

'Take those perfumes,' he said cheerfully. 'They were probably distilled in someone's back shed. Check the packaging – the box colours are never quite right, even though they're colour photo-copied. The real item has tight shrink-wrap film, the fake is usually just a little bit loose. Videos?' He picked up a sample as they passed, juggled with it, then heaved it aside. 'Maybe the stick-on label is a damned good copy, but they are nearly always stuck on by hand – don't touch the sloppy label. Tell your kids – kids buy more pirates than anyone else, then get a let-down when mostly what they see is a snowstorm!'

Gypsy Adams led the way into his private office. It was a large and shabby top-floor room, littered with files, cluttered with surveillance team hardware from motor drive cameras to massive telephoto lenses. There was a computer terminal screen and keyboard, and a coffee percolator was bubbling quietly on a shelf behind his large museum piece of a desk. The Trading Standards supervisor frowned around. 'I'll get you a chair.'

Adams cleared one by dumping a stack of computer printouts on to the stained, faded carpet. As Thane settled in it, the Trading Standards man lowered his considerable bulk into the king-sized chair at his side of the desk. Opening a drawer, he produced two stoneware mugs, then a crumpled bag of sugar.

'We'll take a break.' He reached over for the percolator. 'Black all right?'

'Fine,' Thane nodded. 'On its own.'

Adams filled both mugs from the percolator, gave Thane one which declared in large letters 'My Boss Got Fan Mail From The Gestapo' and kept the other, which proclaimed 'Stolen From Gypsy'. He poured a torrent of sugar straight from the paper bag into his mug, used a pencil to stir the result, and took a mouthful.

'So.' He considered Thane wisely. 'What do you want from us, superintendent?'

'A spare miracle or two always helps.' Thane sipped his own coffee. It had to be the worst brew he'd ever tasted. Maybe it was counterfeit too. 'Can we start with Terry Anson?'

'I checked. We've nothing on him worth a row of beans.' Gypsy Adams scowled. 'He seems to rate as just one of The Cutters' delivery team. That's all – sorry.'

'I've some other names. Les Harrow, probably in the same league until he fell out of favour, and an enforcer nicknamed Crusher.'

Adams frowned. 'Crusher the bogeyman – he's real, whoever he is. Harrow – let's see.' Hauling himself out of his chair again, he went over to the computer terminal and tapped briefly. The screen sprang to life and Adams peered at the lines of type in a long-sighted way. 'Got him – Leslie Harrow, another Counterfeit Charlie salesman. But no recent update. Mostly works an out-of-town sales circuit. We've an address.' He found pen and paper, scribbled the details, and handed the slip to Thane.

'Anything known about a link between Harrow and Terry Anson?'

Adams looked again and nodded. 'Known associates – nothing more.' He paused. 'Anything else?'

Thane sucked his teeth. 'Yes. A long-shot chance, back to Anson. Three names – Finn Thomas, Gonzo Patrick, and Sweep Lannan.'

'And maybe damn all to do with Trading Standards?' Thumbs hooked into the leather belt around his substantial middle, eyeing Thane suspiciously. 'I've heard those names somewhere else, right?'

'A security van hijack,' said Thane.

'Don't drag me into that kind of scene. I've enough problems – and this won't help.' Adams abandoned the computer screen and went back to his desk. Dropping down in his chair again, he fished in another drawer and brought out a small cardboard box. 'Adams' patent answer to Data Protection – things that don't matter but that I don't want on anybody's screen.' He raised an inquiring eyebrow at Thane. 'How about you?'

Thane grinned. 'I've an old notebook.'

'Then let's see.' Adams opened the box, fingered his way through the neat slips of paper inside, paused at last, and lifted one out between his fingertips. 'Nothing on Thomas or Lannan. But Gonzo Patrick rings a small bell. He was supposed to ride shotgun on a pirate audio scam a couple of years back – we broke up the operation, we got the chiefs and let the Indians scatter.' He looked again at the slip of paper and swore. 'You win a prize.'

'Something?'

Adams sighed. 'Terry Anson is listed as an occasional associate.' He put the paper back in the box, then scowled. 'You've somebody talking?'

'About the little she knows.' Thane abandoned all pretence he might ever drink the coffee and set it aside. 'But Anson was also claiming that he could offer replica new-season women's fashions.'

'New-season –' Gypsy Adams blinked. 'Are you sure?'

'Only that he said it.'

'Damn,' said Adams, making it almost a moan. 'Damn, damn and damn. New season's lines – that's all we need.' He drew a deep breath. 'You're really sure?'

'No. Not yet. Maybe when we find Terry Anson –'

'When or if?' asked Adams bleakly. 'How would you bet?'

'What odds would you give?' Thane shook his head. 'Who's on the inside on the women's scene?'

'Fashion and the boutique trade?' Adams shrugged. 'There are one or two.' He had a thought. 'Start with Emma Raleigh. Remember her – Stewart Rae's up-market honey-blonde?'

'I remember.' Thane grinned a little. Anyone like Emma Raleigh wasn't easy to forget.

'She knows the boutique scene. She had her own bruising in a counterfeit rip-off, so she has an extra reason to help.' Adams cleared his throat, slightly embarrassed. 'I – uh – got curious, so I checked. She has a pretty solid reputation in the rag trade and – uh – '

'She's a good-looking woman,' suggested Thane, his grin widening.

'Go to hell,' growled Adams, reddening. 'Anyway, I'm divorced, but I didn't sign any pledge.' He opened his box again and reluctantly took out another slip of paper.

Ten minutes and three telephone calls later, Colin Thane left the CATS base and set off on foot towards a new meeting. His route took him past a set of landmarks he knew only too well – the red-brick City Mortuary came first, then the Victorian stone frontage of the High Court building. It faced across the busy Saltmarket towards the broad parkland of Glasgow Green, where in the nineteenth century the last public executions by hanging had still attracted holiday-sized crowds. Now it wasn't a place where anyone in his or her right mind wandered alone after dark.

Gypsy Adams had left his guest on his own while Thane made his telephone calls. With Adams so keenly interested in anything that was going on, that rated as the ultimate in hospitality.

Thane's first call was to Emma Raleigh's office number. She was apologetic, but she was about to start a desk-top lunch meeting with a visiting client. Still, she would be clear around two fifteen and could see him then.

He had to check a phone directory to locate the number he needed for his second call. The initials GMB stood for the General, Municipal and Boilermakers Union, and it was a wild card call to someone he knew. There, at least, he got a start to what he wanted.

The last call was to the Crime Squad switchboard to tell them where he was heading and to leave a message for Sandra Craig.

Then he thanked Gypsy Adams, left the Trading Standards building, and began walking through the busy, sun-drenched streets which fringed the riverside.

It took only minutes to reach his destination, an unobtrusive Italian restaurant located one side street back from the Clyde. It had faded paintwork and the windows were grubby on the outside. But the red and white cotton covers on the tables were spotless and the owner made the best lasagne in the entire city.

The man he had hoped to meet was already there, sitting at a table on his own. Thane crossed over.

'You didn't waste time, Liam,' said Thane. Drawing out a chair, he sat down opposite. 'I appreciate it.'

'I'm here because you're buying lunch,' said Liam Riley. 'What worries me is what it's going to cost me.'

'Not a lot,' promised Thane. 'And we'll eat first.'

Liam Riley, slight in build and in his forties, gave a grunt of agreement and reached for the hand-printed menu. He had a bald egg-like head, blue eyes, and a broken nose. They had both boxed as amateurs at around the same time and had met again years later when Thane turned up investigating a break-in at the branch office of the giant General, Municipal and Boilermakers Union. Liam Riley worked there as a full-time official. After that, they'd kept casually in touch.

'You're buying?' queried Riley again.

'I'm buying,' confirmed Thane wryly.

'Then it's on expenses,' grunted Riley. 'Trouble.'

They settled for starters of mozzarella, then the house lasagne verde with a shared carafe of Chianti. Any conversation stayed vaguely general until they had eaten. Then Riley sat back, nursing the last dregs of his wine.

'So what's this about?' he demanded.

'Your outfit keeps swallowing up little unions,' said Thane. 'One of them takes in rag trade workers, right?'

Riley grinned. 'You mean the National Union of Tailors and Garment Workers. Remember I told you about their row with the Boilermakers when the Boilermakers were ready to rivet their knickers?' He frowned. 'So? What have they done that brings you tramping around?'

'Nothing.' Thane leaned his elbows on the red and white checked table. 'Liam, your people don't like non-union sweat shops.'

'Loathe them.' Riley shrugged. 'But there's a lot of unemployment in the clothing industry. We can't stop people working for them.'

'Ever heard of counterfeit clothing?'

'Not totally my scene – I handle the Boilermakers, if you'll excuse the expression.' Liam Riley frowned. 'But I've heard what goes on.'

'And it kills off reputable manufacturers, costs your members their jobs.' Thane let the words sink home. 'We've made the scene a target operation.'

Riley showed surprise. 'Then it's heavy?'

'Heavy and nasty. But you could help.' Thane saw the sudden caution in Riley's eyes. 'Help us, help your members. Maybe even protect some jobs.'

'How?' asked Riley.

'We're working with Trading Standards. Trading Standards say there are counterfeit manufacturers working somewhere around Glasgow or somewhere near. We're talking equipment and we're talking work staff.'

'Meaning trained operatives.' Riley carefully drank the last of his Chianti and laid the glass down. 'What do you want, Colin?'

'To know if any of your people have had job offers.'

'You bought the lunch.' Riley sighed. 'All right, I've maybe heard rumours. Suppose I come up with something, suppose you raid somewhere. What happens to the work-force people?'

'Not a lot. They don't interest us.'

'They interest me,' said Liam Riley grimly. 'I'll think about it. Fair?'

'Fair,' agreed Thane. He glanced at his watch, then signalled for the bill. He knew Liam Riley; he knew it would happen.

4

Sandra Craig had the Volkswagen parked across the street on a yellow No Waiting line when he left the restaurant; she was engaged in eye-contact warfare with a hovering traffic warden. Dodging his way through the traffic, Thane went over and got aboard.

'Been waiting long?' he asked.

'No, sir.' Frost in her voice, his new sergeant considered the restaurant. 'Good lunch?'

'It was business,' said Thane mildly.

'Yes sir.' Face expressionless, she reached for the ignition key and started the Volkswagen. 'Where are we heading?'

Thane sighed to himself. A hungry Sandra was never a happy Sandra. But this time there was something else. 'More your scene than mine. Emma Raleigh's boutique in Sauchiehall Street.'

Sandra nodded, slapped the car into gear, and it moved off with a jerk. From there, the white Volkswagen carved a way through the other traffic in ways that made him wince. When they reached the broad, busy shopping width of Sauchiehall Street they turned away from the pedestrian precinct section and turned west, out past the blocks of large department stores and into quieter territory. Watching the shop signs, Sandra slowed the Crime Squad car and drifted it to a halt at a kerbside space in a line of illegally parked vehicles. At that end of Sauchiehall Street no one worried too much.

'Over there, sir.' She thumbed across and down the roadway.

The shop had a large ivory-white sign with the name 'Emma's' in bold gold script. The frontage had large double windows with the ivory-white theme continued in its pillars and central doorway. What Thane could see of the outfits on display – outfits against background swatches of red and gold velvet – were the kind that cost real money. There was an upper floor which could be office territory.

'Looks like she does all right.' Thane glanced at his watch. They were a good fifteen minutes early. 'We'll just wait.' Settled deeper in the passenger seat, he considered Sandra Craig's grim profile and kept down a grin. 'Any luck at Blenheim Rise?'

'Some.' She gave a slight shrug. 'No real improvement on who grabbed Terry Anson. The best we've got would fit half the faces in criminal records. But your C Block friend Mrs Harvey says Anson sometimes flogged some of his special lines around the Rise – usually when he had run out of beer money.'

'Counterfeits?'

Sandra Craig nodded. 'The usual – casual gear, bargain prices.' Pausing, she reached under her seat and drew out a paper bag. Out of it came a slice of cold pizza. It looked like anchovy and cheese. 'Can I have my lunch, sir?'

'Whatever helps,' said Thane drily.

'Thank you.' She took a first bite of pizza and chewed. 'There were a couple of things.' Sandra Craig licked a crumb out of the corner of her mouth. Thane wondered if the redhead knew how erotic she could make such a simple act, then she was speaking again. 'Last time Mrs Harvey talked with Anson, a few days ago, he told her the same story about maybe soon having a new women's line to sell.'

'Any hint about it?'

'No, sir.' She shook her head. 'Scenes of Crime were also out, having another go over his house and lock-up. The house is clean, but they found something new in the lock-up.' Reaching into a pocket in her denim waistcoat she brought out a small plastic evidence envelope, already tagged. Inside was a soiled and crumpled receipt printout. 'If this is his, he bought twenty gallons of diesel fuel at a motorway service station two months back.'

'Where?' Thane showed his interest.

She glanced at the ticket. 'Southwaite.'

'The M6, south of Carlisle.' He'd used it himself, driving south.

'Diesel could mean something bigger than the Fiat.' She guessed the rest. 'Maybe pick-up and delivery?'

Thane nodded, thinking about it. Sandra Craig had gone back to demolishing what was left of her pizza. She scowled as two teenage girls, smartly dressed and giggling about something, went past outside with their high heels clicking on the concrete.

'All right, Sandra.' He'd had enough. 'What's the rest of it? You're promoted, you should be all singing, all dancing. What the hell's riling you?'

She hesitated, then took a deep breath. 'Your Inspector Moss.'

Thane raised an eyebrow. 'What about him?'

'He's a pig-headed male chauvinist – sir.'

'True,' agreed Thane gravely. 'He also has two commendations for bravery and a gallantry medal.' He saw her blink. 'So what did he do?'

'I – ' She hesitated, then shook her head. 'It's nothing I can't cope with, sir.'

'Good.' If Phil Moss was stirring things, he wanted to stay out of it. Looking past her, he noticed an open-top white Mazda sports coupé pulling in at the other side of the road. Then he saw who was getting out on the passenger side and his eyes widened a little. 'Get down. Now.'

Sandra Craig slid deeper down in her seat. He had already done the same on his side, but was still able to have a clear view of what was happening.

Emma Raleigh was lingering beside the stopped car, talking to the man who was behind the wheel. The tall, blonde boutique owner was smartly dressed in a tailored cream linen skirt and jacket and had a brown leather shoulder bag. The coupé driver looked middle-aged with oddly familiar features and thick curly dark hair. His blue shirt was open at the neck and he had on a blue plaid sports jacket.

'That man – ' began Sandra.

'Stay down,' snapped Thane.

His eyes were on the couple. The Mazda's engine was still burbling and its driver was shaking his head at something Emma Raleigh had said.

Then Emma Raleigh seemed to be trying to reassure the man. Leaning against the car, she laid a hand on his shoulder and said something more. It seemed to work. The man hesitated, smiled, and nodded. Apparently satisfied, she turned away and left him.

Thane watched while the tall blonde walked purposefully towards a plain, dark-painted door located almost next to the boutique. Using a key, Emma Raleigh opened the door and Thane had a brief glimpse of a flight of stairs leading upwards. Then she had gone in and the door had closed again. As the door closed, the Mazda coupé pulled away with a snarl of exhaust. It headed off in the direction of the city centre.

'Sir.' Almost despairingly, Sandra Craig tried again. 'That man –'

'What about him?' asked Thane resignedly.

'I know him – recognise him, anyway.' His new sergeant was on the brink of rebellion. 'That's what I've been trying to tell you. That's Peter Dutch. The television personality – or he used to be. He fronted a lot of local late-night chat shows as presenter.' She drew a deep breath. 'You must have seen him. There were times when it was like he was never off the box!'

'Yes. I remember.' Thane swore under his breath. It should have connected earlier. 'Then he was dropped, right?'

'He went down with his show.' Sandra almost grinned. 'Boyfriend?'

'Maybe.' Emma Raleigh had told him she had to stay at her desk through lunch, dealing with a client. 'You got the Mazda's registration?'

Sandra nodded.

'Check it later.' Thane relaxed back in his seat. There was only an empty background hiss of static coming from the car's Crime Squad radio. Sandra's personal portable was softly playing more gentle jazz, an unhurried version of 'Poor Butterfly'. The music was totally soothing. 'We're due there in ten minutes. We'll give her twenty – then make apologetic noises about being delayed.'

Sandra Craig raised an eyebrow, but nodded. 'You're the boss, sir.'

'Item number one in becoming the ideal sergeant.' Thane chuckled. 'Item number two is don't quarrel with Phil Moss. I've seen him eat new sergeants for breakfast, then spit out the buttons.'

She was ready to protest. But Thane had closed his eyes, had folded his arms, and his chin was on his chest. Sandra Craig sighed.

Then she let 'Poor Butterfly' rule.

Exactly on Thane's twenty minutes they left the Volkswagen, crossed the road, and went in through the boutique's ornate glass entry door.

To enter Emma's was to go into a small, private world of thick wall-to-wall carpeting, of mirrors and changing booths, of displays which ranged from bridal dresses to fashion trousers. More garments waited all around on discreetly curtained racks. The air was lightly perfumed, low, throbbing Muzak came from hidden speakers, and staff in white blouses and narrow black skirts outnumbered the only customers, who looked like a mother and daughter.

'To see Emma Raleigh.' Thane showed his warrant card as they were intercepted by the head blouse and skirt, who was smartly full-figured and raven-haired. 'We're expected.'

The woman nodded, glanced at Sandra in a way that indicated she was pricing everything about her including her underwear, then went off and used an internal phone.

'Superintendent.' The woman beckoned.

They followed her to a door to one side of the boutique. Opening it, she indicated a flight of stairs but didn't follow as they went up. At the top, Emma Raleigh was waiting. Her husky voice greeted Thane brightly; she nodded to Sandra Craig as Thane made introductions, and then led them through a deserted outer office area where there were a couple of desks and a scatter of modern office equipment including a word processor.

'Lunch-break.' She indicated the empty desks. 'Really change-over, in fact. I've slimmed down to two job-share secretaries, one morning, one afternoon.' As she spoke, she opened another door. 'This is where I hide.'

Her private office overlooked the street and was expensively finished with oak-panelled walls, cream carpeting, and a scatter of leather-backed chairs. She had a king-sized executive desk in dark oak with a swivel chair to match.

'Nice,' said Sandra politely, looking around. The walls were decorated with framed reproductions of old fashion sketches from between the wars. Two matching ivory telephones on the boutique owner's desk were old in style but with modern touch pads. Then Sandra noticed a framed photograph on the wall behind the desk. It showed a model on a catwalk, and she took a couple of steps nearer for a closer look. 'You, Ms Raleigh?'

'From a few years back, sergeant,' said Emma Raleigh drily. She saw them seated, then went round and settled in her own swivel chair. 'Well, superintendent, you said you needed help. What kind?'

'Your kind – where you're an expert.' Thane gave what he hoped was a friendly smile. 'Thanks for seeing us. Did you have a good meeting?'

'And a good order from it.' She brought her fingertips together under her chin, then looked across them. 'I've a regular customer, a woman who runs an hotel shop near Perth. She wanted to see a new line in a make of French blouses I wholesale.'

'Worth a desk-top lunch?' asked Sandra mildly.

'Coffee and sandwiches.' Emma Raleigh shrugged. 'Part of the job, detective sergeant. Nobody hands me a weekly wage packet.'

'Then we come along,' said Thane sympathetically. 'So you're still trapped inside. No chance to get out in the sun.'

'Not so far.' She lowered her hands with a gesture. 'Maybe later. Let's get to what you want, Superintendent Thane.'

'All right.' They had the woman hooked for lying, whatever the reason. 'You told me you loathe counterfeiters. Stewart Rae told me why.'

'Then you know they nearly destroyed me.'

'We've information that a counterfeit range of women's new-season fashions is ready to roll. Very soon, copying top names. At bargain prices.'

'If it's true, that's bad news.' Emma Raleigh's smile had vanished. She frowned, toying with a small paperknife from her desk. 'Any hint about the designer's name, or the make?'

'None.' Thane shook his head. 'But you know the trade. Maybe you can help.'

'Help? Like that?' The woman stared at him in what could have been near disbelief. 'Superintendent, at this time of year the fashion houses are launching their summer styles. They're already having trade showings for some of next winter's lines. You're talking any number of firms. You've no lead at all?'

'None.'

She sighed and turned to Sandra. 'I don't suppose policewomen are much interested in fashion, sergeant – '

'Does it show?' Sandra, who spent most of her spare cash on clothes, said it sweetly.

'You know what I mean.' Emma Raleigh twirled the paperknife in her fingers. 'Look, everybody knows there's a new style in cutaway velvet jackets coming from Dior. Then there are others, some more down-market.' She looked at Sandra again, then changed her mind about whatever she'd been going to say and switched back to Thane. 'Let me think about it. I could speak to a couple of people I trust and who might have a lot to lose.'

'How many other Emma shops do you operate?' asked Thane.

'This and three others – the others are smaller.'

'At the up-market end of the trade?'

She shrugged. 'We like to think so, superintendent. Ask your wife – or your sergeant.'

'You're sole partner?'

She nodded.

'But is there a Mr Emma in the background?' Thane made it casual interest.

'You mean this?' Emma Raleigh let the light play on her gold and diamonds wedding ring. 'It's a long time since I knew where he was.'

Sandra gave a tut of venomous sympathy. 'You mean he did a runner?'

'Thank you, sergeant,' said Emma Raleigh, her husky voice cold. 'Do you have a partner? Or just a pet of some kind?'

'I know a rat or two.' Sandra Craig's eyes glittered like steel.

And the nearer of the two telephones rang.

Emma Raleigh answered it, then looked at Thane. 'For you, superintendent.'

Thane took the handset with a warning glare at Sandra.

'Thane.'

'Sir.' It was Joe Felix, at headquarters. 'Message from DI Moss. He couldn't raise you by radio. The Fiat van has turned up, and a body with it. He asks if you'll meet him.'

'Yes.' It was the kick in the stomach he'd been expecting. But Thane kept his face expressionless, conscious of his audience. 'Where?'

'Off the A77 Ayr road, near Loganswell. Dark Loch.'

'On my way, Joe.' He hung up and gave a slight nod to Sandra. 'Time to go.' Then, as she rose and put her unused notebook away, he made an apologetic shrug to Emma Raleigh. 'Sorry. Something has turned up. But if you hear anything – '

'I'll be in touch,' she promised and rose to see them out. Her attention flickered to Sandra again. 'That's a nice little blouse, sergeant. Rather like one of ours. Where did you get it?'

'Oxfam,' said Sandra Craig with a thin smile. 'Goodbye, Ms Emma.'

They went out the way they'd come in, through the boutique. Thane waited until they were in the street, then turned on the redhead with a snarl.

'What the hell got into you back there?'

Sandra Craig grinned. 'We didn't hit it off, sir. A female

thing you wouldn't understand. She as good as called me a Sinbad.'

'A Sinbad.' Thane raked his mind and drew a blank, and decided not to ask. 'That can wait. We've got ourselves a body. Let's see if it really belongs to us.'

A fast half-hour drive out from the city, Loganswell was a minor turn-off on the main A77 Glasgow–Ayr artery. Marked by an old monument to a long-dead poet, backed by low green hills and a scatter of small sheep farms, it was the beginning of the broad, empty sweep of the Fenwick Moor. About another mile along the A77, close to one of its forest of 60 mph limit signs, a patrol car was parked inconspicuously at the start of a tarmac track on the right.

The VW crossed the busy stream of oncoming traffic, exchanged a headlight flash of recognition with the patrol car, passed it, and stayed in third gear along the climbing, winding little route. Sheep and cattle grazed in fields on either side.

Thane knew where they were going, although it was long years since last time. His mouth softened. The Dark Loch, a long mile into the hills, was where he and Mary had one of their private places before they were married. It had been empty, it had been lonely –

This time it wasn't.

The car topped another rise of tarmac and the Dark Loch, named for its peat-black water, lay ahead. It was a modest size, reasonably attractive, and a gently sloping stretch of grass and scrub edged one curve. There was a bleak rise of raw rock on the far side, and the rest was an edging of reeds and shingle backed by a straggle of thin trees. There was purple heather in bloom around the outcrop of rock and out on the loch there were ducks floating on the water.

Harsh reality was the two burned-out vehicles lying between the track and the loch, one on its side in a hollow of ground where flames had scorched the vegetation to black ash, the other a gutted skeleton lying on its roof.

Yellow police tapes marked off that area of lochside and a second area nearer the reeds where a brown canvas screen had been erected on poles. Several police vehicles were already parked inside the tape, and Sandra crawled their Volkswagen through a gate-like gap guarded by a uniform constable.

'Pull in anywhere.' Thane waited until she had brought the car to a halt near some of the Crime Squad's contribution to it all. One was his black Ford Mondeo, sadly mud-spattered, the other was Jock Dawson's even grubbier-looking Land-Rover dog-van. Both were empty. As Sandra killed the engine, he looked along the lochside to where Phil Moss stood talking to a gloomy-faced stranger.

'Sandra.' He glanced at her. 'Ease back. Understand?'

She gave a wry grin but nodded.

Moss had seen them. He raised a hand in greeting as they left the car and set off towards him.

There was a light, cool wind. Some clouds had appeared out of nowhere and sent shadows sweeping across the loch. For the rest, the surroundings might be different but the main ingredients were familiar. A mortuary wagon was parked to one side, its crew relaxed, smoking cigarettes, patiently waiting their turn. A big grey Rover coupé belonged to Doc Williams, the police surgeon. A Strathclyde major incidents van was further along, the back doors open, two technicians beside it wearing rubber boots and protective overalls and sipping from coffee mugs. There was no sign of Jock Dawson or his dogs, but a team of uniformed men were making a slow search along the water's edge. A scatter of other people were moving around, each with his or her own job to do and getting on with it.

When they reached Moss, he introduced the stranger to Thane with a faint, warning wink.

'Inspector Torrance, sir. Divisional CID,' said Moss drily. 'His superintendent was here, but couldn't wait.'

'Bill Torrance?' Thane made the connection. 'Springburn, when we had that arson job?'

'Sir.' It helped, but Torrance, a tall, unhappy bean-pole of a man, still had a stiff handshake. Like Moss – like everyone else around, Thane realised – Torrance wore rubber boots. But his were teamed with a blue business suit, a white shirt, and a Scottish Police Federation blue and red tie. 'My super's apologies. Pressure of duties.

'He's presenting prizes at a Community Involvement flower show,' said Moss helpfully.'

'It happens.' Torrance was embarrassed. 'Like I should be in court, giving evidence.'

'All right.' Thane saw Torrance's gathering uneasiness and knew what else was wrong. 'Let's get to it, inspector. So you're standing in for your boss, and this is your territory. But maybe we've a prior claim.' He stopped the man's protest with a gesture. 'Suppose we simply call it mutual aid for now, nothing more final, and let someone else sort it out later?'

'Mutual aid?' The divisional man hesitated. But it was a formula that soothed most ruffled feathers. He relaxed a little more and nodded. 'Done, sir.'

'Good.' Thane glanced at Moss. 'We're certain about the van?'

Moss nodded.

'And the body is Terry Anson?'

'One of them.' Moss gave the smallest of shrugs, his thin, lined face expressionless. 'We've – uh – got two bodies now.'

Momentarily speechless, Thane stared at him.

'Two and counting,' grated Torrance. 'We're still looking.'

A pace behind them, Sandra Craig gave an audible gulp. For Thane, the light hill wind had suddenly taken on a new chill.

'We had Anson first.' Moss shrugged almost apologetically. 'Number two turned up a few minutes ago, when you were on your way. Jock's dogs found it – he's taken them for a wider sniff around.'

Thane sucked hard on his teeth, mind struggling to cope with what he'd been told. A baa-ing near his feet startled him, then a stray sheep wandered past. He saw a few more around, escaped from one of the surrounding fields.

'Both probably shot through the back of the head,' said Moss mildly. He gave a slight smile towards Sandra. 'Or it looks that way. Maybe Doc Williams can say more – he's down with them now.'

'Two,' said Thane heavily.

'So far.' Torrance nodded miserably.

'Thank you,' snarled Thane. He drew a breath. 'Phil, what do we know?'

'We've a witness,' said Moss. The scrawny, unkempt addition to the Crime Squad strength had a speckling of dried mud on his face and small splashes on his clothing. 'He's a farmer. He's here.'

'He'll keep,' said Thane. 'Basics, Phil.'

'No problem.' Moss took a moment to fish a loose and grubby-looking pill from a jacket pocket, flick it into his mouth, and swallow. 'Our farmer is local. He was driving home along the single track around 4 a.m. He was in a Volvo station wagon – that's the wreck furthest from here, the Fiat is the other burn-out lying on its roof. There was moonlight. Our farmer sees a van without lights stopped off the road, near the loch. He saw men moving around it.'

There had been a recent history of night sheep-rustling raids on farms around the Dark Loch. The farmer had his shotgun in the Volvo. He stopped, got out, challenged the strangers, fired a warning with both barrels 'over their heads', then they were shooting back, for real.

'That's when it gets chaotic,' said Moss sourly. 'Our farmer's car had been hit and wouldn't start, so he does a sensible runner on foot. His "sheep-rustlers" come looking for him, he finds a hole and lies very low. After a spell his "sheep-rustlers" try to drive the van away but overturn it on the way back up to the road. Next thing, he's looking at his Volvo and the van both burning.'

He had seen at least four men. At least one had an automatic rifle. Eventually the farmer heard another car start up and drive away. But he had still stayed in hiding, watching the two torched vehicles burn themselves out. He eventually risked making his way home at around dawn.

'He called the police.' Moss passed it to Torrance.

'We sent a traffic car to have a look.' Torrance shrugged. 'They checked things out, reported back to Division – the usual.'

'Then?' Thane waited stonily.

'There was a road accident on the A77, further out – a fatal. Division ordered the traffic car to sort it out. Then as soon as there were a couple of CID officers available, they were sent here.' Defensively Torrance scowled. 'Rustlers, guns, burned-out cars – hell, superintendent, we've heard it all before around here. Every-thing bar the bloody Seventh Cavalry coming over the hill.'

The CID men had spoken to the farmer, had gone on to the Dark Loch, had taken a routine look at the two burned-out vehicles, then had been curious enough to make a reasonably careful search around the shoreline. They'd found the first body dumped in a partly dug grave, some loose soil shovelled hastily on top of it, but a shoe and the foot inside it protruding in a way that had been hard to miss.

'So then it was different.' Torrance avoided Thane's eyes. 'What went wrong was that it was a reasonable spell before anybody realised that one of the torched vehicles might be the Fiat van in your special search request.'

'How long?' snarled Thane. He saw Torrance's hesitation. 'From when the shots were fired, man!'

'Nine hours.' Torrance scowled down at the mud, obviously as sick as anyone. 'Six hours from the time the farmer reported it.' He shook his head. 'It was a foul-up. Wrong priorities, a scrappy start-off incident report for the computer. A total damned glitch. If we'd had a decent incident report – '

'Happens,' said Moss with an abrasive sympathy. He glanced at Sandra Craig. 'Doesn't it, sergeant?'

She flushed.

'The idiot responsible for this one goes to school crossings duty tomorrow,' said Torrance grimly. He looked for a chance to escape. 'I'm due to make a check back to Division. Can I?'

Thane nodded and Torrance strode away.

'Phil.' Thane glanced around. 'Where's Francey?'

'With Doc Williams at the graves.' Moss gave a mild, low-key belch and considered Sandra with some care. 'How are you around bodies, sergeant?'

'You mean dead ones, inspector?' said Sandra Craig with a caustic innocence.

Moss scowled and turned to Thane. 'Them next?'

Thane nodded.

'Then over here first.' Moss led the way across to the major incident van. Going in, he came out again with two pairs of rubber boots. He handed one pair to Thane and tossed the other pair towards Sandra Craig. 'You'll need them.'

They exchanged their shoes for the boots, and set off towards the shore of the loch and the canvas screen. After a few paces, they began squelching through a mixture of mud and gravel.

When they reached the screen, the breeze was making the canvas shake and ripple while Thane led the way past. Then they stopped.

Two shallow, partly waterlogged graves lay opened in the sunlight in front of them. There were several people standing around, including four uniformed men in overalls, the digging squad, still leaning on their spades. Close by, a Scenes of Crime photographer was sharing a flask of coffee with another technician.

But only the graves mattered, each still containing a mummy-like shape wrapped in coarse, mud-stained cloth. Doc Williams, slim, dark-haired and inevitably as immaculate as ever even in overalls and white hospital-issue boots, was squatting in the nearer grave, Francey Dunbar beside him. The Crime Squad's new acting detective inspector saw Thane and nudged Williams, who looked round, then nodded a cheerful greeting.

'I thought you'd got lost, man!' The police surgeon rose, splashed his way out of the shallow grave, and came over, wiping his hands on a piece of waste rag. He gestured around. 'Nice place for it, right?'

'True.' Thane liked Williams and knew his ways. 'What have we got, Doc?'

'Medical?' Williams shrugged. 'Not a lot. Two males, each apparently killed with a single gunshot through the back of the head. Execution style. He thumbed at the shapeless bundle at his feet. 'I'm told this one is yours. Want a look?'

Thane sighed, nodded, and followed as Williams splashed back down into the shallow trench again.

'He was killed somewhere around thirty-six hours ago.' Squatting down, the police surgeon gave an almost apologetic shrug. 'A loch site like this knocks hell out of time-of-death arithmetic.'

'It's near enough for now.' Thane knelt beside him, mind registering the way the dead man had been neatly parcelled head-to-foot then tied with cord. He glanced across at the other grave.

'Same kind of packaging,' said Francey Dunbar softly, reading his mind.

'So – ' Doc Williams carefully lifted open a layer of cloth which had been covering the dead man's face and held it back. 'Has Francey got it right, Colin?'

Thane looked for a long moment, then nodded. Terry Anson's thin face was slack-jawed in death, his blue eyes stared lifelessly, his mousy brown hair was matted with blood from the crater-like exit wound on the left frontal side of his skull. In life, a man's face didn't too often match his SCRO record picture.

In death, Terry Anson did.

Something small and grey moved cautiously around the edge of Anson's mouth. Before Thane could do anything about it, Sandra Craig silently reached past him and flicked the crawling water snail away.

'Thank you, sergeant,' he said formally.

'Sir.' Her face was pale.

Doc Williams covered the dead man's face. 'Now the other one, Colin.'

They went over to the second grave. This was different. Thane knew it from the faint, sweet-sour smell of decay that immediately met his nostrils.

'Looking for anyone else?' asked the police surgeon.

'From how far back?' Thane thought of Les Harrow.

'Six months, maybe more.'

'Too long.' Thane shook his head.

'A pity,' mused Doc Williams. Stooping, he lifted a cut flap of cloth from the other wrapped body. 'We've a problem.'

Colin Thane felt his stomach heave. A rotted nightmare of a skull stared up at him, most of its flesh and soft tissue long since rotted away or infested by small, squirming white maggots. He saw long, dark hair. A couple of gold fillings glinted from grinning teeth.

'I'd say European, maybe in his late twenties, probably fairly tall – guesswork, of course.' The police surgeon used a blue ballpoint pen as a probe. 'Bullet holes here – and here. Same as before, shot from behind, then your exit wound in this frontal area. He removed the ballpoint, frowned at the way a fragment of rotted tissue came with it, wiped the ballpoint clean on a leg of his overalls, then grimaced mildly towards Sandra Craig. 'Well past his sell-by date. Agreed, sergeant?'

Sandra Craig's face had gone several shades paler. Suddenly she turned, made a gagging noise, then almost ran out of their sight to the other side of the canvas screen. They heard her vomiting.

'Ah well.' Doc Williams covered over the horror at his feet, and gave an apologetic shrug. 'She's young.'

'She'll learn,' said Thane quietly. He glanced at Moss. 'Plenty of photographs?'

Moss nodded.

'I want a full forensic team search around both graves as soon as we've moved the bodies. Soil samples, the lot.' He swung back to Doc Williams. 'The usual, Doc.'

'I may have the odd miracle left,' said the police surgeon modestly.

'When?'

90

'When I'm ready,' snarled Williams. 'Don't push your luck.' He frowned suspiciously as Francey Dunbar prowled around him again. 'And what's your problem, laddy?'

'Just curious.' Dunbar gave an apologetic grin. 'I suppose the way they're both parcelled could be interesting.'

'Uh-huh. Could be.' A wisp of approval showed on Doc Williams' face then had gone. He glanced at his wrist-watch. 'Now will you will get the hell out of my way? I've an appointment in town with a patient.'

'A live one?' Moss raised a derisive eyebrow. 'Do you wash your hands first, Doc?'

'And stuff you,' scowled the police surgeon.

They left him and collected Sandra Craig. Her face was still pale, but no one said anything.

'The farmer next,' decided Thane. 'But not you, Francey. Keep the troops searching along the shoreline. We've got two bodies, let's be very sure that it ends there.' He paused and looked around the sweep of empty loch and moorland. 'And find Jock Dawson and his four-legged friends. I want to know what the hell he's been doing. Try barking at him.'

'Barking. Like in mad.' Dunbar grinned and left him, striding briskly across the rough ground.

'He's right about the way they're wrapped,' mused Moss, watching him go. He grimaced. 'Packaged like twins.'

'A rolling hitch,' said Sandra Craig almost to herself.

They stared at her.

'It's a seamen's knot.' She tried a faint smile. 'Used on both of them.'

Moss frowned his doubt. 'And how do you happen to know about seamen's knots, sergeant?'

'I've done some sailing, inspector,' said Sandra Craig coldly. 'With a friend.'

Thane nodded. He had met him, a Royal Navy lieutenant commander who laid siege to the redhead every leave. Currently his ship was on patrol in the Gulf.

'A rolling hitch. You're sure?' he asked.

She nodded. 'It's quick and easy. It won't slip, it takes a lot of strain. Somebody knows how to use it, and neatly.'

So a seaman could be involved somewhere in both murders. Small pieces always added together sooner or later, even if in

91

ways that weren't expected. They followed Moss across the rough grass and low scrub towards one of the parked police cars. When Moss reached it, the sole occupant emerged warily.

'This is Hugh Flood,' said Moss drily. 'Mr Flood, this is Detective Superintendent Thane and Detective Sergeant Craig.'

They exchanged handshakes. The farmer was a tall, lanky man in his late thirties, still red-eyed from lack of sleep, in need of a wash, a shave, and a change of clothing. His heavy tweed suit was mud-stained and had a long tear down one shoulder. His white shirt, badly stained and crumpled, was fastened at the neck but without a tie. There was more mud on what had been well-polished brown boots.

'You had a bad time,' said Thane sympathetically.

'My own fault. I was a pure bloody fool,' said Flood. His stale whisky breath hit Thane like a wave. 'They might have killed me, right?'

His farm, which he ran with one helper, was named Highshiels. He described it as 'a slice o' rocky moorland and a few hundred sheep'.

'Do you live on your own?' asked Thane.

'I'm married. She's on holiday with her sister.' Flood hauled a crumpled pack of cigarettes out of his pocket and lit a cigarette with a bookmatch. 'She's going to give me hell over this, man.'

Thane gave a small shrug in mild sympathy.

'Why so late on the road, Mr Flood?'

'There's a wee poker game at one o' the farms, once a week.' Flood blinked as some of his cigarette smoke caught at his eyes and made them water. 'Just a friendly game, the same lads, a few drams. We're all farmers.'

'A good night?' suggested Moss, a small twinkle in his eyes.

'Damned good night,' agreed Flood. 'Win a little, lose a little. Nae women allowed.' He glanced at Sandra. 'Nothing against women, sergeant. Just a wee break from them.'

'But did it go on until 4 a.m.?' pressed Thane.

'Only till two. But I'd had more drink than I could handle,' admitted the lanky farmer sadly. 'I nearly put the car into a ditch a couple o' times when I tried for home. So I stopped – for a wee rest, right? When I woke up again, the time was 4 a.m.' He sighed. 'It was the drink, superintendent. If I'd been sober, I wouldn't have stuck out my damned fool nose the way I did. But now?' He scowled. 'I've lost my car, I'll get an all-round bollocking from the wife, and there's you folk too!'

'How was your poker luck?' asked Sandra mildly.

'Three aces always beats three jacks,' grunted Flood. 'I had the jacks.'

His story was basic. Finally driving home, he had seen the parked, unlit van in the faint moonlight and figures moving around it. He had stopped, had decided they were rustlers, had shouted a warning, then had fired his shotgun as a warning.

They'd promptly terrified him by firing back. He couldn't give descriptions. From that moment on, his only interest had been in hiding. Yes, he was sure there had been a third vehicle but he hadn't seen it, had just heard the sound of it eventually starting up and pulling away.

'I lost ten sheep in one raid last summer.' Gloomily, he removed the final stub of cigarette before it singed his lips. 'But last night's bunch weren't rustlers, were they?'

Thane shook his head.

'Aye.' Flood rasped a dirty thumbnail across his unshaven chin. 'These days I'm a sheep farmer. But I know my weapons, superintendent. I was a platoon sergeant in the best damned infantry regiment in the world, the Royal Scots. I served out in Desert Storm. For certain, one of that bunch last night, this mornin' – or whenever the hell you want to call it – had an automatic rifle. Had it, an' knew how to use it. You'd better remember that.'

They were finished with him. A divisional car was organised to take him home.

Once he'd gone, Thane walked the rest of the distance towards the two burned-out vehicles with Moss and Sandra following. As they went, they disturbed a few of the stray sheep which were around; the animals scattered back where they belonged.

When he reached the vehicles, he grimaced. Both had been reduced almost beyond recognition. Only the engine block identi- fied the van as having been a Fiat. For Fiat and Volvo alike, the rest was mainly distorted metal, destroyed glass and the spider web remains of what had once been main wiring harnesses. The scorched ground around each was thick with grey ash and black soot, and a clinging smell of burning still hung in the air.

They retreated back towards the police vehicles. Beyond them, behind the canvas screen, an electronic camera flash was blinking. In the background a line of uniforms had resumed their step-by-step search along a fresh stretch of lochside. There was no sign of Francey Dunbar, whatever direction he had taken. But two Scenes of Crime men were doing things with a measuring tape.

One tall and thin, the other small and fat, everyone knew Boomerang and The Pawnbroker. They always worked together, two sergeants whose real names were almost forgotten. They seldom missed anything.

Thane went over to them. He asked, 'What have you got so far?'

Boomerang and The Pawnbroker exchanged a cautious glance which was part of their don't-tell-them-much outlook. Then Boomerang relented a little.

'Ballistics are going to be interested in these.' He dragged a plastic evidence bag from one pocket and the capricious sun glinted on an assortment of used brass cartridge cases.

Thane looked and sucked his teeth. 'Automatic rifle.'

Boomerang's long, thin face shaped agreement. 'Like the farmer said.'

That was the apparent ration of information they were prepared to give out. They had plenty still to do.

'But we'll get back to you, superintendent,' promised the tall, thin sergeant.

His small, fat companion beamed on time-honoured cue. 'Leave it with us, superintendent.'

Boomerang and The Pawnbroker had struck again.

Swearing softly, Thane led the others over to the major incident van. The woman constable running the communications desk had a supply of coffee and doughnuts on offer, and they were glad to see them. Thane told Sandra to check back with Joe Felix at headquarters, then beckoned Moss through to the temporarily unused briefing room further along the big, box-like vehicle.

'It looks an all-round nasty, Phil.' He took a swallow of coffee, following it with a first bite of doughnut. 'We've got trouble.'

'Odds-on trouble.' Moss gave a dyspeptic scowl. 'Why the hell did they kill Anson?'

'Because we knew about him, maybe. If he also knew enough to matter.' Thane shrugged. 'What's the best way to stop a leak?'

'Before it happens.' Moss gulped his coffee. The hot liquid had steamed the van window beside him and he cleared a sweep with his hand to look towards the lochside. 'We're not doing too much winning anywhere. SCRO ran a full computer check on any Crusher listing like you asked. Total zero.'

Thane nodded his acceptance. Scottish Criminal Records had 680,000 names on its big mainframe Bull computer, several times that number of listings again in terms of details from scars and tattoos to nicknames and known MOs. If they said they didn't have something, they meant it.

'Phil.' For a moment, he forced his mind away from the two packaged bodies in those graves, one with its dead face, the other with its decomposed head. 'How hard did you lean on Sandra?'

A wintry grin touched Moss's lips. 'Hard enough. You gave me a free hand, remember?' Then his eyes narrowed. 'Why?'

'She may go for your throat.'

'Good.' Moss chuckled, relaxed, swallowed more coffee, and gave a raucous two-tone belch. A sheep outside the window decided to scurry. 'Knock her into shape, and you've got a damned good sergeant. Maybe accelerated promotion material – and to do that when you're a woman you've got to be the best. But right now she needs her backside kicked.'

Thane frowned. 'Why?'

Moss shook his head. 'That's for me to know, me to sort out.'

'All right.' Thane knew he was right. 'Something else, Phil. What the hell's a Sinbad?'

'Like in Hello Sailor?' Moss grunted. 'No idea.'

Sandra Craig joined them. She had her own ration of coffee and a massive slab of cherry cake. Most of the colour was back in her cheeks.

'Anything?' queried Thane.

'Nothing that can't wait, sir.' She shook her head.

'Any word back from London on the other name, this Les Harrow?' asked Moss.

'Not yet.' Sandra's manner was still cool. But Thane gauged the worst was over. 'We have him listed in Glasgow for a couple of small convictions for theft. But nothing recent.' She turned to Thane again. 'Joe wants to know if we'll want Terry Anson's wife for an ID. If we do, he says not to expect a broken heart.'

'It can wait.' Thane stayed at the window. He could see the tall, gloomy figure of Torrance, the divisional DI, plodding across the grass towards the major incident van. 'But we'll need to tell her. I don't want some all-singing all-dancing journalist getting in first.'

Torrance reached the van steps and they felt the big trailer rock as he stepped aboard. In another couple of minutes he joined them. He had done his rounds and the officers he'd sent visiting the scatter of isolated farms and the few private homes within a reasonable radius had returned from that task. Other farmers in Hugh Flood's poker game had been interviewed and had confirmed that part of his story.

'Take a stab at something for me,' invited Thane. 'Two executions. Why bury them out here?'

'It's lonely, yet not far out of town. Easy to reach by road.' Torrance sighed unhappily. 'Wild, yet easy digging with a shovel. Just my bad luck it's on my patch.'

'Then what about the van?' demanded Thane.

'Uh – ' Torrance hesitated, puzzled.

'Why bring the Fiat out here?' persisted Thane.

'To dump it in Dark Loch?' suggested Moss.

'No.' Torrance snorted at the idea. 'Too shallow. Do that, and you could still dance on the roof. But we've a couple of old deep-hole quarries, not far from here – so many vehicles get dumped there that we just clean them out every few months.'

'Months?' Sandra Craig frowned. 'Environmentally – '

'Stuff the environment, sergeant,' snarled Torrance. 'We've a tight budget.' He scowled out at the landscape. 'There's your doggy man coming.'

They looked. Jock Dawson was striding over the rough moorland towards them. The lanky Crime Squad dog-handler was throwing a stick ahead of him as he came, for the benefit of the two dogs bounding energetically around him.

'Time I tried to contact my boss again.' Torrance made it almost a challenge. 'He should be back at Division by now.'

'Let's hope he enjoyed his flower show,' said Moss blandly.

'Go to hell.' Torrance turned on his heel and left them.

Gesturing Moss and Sandra Craig to follow, Thane went out to meet Dawson in the open.

'We practically posted you missing,' said Thane. He saw Dawson was carrying a crumped bundle under one arm. 'What's that?'

'Found it, sir,' said Dawson laconically. The dog-handler was in his early forties and he had a sleepy, lived-in face which showed no particular emotion as he gave a flick of his arm and revealed his bundle. It was a man's grey blouson jacket, muddied, heavily stained red with blood down one side. 'A fox had dragged it around. That's why I brought it in.'

'From where?' Thane was aware that, without any command,

both dogs were now crouching down beside Dawson, bright-eyed, totally watchful.

'Back there a bit, sir.' Dawson thumbed the way he'd come. 'Behind some scrub, near a bend in the road. It looks like a car stopped there for a spell, with people.' He saw Thane's question coming. 'I grabbed a couple of the local cops coming down. They're taking care of the rest.'

Thane nodded. It wasn't the regular way to handle possible evidence, but he wasn't going to argue. Under the blood and mud, the blouson jacket looked good quality – and the blood, though dried, was comparatively fresh with a buzzing cluster of flies busy around it.

'Farmer Flood firing over their heads?' suggested Moss drily. 'This gives them a good reason for shooting back in earnest!' He frowned. 'Francey was sent to find you. Did you see him?'

'No, inspector.' Dawson shrugged. 'Maybe he fell down a hole somewhere.'

'If he did, maybe there's room in it for two of you,' growled Thane.

The dog-handler grinned, unperturbed. The Crime Squad had been conned into taking Dawson and his dogs by a dog branch chief inspector who saw Dawson as beyond any kind of redemption. But Dawson lived for his dogs and the dogs probably felt the same way about him. Rajah, the big German Shepherd, was ten years old, due to be pensioned off on age from police work according to regulations. The only sign Rajah was ageing was a faint trace of grey around his muzzle and he had been Dawson's dog since a pup. The other half of the team, Goldie, was a slim, golden-coated two-year-old Labrador bitch trained for drugs and explosives work, and Rajah's official replacement. But Rajah had been Dawson's first dog. He simply kept them both and gave a two-fingered response to the rules. One look at Rajah, and nobody felt like disputing things.

'Nicely done.' Now, the dogs had scored another small triumph. Thane thumbed towards the Scenes of Crime team. 'Dump the jacket on Boomerang and The Pawnbroker. Tell them the story.'

'Then I'll take a break, sir.' Dawson glanced at his dogs. Goldie promptly scratched herself behind one ear while Rajah gave an awesome grin. 'These two need to be fed and watered.'

'They're not alone,' muttered Sandra Craig.

Thane ignored her and turned to Moss. 'Phil, I'm going back to headquarters. Sandra comes with me. You stay here with Jock until things wind down for the day. Don't forget Francey – and make friendly noises to the divisional team.'

Moss belched. It was comment enough.

Sandra Craig driving the Volkswagen, Thane her passenger again, they left Dark Loch at the same time as a couple of press cars made a wary approach towards the taped-off scene.

The sight made Thane curse, although he was partly surprised that the media had taken so long to find out that something was going on at the lochside. But it also made up his mind in another direction.

A few minutes later, when they were back on the main road and heading in towards the city, he used the Volkswagen's radio. Raising the Crime Squad, he got a patch through to Joe Felix in the duty room.

'There are a bundle of people looking for you, boss,' reported the middle-aged detective constable gloomily. 'Mostly I've been fending them off, answering phones, and scratching. Sometimes just scratching. Not much action here.'

'Enjoy it while it lasts.' They were making good time along the road. Thane could already see the start of the city's skyline in the distance. 'I need the address for Terry Anson's wife.'

He gave Thane the address. Once he had that, Thane wanted something more. 'Put a call into Barlinnie Prison, Joe. Tell them I'll be along in an hour or so, and that it's urgent I talk with their remand prisoner, Freddy Peters. They got him from court this morning.'

'Freddy Peters, the pride of Blenheim Rise?' Felix understood. 'Will do.'

Thane signed off and tossed the microphone back on its shelf.

'You were going to wait before you told Anson's wife,' reminded Sandra Craig from behind the steering wheel, giving him a quick, puzzled glance.

'I changed my mind,' he said shortly. Breaking bad news was a dirty job, but he'd caught a glimpse of one of the journalists in one of the press cars. He was a merciless shark who interviewed without pity.

'Sir, this maybe doesn't matter right now.' Sandra Craig carefully kept her eyes on the road. 'But I got a chance to run that PNC check on the car outside Emma Raleigh's boutique – '

'The white Mazda.' Thane nodded absently. 'Peter Dutch, the TV man – '

'He was the driver, yes.' The redhead frowned. 'But Emma Raleigh is the registered owner.'

'So she loans boyfriend her car,' grunted Thane. He hadn't forgotten Emma Raleigh. He hadn't forgotten a list of other things. But the two bodies by the lochside had set their own priorities. 'All right, find out if there's any gossip. When you've time.'

She nodded, snapped off a couple of squares from a chocolate bar, and popped them in her mouth. The bar was waved in Thane's direction, and he did the same.

Scots knew Castlemilk as one of Europe's biggest local authority housing projects, old enough now to look sad and dreary, a monument to bad planning and the politician's idea that all people needed for improved life-style was a bathroom and flush toilet. The police knew Castlemilk as *Château Lait*, cynical nickname for just another area where ordinary families worried more about the risks of their children playing with discarded drug needles than the lesser chance of being mugged.

Terry Anson's wife Martha lived in a second-floor flat in a long concrete terrace. Both flats on the ground floor were empty, and the housing department had done its usual act of sealing them off with steel doors and metal window grilles to prevent vandals moving in.

A dark-haired young woman, thin, sallow-faced, poorly dressed, she was wary from the moment she opened the door. The four-year-old clinging to her side was equally sallow, fat, and aggressively noisy. Martha Anson took them into a living-room which was shabbily furnished but spotlessly clean. So was her child. She didn't ask either of her visitors to sit down.

'About Terry again?' she asked.

Thane looked at the child, who was staring and had gone silent. 'Would you like a neighbour to come in, Martha?'

'That bad?' She pursed her lips but her eyes stayed steady. 'You've found him?'

Thane nodded. 'We think so. We'd like you to look at him. But not yet.'

'I see.' Probably without realising it, she laid a hand on the

99

child's mop of hair. 'You're not breakin' my heart, superintendent. He did that years ago. What happened?'

Thane looked at Sandra Craig.

'He was shot,' said Sandra. 'Through the head, Martha. I'm sorry.'

'Shot?' The woman gave a short, shrill laugh. 'Too damn good for him. Too damn quick. An' it's like I told the wee detective who came earlier – I haven't seen him, I wasn't lookin' for him. Last time he was here it was my birthday. He was drunk.'

'Celebrating drunk?' asked Thane.

'Like in Happy Birthday Martha?' she asked caustically. 'He beat me up, mister. Knocked out two teeth, broke a rib. Right?'

She had talked enough. The child had begun crying again. They let her lead them back to the door, then she closed the door hard and quick on them.

But not quick enough. Thane had seen the start of tears in her eyes. Maybe for what might have been.

5

It was dusk by the time they drove across the city to its east side and the gloomy grey bulk of Barlinnie Prison. They parked the Volkswagen, then there was the usual routine of going through the gate procedures with guards who were glad of any break in their normal monotony. From the gatehouse, they were escorted across a yard, then through concrete corridors where the air smelled of old urine and cheap disinfectant. They could hear the occasional shouts of men they couldn't see and a clatter of crockery being gathered in after the evening meal.

They were shown into an interview room. Freddy Peters was already there. The spiky-haired Blenheim Rise teenager, still wearing his own street clothing because he was a remand prisoner, sat on a chair at one side of a table. A bored but watchful prison officer leaned against the wall behind him.

'You!' The teenager stared at Colin Thane in surprise. Moistening his lips, he appealed over his shoulder to the prison officer. 'Shouldn't I have a lawyer or something?'

'Depends what they want to talk to you about. Nothing to do with me, Freddy boy.' The guard glanced at his wrist-watch, then at Thane. 'Call of nature, superintendent. Do you mind?'

Thane shook his head. As the guard winked and left, the two visitors settled in chairs positioned at their side of the table.

'Look, mister – ' Peters made one more try at being aggressive. 'I'm not sayin' anything. Not till I'm in court with a lawyer, right?'

'You'd better listen,' said Thane unemotionally. He stretched back in his chair as he spoke. 'You could do yourself a favour, keep your nose clean. There's a good new reason.'

'Like what?' asked the teenager, suspicious but curious.

'Tell him, sergeant,' said Thane.

'Terry Anson turned up,' said Sandra flatly. 'Dead, Freddy.

He'd been shot through the back of the head. Then he was dumped.'

The teenager's mouth fell open, then he swallowed.

'Where – where was it?'

'He was found out on the Fenwick Moor.' Sandra shrugged. 'After they shot him, his friends scraped the start of a hole, then dropped him into it. They didn't do a very neat job.'

'And that's why we're here,' said Thane simply. 'You're still the last person we can name who saw Terry Anson alive. That makes you interesting, Freddy. You say you saw the men who grabbed Anson at Blenheim Rise – but you didn't know them, couldn't identify them again.' He allowed himself to lean a little forward in the chair. 'Any chance you want to change any of that?'

Peters moistened his lips. 'Suppose I don't? What happens?'

Thane sighed. 'Sergeant?'

'What we sometimes do, sir,' she lied with a small smile on her lips. 'Drop any charges against Freddy, have him released, I suppose. Tell people how much he did to help us.'

It was a time-worn routine, but it still often worked.

'You – you couldn't!' The teenager stared in horror. 'I'd be crucified outside!'

'Probably,' agreed Thane. 'But if your memory suddenly improved we'd put in a word at court. You're small-time, Freddy. You might just get community service. Your own social worker, you'd paint public lavatories or dig gardens. But it's up to you.'

Peters buried his thin face in his hands and it was a full minute before he looked up. He gave a slow, defeated nod.

'I knew one of them. I – I'd seen him around Blenheim Rise with Terry.' He chewed on his lower lip. 'Terry called him Duff – that's all I know. For real.'

Sandra nodded. 'Describe him.'

'In his thirties, heavy build, ordinary height. Dark hair but thinnin' a bit – an' a small scar on his nose.' The teenager shook his head. 'He's a smart dresser, and maybe English from the way he talks. That's it, except he drives an old green Mercedes – a banger.'

'Good,' said Thane. 'What about the others with him?'

Peters frowned. 'No. I didn't know any of them.'

They tried for more from him. But anything Freddy Peters could offer in the way of descriptions was vague and unreliable, and he claimed he had no real idea how the late Terry Anson had made his money.

The prison officer returned, humming softly under his breath, and asked, 'Finished with him, superintendent?'

'For now.' Thane nodded.

'Eh – can I ask you something, Mr Thane?' The man lowered his voice. 'There's a story goin' around in here that three prisoners in the untried wing could walk. You know them – the three your people nailed for the security van hijack. Something about a witness you need who has done a runner.' He gave a small, warily apologetic grin. 'Is it true they could walk?'

'Wishful thinking,' said Thane grimly.

'Glad to hear it. They're three real awkward bastards.' The prison officer glanced at Freddy Peters and beckoned. 'Right, son. Heel – let's go.'

The moon was partly obscured by cloud and there was a definite hint of rain in the air by the time the Volkswagen arrived at Crime Squad headquarters. They left the vehicle in the floodlit parking lot, then went into the brightly lit, still busy building. Sandra headed straight towards the main duty room but as Thane passed the reception area he saw Commander Hart coming along the corridor towards him.

'The return of the wanderer,' Hart greeted him with a wry nod. 'You owe me, Colin. I'm talking serious owing.'

'Like what?' Thane was puzzled. Hart, carrying his briefcase, was obviously on his way home. 'How?'

'Like I spent half an hour keeping that little tyke Hilson off your back.' Jack Hart's lined, habitually sad-eyed face shaped a grimace at the thought. 'He gave me a headache beating a big drum about how you would have to drop charges against his man.'

Thane shaped a grimace of his own. Calling Martin Hilson a tyke was unkind to tykes. Hilson was the defence solicitor for Gonzo Patrick, the one name among the three in custody for the security van raid who was linked to Terry Anson.

'I sent him on his way, no rejoicing,' said Hart bleakly. 'But he'll be back, snapping at our heels.' He paused to acknowledge the nodds from two plain-clothes men who were heading out. They were shabby and unshaven, in old leather jackets and army surplus khakis, the night half of a team tagging a mini-sized drugs baron. He was aged fourteen, he sold around five city schools, and it was known he was waiting on an Ecstasy delivery. When it arrived, he would be grabbed. 'I've also had HMCI twittering at me.'

That mattered more. 'Wanting what?'

'We're his flavour of the month, the sharp end of his personal crusade against counterfeiting,' said Hart wearily. 'Whatever happens, he wants a constant update. Make sure he gets it, Colin – for all our sakes.'

'I'll try.' It was something Thane could have done without. The Cutters and their brutal piracy operation were interesting too many people who could throw weight around.

'Good.' Hart stopped what might have been a yawn. 'I've seen Moss since he got back. What about you? Anything new to add?'

'A few more things we can start running.' Thane left it at that. 'Some of them can be dumped as inquiries on the night shift.'

'But don't expect miracles?' Hart understood. It was part of his job to know the signs. He took a deep breath and hefted his briefcase. 'Well, I'm heading home. You know why? Because I've a wedding anniversary to celebrate – mine, and I'm already tight for time. If I'm any later, blood will flow.'

Thane grinned. He knew Hart's wife, liked her. Even so, she was a woman with enough of a temper to worry most men.

Once Hart had left, Thane went along to the duty room. It was that early evening time when it was always busy, as the night shift took over, but his team had seized a corner as their own and were there complete with Jock Dawson and his dogs.

'Update time,' Thane told them, and met a set of resigned faces. Even Moss didn't look particularly keen. 'What have we got?'

'Mainly mud by the look of things, sir,' said Jock Dawson laconically.

Francey Dunbar scowled at the dog-handler. Dunbar had a thick coating of dried mud on his shoes, more mud or worse on his trousers all the way up to the knees, and dried splashes on his leather jacket. He also smelled distinctly foul.

'Where did you find him, Jock?' asked Thane, fighting down a chuckle.

'Up to his middle in a patch o' bog and sheep yuck, sir,' reported Dawson cheerfully. 'He'd got himself lost. I brought him back in the van, though the dogs didn't like it.'

'Stay upwind of him,' advised Moss acidly. 'It's better that way.'

'Believe it, sir,' contributed Sandra Craig.

'What's so damned funny?' complained Dunbar. His thin face was indignant. 'That stuff could have swallowed me for ever.'

'We'd have missed you,' said Joe Felix, his eyes twinkling. 'Never mind, Francey. We'd have chipped in for a marker stone. You know the kind of thing – "Our poor Francey lost his way, now he's under the mire to stay."'

'Stuff your poetry,' snarled the new acting detective inspector. 'I'll need to scrape some of this stuff off with a knife.'

'Enough,' Thane told them. He glanced at Felix. 'What have you got, Joe?'

'Some more detail on Les Harrow, sir.' Felix perched on the edge of a desk and glanced at his notebook. 'Yes, he took off for London, like you were told. But then it seems he got himself killed under a bus.' He shrugged at Thane's disbelief. 'It looks kosher, sir. The Met officers who handled it say it was a straight accident with formal coroner's inquest, everybody satisfied.'

'Except Harrow,' muttered Thane.

Felix grinned and nodded. 'That's about it so far, sir. We've nothing on any heavy called Crusher, nothing more on the Cutters team. At least not yet.'

'Feed the name Duff to the computers,' Thane told him. 'He's probably a ned, it's probably another nickname.' He felt an irrational anger at the report of Les Harrow's death, even in an accident. It was just one more blank wall. 'Anything else, Joe?'

'Some phone calls for you.' Felix turned a page of his notebook. 'Gypsy Adams at Trading Standards, twice in the past hour. He says call him. Then I had that Reebok man, Rae. He said it wasn't urgent, but would you call him at home.' He had the phone number on a slip of paper, which he passed to Thane. 'There were others, but you can forget them.'

'I will.' Joe Felix could be relied on as a filter. Thane glanced at Moss. 'Phil?'

'I've made a few calls.' Moss's lean, leathery features twitched in a momentary frown and he scratched hard under one arm. 'Uh – Doc Williams says he'll have some kind of an autopsy report on both bodies put together by 11 a.m. tomorrow – no earlier. Forensic says they're trying for the same kind of target.' He paused, frowned again, scratched again, then glared first at the dogs and then at Dunbar. 'Hell, I'm being bitten by something!'

'It's not from my dogs, inspector!' Indignantly, Jock Dawson called his dogs closer to his feet and away from Francey Dunbar.

'Now wait a minute – ' began Dunbar, scowling.

'Not now, Francey.' Thane cut his protest short. 'Later, all right?' He turned back to Moss. 'What else?'

'Some good news,' said Moss, looking happier. 'Scenes of Crime say they've managed partial fingerprints off body number two, maybe enough to try for an SCRO scan through records. And Ballistics are positive that there was an automatic rifle used out at Dark Loch. Probably a Kalashnikov.'

'Thoughts?' asked Thane, considering the faces around him.

'It might be worth trying the Met again about Les Harrow's death,' suggested Francey Dunbar. 'All right, it was an accident. But there might be something in the details.'

'Try it, Joe,' Thane told Joe Felix. 'Then keep searching every force report you can lay your hands on that says "counterfeit". Look for anything that might interest us.'

'There's the Emma Raleigh angle,' suggested Sandra, chewing on a pencil. 'And boyfriend.'

'Yes, but tomorrow,' qualified Thane. 'They're not high priority as things stand.' He glanced at Moss. 'What have we put together on them so far?'

'Emma Raleigh seems clean.' Moss shrugged. 'By tomorrow we can have checked this – uh – '

'Peter Dutch,' reminded Felix helpfully.

'The TV man.' Moss paused, then added darkly, 'Talking of tomorrow, a reminder for everybody. Reports, please. Up-to-date, first priority. Don't think it's just you. I'm chasing every team in this building. You lot just happen to be the worst.'

'Everybody's priority,' agreed Thane, knowing the support was needed. 'We're all being leaned on.' He paused, sadly considered the muddy, evil-smelling Francey Dunbar, then his mouth twitched as he nodded to Jock Dawson. 'Jock, take Francey home in your van. My apologies to the dogs.'

'Try putting him through a car wash on the way,' grunted Moss.

'Back to work.' Thane ended the grins around. 'Phil, I want you to go out and talk with Liz Hill. Take Sandra.'

'I could do it on my own, sir,' protested Sandra Craig. 'I don't need an escort, not with Liz.'

'You could do it,' agreed Thane. 'But I want Phil Moss to have a try at her.' He ignored her frown and focused on Moss again. 'I'll be here, Phil. Remember that this woman shouldn't know that either Anson or Harrow is dead. So play it gently at first.'

'Then see what I can shake loose.' Moss nodded his understanding, then tossed Thane the Mondeo keys. 'You'd better have these back.' He rose, beckoning to Sandra. 'Let's do it, sergeant. Take the Volkswagen.'

They left, Sandra still unhappy. Joe Felix had already vanished, and suddenly Thane was totally alone in the duty room except for a woman constable in another corner, speaking quietly on a telephone. The atmosphere was so quiet it was unnatural.

He had a few things of his own to do. He left the duty room and went along the corridor to his small office. Lifting the telephone, he dialled Gypsy Adams' number at Trading Standards. Within seconds, the CATS supervisor was on the line.

'Thanks for calling back,' said Adams. 'I've heard some of what's happening. Two bodies, one of them Anson for sure, the other an unknown male who has been buried for a spell. Right so far?'

'That's how it stands,' agreed Thane.

'Two.' Adams made a tooth-sucking noise. 'Are we talking Cutters?'

'It looks that way,' agreed Thane. 'We've also a third death, apparently accidental. Not here.' He told Adams about Les Harrow's death in London.

'A pity. He might have been useful,' mused the CATS supervisor, then brightened. 'Well, I maybe have better news – something shaping for tomorrow or the day after. If it comes off, I could use some of your people as back-up muscle.'

'For what?' Headlamps flickered past outside his window, another Squad pool car on its way somewhere.

'Remember Mega Mickey, the computer game king my boys hauled in this morning?' Adams made a happy noise over the line. 'Thane, he's offering to do a deal – we let half of his fake discs walk out again by the back door, and he says he can give us a lead on a Cutters' counterfeit factory base. He says it's new and it's not far out of town.'

'Why the offer?'

'It's not Mickey's usual style,' admitted Adams warily. 'But our raid knocked him back for just about everything he's got. He says he's desperate.'

'You'll do the deal?'

'We'll talk about it,' corrected Adams. 'Beyond talk, it's my boss to your boss. Let them do the worrying. Agreed?'

'Agreed,' said Thane and hung up.

He'd wait and see what happened. After a moment he tried his second call, Stewart Rae's home number. It rang out a few times, then a woman answered. She had a pleasant, oddly familiar voice and he could hear a TV set playing in the background.

'He's here,' she agreed when he asked for the sports goods agent. 'We met yesterday, superintendent. I'm Sophie – wife after hours, underpaid warehouse staff the rest of the time.'

'That's right!' Stewart Rae came on the line with a boom of a laugh. 'Why else would I keep the woman? Sophie, get the hell out of that!' There was the noise of a brief horseplay scuffle, then Rae was on the line again. 'So, how are things now, Thane?

'We found Terry Anson,' said Thane bluntly. 'He was dead.'

'Uh?' Stewart Rae sobered instantly. 'What happened?'

'He'd been shot. Through the back of the head. They'd tried to bury him.'

'Dear God!' Rae gave a distinct swallow. 'But – '

Thane stopped him. 'We don't know much more. We're still working on it.'

'I understand.' Rae made it clear he wanted to ask more, but wouldn't. 'This is maybe wrong time, wrong mood, but it's why I called you earlier. You said you wanted to know more about the local fashion world. Does it still matter?'

'More than ever,' agreed Thane.

'This is something I'd forgotten about, because it isn't my normal scene.' Rae was apologetic. 'There's a Trade Only fashion showing in town tomorrow evening. Free drinks, live music, catwalk models, latest collections on display, all the rag trade and their gossip gathered under one roof. Everyone who thinks they matter in the local fashion stakes will be there.' He paused. 'Sophie managed to get some late tickets. They're free – one of the big multiples picks up the tab. Would you like a couple? Bring your wife.'

'It could be useful. Yes, thank you.' There was a new bright glare of headlights outside in the parking area as two cars arrived. They stopped in a scatter of gravel; he heard doors open and slam, the sound of voices. 'Stewart, you could maybe help me in another way.'

'Name it.'

108

'Emma Raleigh.'

'What about Emma Raleigh?' Rae was suddenly cautious. 'We do business, and that's it. Ask Sophie.'

'What do you know about Emma Raleigh and her friend Peter Dutch?'

'The TV front man?' Rae gave an almost derisive grunt. 'I've seen them around together, I suppose they fall in and out of bed sometimes. But it's not searing passion – I've heard that Emma can play the field.'

'Has Dutch any rag trade interests?'

'I know who to ask. Hold on.' Stewart Rae shouted the query at his wife, wherever she had gone, then came back on the line. 'He knows people, he picks up personal appearance money when some of the big stores have a sales event.' He stopped for another shout from the background, then grunted, 'Sophie thinks he's still sexy, for what that's worth. Uh – anything else?'

'Not right now.' Thane thanked the man, said he'd look out for the tickets, and ended the call.

The offer was a surprise, one that might be useful.

He lifted the phone yet again, and this time dialled his home number. It rang engaged, the way it did more often than not when two teenagers were home from school.

He hung up, used a few minutes to scan through the collection of fax and telex messages which had gathered while he was away, then tried his home number again.

This time he got through. Kate answered the call, made her usual disappointed noise that it wasn't anyone more exciting, then yelled for her mother. There was a short pause with a background of a heavy metal tape being played somewhere, then Mary was on the line.

'All quiet?' he asked.

'So quiet I'm sewing buttons on one of your shirts,' she said wryly. 'How about you?'

'Busy.'

'I heard.' Cops' wives had their own grapevine. 'Rough?'

'All I want. I'll be late.' He shifted his grip on the receiver. 'We've got an invitation for tomorrow night – line of duty, but you'd maybe enjoy it. It's a fashion trade bash in town. Drinks and music, all the new styles on parade. Free tickets.'

'So I get taken?' She gave a groan of mock ecstasy. 'Dear God, the man cares! Do I get to buy if I see anything I like?'

He grinned. 'No.'

'That's living dangerously. But I'd like to go.' She sighed. 'Except what do I wear?'

'Try your friends. Borrow something,' suggested Thane. He heard the start of a dangerous splutter and quickly moved on. 'Translate something for me. If one woman calls another woman a Sinbad, what does it mean?'

'A Sinbad?' Mary was puzzled. 'No, I don't know. Does it matter?'

'Not a lot.'

'I'll find out.' Her mood changed. 'How's your Sergeant Sandra?'

'Acting Sergeant.' The network had been very busy. But it had to be a coincidence she'd asked straight after his own question. 'Fine.'

'It sounds like all-change time. Sandra, Francey – and Phil.' She gave a soft chuckle. 'About tomorrow evening. I had a clinic meeting scheduled. But I can do some shaking and moving, shift it along. Now say goodbye – Kate's getting anxious. Monkey the Boyfriend is due to call.'

Thane grinned and hung up. Then he went back to the messages on his desk and combed his way through them again, redirecting some, marking others. But there was also a promise he'd made to himself. He took a few minutes to put together some scribbled notes of names, places and times.

Even after so many years, it was still a job he loathed. Lifting his telephone again, he tapped an internal number which connected him to the Squad's digital dictation system. A soft beep signalled he was connected to the computer and he started dictating. As a system, it had all the charm and warmth of trying to relate to a brick wall. At the other end, he knew he was being recorded straight on to hard disc – the old audiotapes system had been dumped when it was realised that hard disc allowed any-time access to add or edit.

It took time, and he was hoarse when he had finished. He was also beginning to feel hungry. Joe Felix hadn't surfaced; he could only wait for word from Moss and at the same time hope that someone else somewhere was going to come up with something. Surrendering to his stomach, Thane went along to the Squad canteen. He queued behind a couple of uniformed traffic officers, then collected and paid for a greasy hamburger and fried egg sandwich, black coffee, and a side plate of biscuits and mousetrap cheese.

It was about eight in the evening and at that hour most of the tables were vacant. He chose one which would give him a view of the canteen's TV set, which was showing live football.

'Can I join you?' asked a voice.

Tina Redder didn't wait for an answer. One leg reached out in a way that made a sergeant two tables away almost choke on a sausage. The slim, dark-haired chief inspector hooked out a chair for herself, dumped her tray of food beside Thane's food then plonked herself on the chair.

'Not a happy day for you, is it, Colin?' She gave him an urchin-style grin across the table, then neatly spread out her meal. Predictably, it was a salad with cottage cheese, thin-sliced wholemeal bread, and a tub of low-fat yoghurt. 'You keep finding bodies, right?'

'Drop dead, Tina,' said Thane dispassionately.

'On your kind of diet, I know who'll go first.' She reached over and took a sample of his hamburger, chewing it delicately. 'Incidentally, do you know you're putting on weight?'

Thane grunted, trying to both eat and watch football. Tina Redder nibbled her salad for a moment, obviously in a cheerful mood.

'So ask me how I'm doing,' she invited.

'No.'

'I knew you'd be interested.' Tina grinned and tried the wholemeal bread. 'We rounded up most of my dynamite bunch as planned this morning. Jock Dawson and his dogs were a big help.' She beamed. 'We only missed out on one, and we've just brought him in.'

Thane nodded, remembering the headlamps. 'How did you find him?'

'Back to basics.' Tina waved the bread for emphasis. 'We had a name, we knew he lived somewhere not too far out of town. What's the first thing we teach a probationer cop to do when they want to find someone?' She gave her own answer. 'We checked a couple of phone directories and he was hiding at his mother's place, keeping detonators in her freezer.'

'Why try to be clever?' agreed Thane. Time after time, the simple approach scored. 'So everything's wrapped up?'

'You should ask!' She grimaced. 'This one is going to take a

111

couple of miles of damned arrest sheets, statements, and court reports to wrap up. I'll keep things rolling for a couple more hours tonight, then everybody can sweat on it again tomorrow.'

The home team scored an unexpected goal on TV while Tina Redder made a new inroad on her salad. Most of Thane's mind was on the football action, but he also spared Tina some sympathy.

Except that it had become the same for any cop anywhere. A bureaucracy that was an unholy alliance of the law and the demands of civil rights activists had created a procedural nightmare of a system. Even under Scotland's reasonably enlightened legal system a simple shoplifting arrest could create a need for as many as fifteen different forms and documents, a good two and a half hours' work. There was a classic case involving a juvenile on a minor offence where the number of forms had topped seventy.

A new attack on goal came up and was cleared by a player built like the Rock of Gibraltar. Thane sighed as he watched, then brightened. Another chance for a goal was coming up on the TV screen –

'Colin.' Tina Redder nudged him hard.

'Huh?' He kept his attention glued to the screen for a few seconds more. Then, from a full fifteen yards, an attacking wingman slammed a shot which scorched past the opposing keeper in a way that bulged the back of the net. The home crowd rose with a vicious roar of triumph. Thane relaxed back as the teams prepared to kick off again.

'Phone.' Tina Redder used her fork as a pointer. The duty supervisor at the canteen cashdesk was signalling for him with her desk telephone.

'You should have told me, woman.' Taking another mouthful of hamburger, Thane rose and went over. Still chewing, he took the call. It was Moss on the other end of the line.

'Trouble,' reported Moss unemotionally. 'I'm at Liz Hill's place at Flannan Street. We were beaten to it, Colin. Somebody did a full slashing job on her face, the house was trashed.'

Thane cursed. 'How is she?'

'Like someone enjoyed what he did,' said Moss bleakly. 'But no other injuries. Sandra took her to Casualty at the Royal, I've stayed on.'

'Anyone with you?' Thane ignored the canteen supervisor's eavesdropping interest.

'A couple of local uniforms.' Moss didn't elaborate. He paused for a moment as another voice muttered at his end, then was back on the line. 'Scenes of Crime are on their way. Before you ask, she was in no state to tell us much what happened.'

'I'll come out,' Thane told him.

'Right. I'm trying neighbours.' Moss gave a sardonic grunt. 'Wish me luck. I'm not getting far.'

Thane hung up, thanked the canteen supervisor, and strode back to his table.

'What's wrong?' asked Tina Redder as he wrapped the remains of the hamburger in a paper napkin from the table-top dispenser.

'We've had a witness done over.' Thane didn't waste words. 'A woman.'

The slim, dark-haired detective chief inspector halted a forkful of salad in mid-air. 'Your missing one from the bank van job?'

'No.' He said it bitterly. His record with women was hitting rock bottom. 'Another one. She was slashed.'

She laid down her fork with a small grimace of disgust. 'Need any help?'

'No.' He shrugged. 'Unless you find Joe Felix and tell him I've gone out.'

He drew a quick nod of agreement from Tina, then hurried from the canteen, out along the corridor, past the front desk and out of the building towards the parking lot. The Ford Mondeo's keys were in his pocket and he spotted the black car glinting ahead under the security lights. Someone had washed the worst of the lochside mud away from it.

Still clutching the half-eaten hamburger, Thane got aboard the Ford and started it up. Putting the car into gear, setting it moving, he returned to eating while he headed towards the lights of the city.

A blend of hard driving and not too much other traffic on the roads got him across to Flannan Street in under twenty minutes. When he pulled in at the kerb outside number thirty-four, the old grey stone tenement looked deceptively quiet and most of its windows were in darkness. But as he got out and locked the car, spectators were silently watching from across the roadway.

Thane went into the tenement close and toiled his way up the ill-lit stinking stairway to the top floor. A beat man was on duty outside Liz Hill's door and straightened with a nod

113

of recognition. Thane could see the fresh white of recently splintered wood around the forced door locks and smashed security chain.

He pushed the door open and went in. The second beat man was in the kitchen, boiling a kettle and making tea. Phil Moss was in the shabby living-room, wearily going through a rubbish-tip collection of papers and dumped clothes under the glare of an overhead light. An upturned table had lost a leg, a couple of drawers from a sideboard had been broken. Photographs and ornaments had been smashed. The dead parrot's empty cage lay on its side at the window, trampled flat.

'Bastards,' said Moss softly, looking up at him. 'Pure bastards, whoever they were.'

Silently, Thane looked around. His mouth tightened as he saw the bloodstains everywhere – some spattered, some long smears. More of it in small pools on the floor or as dark stains which had soaked into towels.

'You saw the door?' asked Moss.

Thane nodded. 'Sledgehammer?'

'Neighbours saw nothing, heard nothing.' Moss made it a snarl of near-rage. 'Either they were asleep or watching the damned TV – they say.'

'Sir.' The second beat man came in, nursing two large mugs of tea. He gave the first to Thane, the usual wry protocol of rank, the other went to Moss. Then the man ambled off again.

'What's the rest of it?' asked Thane, tasting the tea. It was tarry strong, the way night-shift cops always make it.

'Not a lot.' Moss shrugged. 'We got here, we found the front door smashed, we went in. The woman was lying on the floor near the window. She was moaning, there was blood every damned place, her face was a nightmare, and the rest is as you see it. They did the same kind of job in the bedroom.'

'They?'

'Two of them. We got that much out of her – not much more.' Moss released a long, soft burp, then gave an odd grin. 'Your new baby sergeant did well. Grabbed towels, soothed the woman. Then it was her idea to say to hell with waiting for an ambulance. She took her off to hospital in the Volkswagen.'

'Sandra will shape out.' He saw Moss was wearing a pair of the thin plastic disposable gloves most officers now carried in the

114

world of HIV and Aids, and knew he didn't have to ask about Sandra Craig. A different question was how the Crime Squad motor pool sergeant would react to smears of blood on the Volkswagen's upholstery. But that went with the territory. Pursing his lips, he considered the smashed-up room. 'Phil, how do you read it?'

'This was a wrecking crew. They weren't searching for anything.' Moss took another gulp of tea from his mug. 'Not the way this was done.'

Slowly, Thane nodded. He felt the same. 'The Cutters handing out a general frightener?'

'I'd put money on it. Except – ' Moss gulped at his tea again, his tired eyes glinting in the harsh glare of the overhead light. 'Yes, except maybe they did us a favour.' He beckoned. 'Look at this.'

Thane went over and joined his scrawny second-in-command in kneeling beside the spilled contents of a smashed drawer. One edge of a slim pad of printed forms protruded from under some faded, crumpled blouses. Silently Moss brushed the blouses to one side.

'So how did she get these?' asked Thane softly.

It was a pad of blank vehicle service reports headed Pizzaro Truck Rentals. There was no address, but the telephone number below was a Perth county code, somewhere at least a couple of hours' travel north of Glasgow.

He had been seeking a lead to tie in with that diesel fuel receipt from the lock-up garage at Blenheim Rise. Maybe he had just been handed it on a plate. There was only one way to find out. Meantime, they could leave the rest to Scenes of Crime, who tackled a situation like this in clockwork style.

'Let's move.' He tore the top Pizzaro sheet from the pad, folded it, and tucked it away. 'We'll see how things are at the Royal.'

The two beat men didn't argue about being left to hold the fort. Drinking tea and waiting was better than plodding their way around the Flannan Street area after dark.

It was only a few minutes' drive to the Royal Infirmary. It was years since Thane had last been there, but the hospital complex was still the same mix of old Victorian stonework overshadowed by modern concrete with a night-time silhouette which emphasised how badly they could clash. Parking was still as impossible as ever.

Thane tucked the Ford into the space behind an empty, off-duty ambulance. He waved his warrant card under the nose of an aggressive hospital porter who appeared out of nowhere, and didn't stop to argue. Moss beside him, he walked through the main reception doors into Casualty reception. It had been given a facelift and new paintwork.

But the rest didn't look much different from the area he'd known back when he was a beat man in the old Central Division, down to the inevitable queue of damaged humanity waiting to be repaired. A couple of noisy drunks were comparing head wounds. Some white-faced, frightened teenagers were being quizzed by a uniformed constable for some reason that had to matter. An old lady with a bandaged ankle in a wheelchair clutched a small dog that should never have been allowed in. Next to her a plump, middle-aged woman sat comforting a child, never taking her eyes off one of the closed sets of cubicle curtains.

Moss stopped a passing nurse. They spoke. She nodded, led them to another set of closed curtains further along, checked inside, then beckoned. Sandra Craig was there, watching while a doctor and a staff nurse worked on Liz Hill, who was lying propped up on a treatment couch making faint whimpering noises.

'Yours, sergeant?' the doctor asked Sandra with a glance at his visitors.

She nodded.

'I'll be right with you.' He switched back to his patient.

The worst of the bleeding had been staunched. But the long twin-track slashes across Liz Hill's face were cruel. One set raked across from her right ear. Another had sliced open part of a nostril, then cut downwards from there, across her mouth to her jaw-line. There were at least half a dozen separate slicing wounds.

'Right.' The doctor rose from his stooping position, stretched gladly, and nodded to the staff nurse. 'Take a break.'

'How is she?' asked Thane quietly.

'Not exactly ready for singing or dancing,' said the medical man drily. He had a young face already old with experience. 'She lost blood, she's still shocked. I've given her a local anaesthetic. But she's going to need a lot of stitching – a hell of a lot.'

116

Liz Hill's eyes had moved from the ceiling and were now focused on Thane. Her whimpering had stopped.

'Can we speak with her?' asked Thane.

'Go ahead.' The doctor nodded and stepped back to let Thane nearer to his patient. 'Don't push her.'

'Liz.' Thane sat on the edge of the couch and leaned over the thin, raw-boned woman with her dyed blonde hair. 'Did you know them?'

Liz Hill gave the faintest of headshakes.

'I've got some of it from her,' volunteered Sandra. 'They just burst in through her door.'

Liz Hill gave a slight, painful nod in agreement. Her words came as a painful whisper. 'Said . . . said I'd earned it, Mr Thane.'

'Nothing more, Liz?'

'No.' Some fresh blood showed along one of the slash tracks. The staff nurse made a protesting noise.

'Almost finished, Liz.' Thane produced the sheet of Pizzaro Truck Rentals headed paper. 'You had these. Where did you get them?'

She peered, trying to focus. 'Terry Anson.' Thane had to bend close to catch her words. 'He left them in my place once . . . a while ago. I kept them. I used some. For the bottom of Ringo's cage.' She stopped, winced, and looked away.

'No more,' said the doctor. The staff nurse had already moved in. 'Not tonight.' Curiosity got the better of him. 'You know this Anson?'

Thane nodded grimly.

'And what about Ringo?'

'Her parrot,' said Thane.

'What else?' The doctor was still young enough to sigh. 'Now do you mind leaving?' He followed all three of them almost out of the cubicle, then stopped and grimaced. 'I'll do my best needlework. But she's going to be scarred. Badly scarred. I hate these damned twin-blade slashings. Thank God we don't see too many of them – they're hell to repair.'

Phil Moss broke his total silence with a long muffled belch.

'If that's painful, officer, you should see about it,' murmured the doctor.

Moss glared. The doctor shrugged, went back into the cubicle, and the curtains closed again.

'Why can't people mind their own damned business?' asked Moss sourly

'Maybe he cared,' suggested Sandra.

She received a glare all her own.

There was a sudden shouting and a scattering of the waiting queue in Casualty reception. The two drunks were fighting. There was no sign of the uniformed cop, but a nurse was heading to intervene.

That was the moment when one drunk tried to hit the other over the head with a chair, missed, and smashed it on a radiator.

'He's mine,' rasped Moss. 'I need the exercise.'

He stopped and blinked. Sandra Craig was already there. As the broken chair swung again she shoved the second drunk aside, dodged under the flailing chair, grabbed the first drunk. She swung him round in a two-handed wristlock, and the man squealed in startled agony. As he dropped the chair the redhead swung him around again and rammed him face-first into the nearest wall.

'Police,' said Sandra crisply. 'Behave. This is a hospital.'

'Ease up, woman,' said Moss with a small irritation. 'He'll dirty that wall.'

She obeyed, loosening her grip a little.

'You saw that, didn't you?' The drunk twisted his head round. 'The bitch attacked me, right?'

'The bitch is a sergeant, she's good at it, and this is Police Brutality Week,' Moss told him softly. 'You've a choice, sunshine. Either you behave, or I let her kick you up the arse so hard your nose starts bleeding.'

The drunk swallowed, subsided, and allowed himself to be dumped in another chair well away from his equally subdued friend. Hurrying back from the direction of the canteen, the uniformed cop arrived, opened his mouth, then closed it again as Moss showed his warrant card.

'Sort it out, constable,' said Moss mildly. His thin face shaped a small, leathery grin as he turned again. 'Nicely done, Detective Sergeant Craig.'

'Thank you, Detective Inspector Moss,' she said with an equal formality. She switched to Thane. 'Sir, I'd like to stay for a spell. Till I see Liz settled.'

'Do it,' agreed Thane. Then he grinned. 'Just remember, I expect my sergeant to be in ahead of me in the mornings.'

He said goodnight and left the hospital with Moss at his side.

When they got back to the car, a radio check with the duty controller confirmed there was no message awaiting them from anywhere. Starting the Ford, Thane set it moving but pulled in again after a short distance where a newsvendor was already at his pitch selling the early editions of the next morning's papers.

'Let's see what they've got,' he told Moss.

Moss got out, grumbling at having to pay, and returned with a selection. Several had the bodies out at Dark Loch as their lead headlines and two also had photographs of Terry Anson which had obviously been collected from his home.

'I hope the sorrowing widow held out for a decent price,' said Moss cynically. 'What's she like?'

'The kind who'll survive,' said Thane, thinking of the woman and her small son. 'With sense enough to shout that she knows nothing.' He put the car back into gear. 'We'll call it a night. I'll give you a lift home.'

He drove on through the brightly lit streets, his mind on the puzzle of the second body found at Dark Loch and all the tangle of possibilities that were waiting to crowd in. What he needed more than anything was a clear lead that would take him to The Cutters. Maybe Gypsy Adams was going to provide that, but the counterfeit team had already proved themselves more ruthless than he'd expected, maybe better informed in a way he didn't like.

'Hell, it's still early days yet,' said Moss suddenly from the shadows of the passenger seat as if reading his mind. His former second-in-command's teeth showed briefly and white in the dark. 'It'll come together.'

Thane gave a lop-sided grimace. It was a reversal of their usual roles, when he knew that just as Moss was the natural pessimist he had a reputation for an optimistic charge-in-and-chance-it style of action.

They took the Clydeside Expressway route along the north bank of the river. The latest in Moss's regularly changing series of landladies had a Victorian red sandstone house on the fringe of Partick, not far from the boundary of their old Millside Division.

When Phil Moss moved it was usually because yet another landlady had begun proving amorously friendly. A middle-aged bachelor – even of the grubby, down-at-heel variety – who had the prospect of a police pension ahead was always a reasonable

119

catch in some eyes. Two previous landladies had proposed marriage. Another had got into bed with him in the middle of the night saying she was lonely.

They reached King Street, turned off at the second side road along, and the house where Moss now lived was ahead. There was a light burning in the porch, probably a hot supper waiting inside.

'Settled in all right?' asked Thane, letting the car roll to a halt.

'It'll do.' Moss gave a carefully considered verdict. 'She keeps tidying around me and wanting to iron things. But she knows how to make scrambled egg, and that's damned near a lost art.' He opened the passenger door and got out. 'Thanks for the lift.' His face crinkled in a surprising, vinegary grin. 'I feel rusty as hell. But that'll pass.'

'Fine,' said Thane drily. 'Remember you've been transferred to do paperwork.'

'Right.' Moss raised a hand in farewell and started up the path towards the house's front door. Half-way there he paused and released a thunderclap of a belch. Seconds later the front door opened and his landlady was there to usher him in.

Chuckling, Thane drove off again. He took the Clyde Tunnel route across to the south side of the river and was home in another fifteen minutes. It was barely eleven o'clock, but the house was already in complete darkness. He got out, locked the car, and crunched his way over their gravel front path through a faint drizzle of rain to the front door. The dog didn't bother to bark when he went in. When Thane reached the kitchen and switched on the light he still only drew a Boxer glare from the basket beside the refrigerator.

He dumped his jacket on a chair, loosened his tie, and was making himself a pot of coffee and a cheese sandwich when Mary wandered in. She was yawning, wearing a dressing-gown, and helped herself to some of the coffee and half of the sandwich.

'I decided to have an early night. I need it if I've to do my Cinderella act with your fashion people tomorrow evening.' She sat at the kitchen table, resting her chin on her hands. 'Things shaping any better?'

'No. Bad today, worse tomorrow.' He joined her at the table, heard a strange sound, and looked round. Clyde had gone back to sleep again and was snoring. Grinning, he thumbed towards the bedrooms upstairs. 'What about the enemy?'

'All quiet, except for a small war over the dreaded Monkey.'

Thane sighed. 'Does he have a second name?'

'I forget.' She yawned. 'But I solved your mystery. Still want to know what Sinbad means?'

'Tell.'

'Single Income, No Boyfriend, Absolutely Desperate. It's pretty cruel. So who labelled who?'

'Don't ask.' He shook his head. 'But who knew what it meant?'

'Our dear daughter. She says it's the flavour of the month insult.'

'Couldn't you ask someone else?'

'I did. They didn't know – and I wanted to hear.' Mary yawned, put down her mug, and rose. 'Either I go to bed now or you carry me. Choose.'

'I'll think about it,' he said vaguely.

Sandra reckoned that Emma Raleigh had labelled her a Sinbad. That might be just short of declaring war, but the way things were it was almost incidental.

He heard Mary sigh, and her lips touched his forehead. Then she left.

The next day began grey with clouds, the streets still damp from the overnight drizzle. Thane arrived at the Crime Squad headquarters building shortly before 8 a.m., left the pool Ford in his slot in the parking lot, and smiled to himself as he saw Sandra Craig's Volkswagen already lying empty further along.

She was waiting in his room when he arrived. The overnight paperwork on his desk had been sorted into bundles, and his red-haired sergeant looked bandbox fresh in a silky grey rollneck sweater, carefully faded denim trousers and a suede jacket, worn with rubber-soled black jogging shoes.

'Morning,' said Thane. He hung his jacket on a hook, then nodded at his desk. 'What do I need to know that matters?'

'Not a lot, sir.' Sandra shook her head. 'Scenes of Crime drew a blank at Liz's house. Strathclyde are running another check for bodies out at Dark Loch, and you've a letter marked Private.'

'Right.' Thane settled behind his desk, then looked at her hopefully. 'I could kill for a cup of coffee. Like to put a kettle on?'

She stiffened. 'Did Francey make coffee, sir?'

Thane wished he hadn't opened his mouth. 'No.'

'He didn't make coffee, I don't make coffee. Agreed, sir?'

'Fine,' surrendered Thane.

'Thank you.' She used the telephone on his desk to call the canteen.

'When did you leave the Royal and get home?' he asked as she finished.

'Around midnight. The Casualty team did their best.' Her mouth tightened at the memory. 'I phoned this morning and they say she's comfortable. Comfortable? With fifty-six stitches?'

An orderly brought coffee for them. Sipping from his mug, Thane went through the papers on his desk. He blinked at the unusual sight of a set of overtime sheets completed and ready for his signature before he had to shout and threaten for them. There were others in the same category, some organised by Sandra Craig, others already initialled by Moss.

He kept the envelope marked Private until last. It contained the two fashion trade show tickets he'd been promised by Stewart Rae. But the Reebok agent hadn't mentioned that it was being held in the marble-pillared splendour of the banqueting hall at the City Chambers, full dinner-jacket style with a cabaret. He knew he would have to let Mary know.

'There's something I'd like to ask about Inspector Moss, sir.' Sandra looked at him over the edge of her coffee mug. 'I knew he had a stomach ulcer but didn't he have surgery?'

'A patch and weld for a duodenal.' Thane nodded. 'But he reckons it's back again – and this time it will take a lot before he lets anyone else near him with a scalpel. Why?'

'Just curiosity, sir. Know the enemy.' She grinned and used a hand to brush a strand of red hair back from her forehead. 'Anything else for me?'

'When there is, you'll hear,' he promised.

She went out, and Thane took the chance to phone home. The number rang engaged, which hardly rated as the surprise of the year.

Phil Moss ambled in as he put the receiver down. For once, Moss was reasonably clean-shaven but with resultant bloodstains on his shirt front. Inevitably, he also looked as if he had slept in his suit.

'You're early,' accused Moss, propping himself against a filing cabinet. 'Start of a new life-style?'

'Go away,' said Thane grimly. 'Goodbye.'

'Touchy.' Moss grinned in a way which made the lines on his face look more like pleats than wrinkles. 'Maybe this will help. We've another message in from London about Les Harrow.' The scrawny detective sucked his slips. 'The post-morten report on Harrow noted that a few days before he was hit by that bus he appeared to have been slashed across the face with a twin-bladed knife. Same style of attack as on Liz Hill. The wounds had been stitched – they're sending up photographs taken at the autopsy.'

It was another link in a chain which still didn't have a firm beginning or end. But everything helped.

'Anything on Pizzaro Trucks?'

'Francey is working on that.' Moss allowed a gentle burp to pass his lips. 'But something else looks good. Criminal Records think they've got a name for that other body at Dark Loch. They'll get back to us before noon.'

'Any hints?' asked Thane hopefully.

'Only that it could be someone they've been wanting to find,' grunted Moss. 'They're checking something through Interpol. Apart from that, you know what they're like – tight-mouthed devils.'

Thane nodded. He knew from bitter experience. But when SCRO gave an identification it came with a money-back guarantee.

Moss left, and as the office door closed again Thane had another try at getting through to his home number. This time he was lucky, and Mary answered.

'Make it quick,' she warned. 'I'm on my way out and I'm late already.'

He told her the fashion invitation details.

'Dear God!' Mary drew a deep breath. 'It's way up-market! Thanks for the warning – and here's one for you. This is going to cost us!'

She hung up. After a few minutes Thane made another couple of calls out, the first to the forensic laboratory at Strathclyde's headquarters building where he was told to try again later, the second to Trading Standards where Gypsy Adams quickly came on the line.

'You're mind-reading, Thane!' The gruff-voiced CATS supervisor sounded elated. 'Have you heard?'

'Heard what?' asked Thane.

'We're in business,' declared Adams. 'Another couple of minutes and I'd have called you. It's the way our little friend Mega

Mickey promised. We've done a partial deal with him, we've got what looks like The Cutters' base on a plate. Everything checks out and my boss is on his way to talk to your boss.'

'I'm happy for them,' said Thane sardonically.

Adams chuckled. 'They can take care of the red tape. You and I can sort out the real details. The target is a factory out of town, near Belshill.' Thane heard someone speak to him in the background. 'Hold on a moment.'

It took nearer a couple of minutes with more background voices on the line, then Adams was back. 'It's for real. My people saw the work-force being bussed in, they're keeping the place under observation, I'm planning to raid at noon, and I want everyone in position fifteen minutes before that.'

Thane frowned as he replaced the receiver. Somehow it seemed too smooth, too simple. But if the CATS team really had located their counterfeit factory then the day was certainly going to be busy.

He was still thinking his way through what could be involved when his telephone rang.

'The commander wants you,' said Maggie Fyffe when he answered. 'Now – and God is back again.'

Thane swore softly and hung up. Rising, pulling on his jacket, straightening his tie, he went along the corridor to Jack Hart's office. On the way, he passed a window which gave him a full view of the Crime Squad parking lot. There, close to the building's main entrance, the white 4.2 litre Jaguar used by Her Majesty's Chief Inspector of Constabulary waited with Patrick Ronaldson's sergeant driver reading a newspaper behind the wheel. When he reached Jack Hart's office, Maggie Fyffe gave him a quick wink and ushered him straight in.

Hart and Ronaldson were both standing studying a wall map when Thane entered. Ronaldson greeted him with a half-smile, but left the immediate talking to Hart.

'You've heard what's happening?' demanded Hart. 'Trading Standards think they've struck it lucky.'

'Gypsy Adams just told me,' nodded Thane.

'Peerman is on his way over now.' Hands clasped behind his back, Hart frowned. 'Obviously, if it is true, it's good news.'

'For once, I'll be an optimist,' murmured Ronaldson, with one of his stock thin smiles. 'I know Peerman, he phoned me. But one could say I'm not officially here, superintendent. I'm being – ah – a fly on the wall. You understand?'

'Yes, sir.' Thane left it at that. HMCI could do no wrong. But he felt a sudden sympathy for Jack Hart, lumbered with both Ronaldson and the Trading Standards deputy.

'We'll co-operate in the raid, of course,' said Hart. He sucked briefly on his teeth. 'But we're also talking murder, talking assault, God knows what else apart from counterfeiting. Go carefully, Colin.'

'Walking on eggshells,' agreed Ronaldson briskly. 'Of course, you've got my total confidence.'

'We appreciate that, sir.' Hart said it deadpan, but his eyes glittered their own warning to Thane. 'The bottom line, as I'll spell it out to Peerman, is that we have our own priorities.' He let a small, cynical grin cross his face. 'Use your well-known diplomacy.'

'Or try.' Ronaldson nodded. 'Pleased you've got Moss with you again, Thane?'

'Very,' agreed Thane. 'Thank you, sir.'

'I had to do something, eh?' Ronaldson dismissed the matter. 'Any progress in getting a name for that other body?'

'There's a prospect,' said Thane.

'As long as no more turn up, eh?' Ronaldson glanced at his watch.

It was an effective dismissal. Thane left them, shrugged at Maggie Fyffe on the way out, and kept on walking. He was at the reception area when a small, thick-set man he hadn't noticed almost bounced from the depths of one of the reception chairs and bustled forward to intercept him.

'Superintendent, we have to talk.' Dentures gleaming in a quick grimace of a smile. 'That shouldn't surprise you.'

'It doesn't particularly, Mr Hilson.' Colin Thane considered the man without emotion. Martin Hilson was probably the smartest criminal lawyer in Glasgow and knew it. He wore a dark suit, white shirt and grey tie like a uniform, and as always he had a carnation buttonhole. He had a heavy, usually brooding face. One day a court somewhere would pin Hilson against a wall for some of his tactics, but until that happened it always paid to be very careful around him. 'What's your problem?'

'Your problem, not mine, superintendent.' Hilson pursed his lips. 'I hear you've – ah – lost your key woman witness in the security van hijack case. You've still got my client Gonzo Patrick in custody.'

'Where he stays,' said Thane shortly. 'Whatever you've heard.'

Hilson glared. 'I also understand that your people are going around trying to link my client with another possibly serious matter. They made one mistake, Thane. Now they're making another. You can tell them they have it wrong. Gonzo Patrick is clean.'

'That's good to know,' said Thane sardonically. 'Thank you, Mr Hilson.'

'Superintendent, face facts,' said the lawyer curtly. 'You don't have any kind of case left to bring any of the three you've charged to court. Any judge will throw it straight out and want to know why you wasted his time.'

'He stays,' said Thane. He glanced at his wrist-watch. 'Nice seeing you, Mr Hilson.'

'Don't mess me about, Thane,' said Hilson acidly. 'This is a warning. Gonzo Patrick and the other two have been advised of their rights. Give up any thoughts you have about any kind of question session in a prison interview room.' He gave a warning, weasel smile. 'You know, even detective superintendents can end up to their armpits in trouble. You understand me?'

Thane looked at the small, thick-set lawyer in silence for a long moment and fought down what he really felt like doing.

'Thank you, Mr Hilson,' he said unemotionally. 'See you in court.'

Martin Hilson flushed angrily, then spun on his heel and marched away. Thane watched him leave and climb into a large red BMW. It had a bumper sticker, 'Support The Law, Sue Somebody'. The lawyer started the car, revved the engine angrily, then sent it moving in a scatter of gravel. As it passed the front door of the building, Hilson raised one hand in a viciously derisive two-fingered gesture.

'You too,' said Thane softly, and felt slightly better for it.

It was still only the beginnings of a hunch. But he had a growing feeling that between them CATS and Crime Squad might now have the start of a winning hand. The Cutters counterfeit killings had created protection through fear.

That had to be beaten.

One was a woman who now had her face held together by fifty-six stitches.

6

When Thane reached the duty room he found everyone gathered at its broad sweep of window. A line of mounties were trotting their horses through an elaborate weave of a drill sequence through a peg-marked course in the field outside. They were carrying the long, spike-tipped lances they used on ceremonial parades.

'Show-time,' snorted Phil Moss, appearing from a cupboard-sized corner office he had somehow acquired. He scowled towards the horses. 'Chocolate box stuff.'

'There are times when a damned great spear could be pretty useful,' mused Thane.

'True.' Moss gave a cynical grin and slapped a tight fist into an open palm. 'Trot, gallop, charge – splat! We could get rid of a few problems.'

Face pressed against the window, Francey Dunbar gave a sudden howl of disappointment. Further along, a young, blonde woman officer laughed. Thane gave Dunbar a sympathetic shrug at losing. It was a favourite Crime Squad gamble when the mounties were around – drawing lots to sections of the field, then watching to see where the most horse manure landed within a fixed time. It wasn't the first time he'd seen the blonde girl be lucky.

'I saw you with a visitor,' said Moss drily. 'The original legal vulture.'

'If you saw, why didn't you come to help?' demanded Thane.

'My old mother always told me it was rude to interrupt your betters,' said Moss maliciously. He gave a low belch. 'So what did he want?'

'He says it's time we released Gonzo Patrick. At very least, we've got to stop annoying Patrick in his nice cell. The same obviously goes for his friends.' Thane's mouth tightened. 'They know we've a witness problem.'

'Only temporary,' murmured Moss. 'She'll turn up – I'd put money on it.' A burst of cheering from the window told them someone else was in the hunt. 'So what do we do about it?'

'Gonzo stays in Barlinnie.' Thane sucked his teeth. 'We leave him alone, we let him worry – at least for now.'

'I can live with that.' Moss gave a grunt of approval. 'But Hilson won't like it.'

'All the better,' murmured Thane. He glanced towards the window and raised his voice. 'Everybody, it's finished. Can we get some work done?'

Somehow, his team crammed together into Moss's cramped corner room. There was one absence.

'Where's Jock?' asked Thane, looking around for the lanky dog-handler.

'Gone walkies,' said Sandra. 'He asked, I said he could. The dogs needed it.'

'Next time I'll be a dog,' declared Joe Felix fervently. 'They get the best deals.'

They listened while Thane briefed them on the proposed CATS raid. Then they took turns to make their own reports. There was still no further word about the name for the second body from the lochside. There was still nothing new tied in with The Crusher or a Duff. None of the usual contact sources had even a squeak to offer about who had done the butcher-shop job on Liz Hill's face.

But Francey Dunbar, working hard to earn his new acting inspector status, had done a little better when it came to Pizzaro Truck Rentals.

'It's a long-distance haulage outfit, located near Crieff,' he reported. Crieff was in Perthshire, a small town buried in sheep and heather country about fifty miles out from Glasgow. Small, but busy. 'They've got a handful of truck and trailer rigs, mostly they haul whisky for some of the highland distilleries, and they've only been on the scene for the last couple of years. So far, they've kept their noses clean – or it seems that way.'

'Who says?' asked Moss, frowning.

'Mack Green, one of the cops at Crieff. He's their Federation rep, we're on the same Pay and Conditions Committee.'

Moss grunted. 'Another rabble-rouser?'

'Maybe. But he knows his area,' countered Dunbar without rancour. He switched his attention to Thane. 'I spoke with a couple of names he gave me. Nobody knows much about the Pizzaro set-up. Basically, they operate with an office manager and a couple of mechanics, they mostly use casual drivers, and they don't particularly welcome visitors.' He fiddled absently with the silver identity bracelet on his wrist. 'They could fit what we're after, boss.'

'Who owns it?'

Dunbar shrugged. 'A private company, Edinburgh-based. Joe and I are still digging.'

'Keep at it.' Thane looked around. 'What else?'

As he'd almost expected, Sandra Craig raised a hand. 'What about Emma Raleigh and boyfriend, sir?'

'What about them?'

'I think they could stand a closer look.'

Thane raised a deliberate eyebrow. 'Anything personal in this, sergeant?'

She pursed her lips, then shook her head. 'No. Call it a hunch.'

'I see.' Thane took a deep breath. 'A hunch.'

Beside him, he saw Phil Moss's thin, lined face was suddenly empty of expression. Colin Thane knew why – just as he knew all about hunches. For Thane, several purple patches in his police career had revolved around pursuing hunches, wild or otherwise. Sometimes his fingers had been burned that way – sometimes, but not always. More often than not, Moss had been there too, gloomily accepting his share of the nervous trauma involved.

So his new sergeant had a hunch. He let the breath out as a sigh.

'What would you do, Sandra?' He paused and silenced the start of a snicker from Francey Dunbar with a glare. 'I'm listening.'

'Have a go at the boyfriend.' Sandra grew bolder. 'Shake him up, see what falls out of his tree. We might get lucky.'

'Female intuition?' asked Moss cynically.

The redhead gave him a cool frown. 'Mainly gossip I picked up. He seems to know some heavy company.' She glanced apologetically at Thane. 'That's through a friend of a friend, sir. Someone in television.'

'All right.' Thane glanced at his watch and decided. 'But we nurse him along. Try phoning him at home, say we're looking for help, and that we'll come right out.'

She grinned and left the little room. Within a couple of minutes, she was back.

'Got him,' she confirmed. 'He's getting ready to leave, but he'll wait for us.'

'Let's do it.' Thane glanced at Moss. 'I'll pick up the autopsy results and anything Forensic have afterwards. Keep in touch with Gypsy Adams about his CATS raid – and tell Jock Dawson we want his dogs along.'

He took the Mondeo and did the driving, Sandra Craig in the passenger seat. She had Peter Dutch's address over the north side and used a street map as they headed out. His sergeant seemed content to stay silent, munching on an apple, and Thane had enough of his own thoughts to sort out while they went along with the traffic flow.

It was about a twenty-minute drive across the city. They wanted Horsehall Avenue in Abbotswalk, a prosperous slice of middle-income suburbia where gardens weren't allowed to have weeds and where the local amenities included a golf course and part of an old Roman fortified wall which dated back to the second century AD.

Horsehall Avenue was quiet and tree-lined. They parked outside Peter Dutch's house, which was single-storey and modern with a large satellite dish on its flat roof. There was a separate garage to one side and the garden had an ornamental fishpond with a fountain jet. It was strange, but it wasn't a crime on its own. They left the car, walked the slabbed path to the oak front door, and Thane pressed the bellpush. The door opened after a few moments and Peter Dutch looked out at them.

'Police?' He gave the kind of smile which Thane remembered from at least a decade of chat shows, then glanced at Sandra. 'Sergeant Craig, who telephoned?'

'And Detective Superintendent Thane.' Thane showed his warrant card.

'Come in,' said Dutch easily. 'No law against being comfortable.'

They went in. Dutch closed the oak door then led them along a bright hallway into a lounge where glass patio doors looked out on a barbecue area backed by shrugs. The room had big, cowhide-upholstered armchairs and Scandinavian-style teak furniture, with a matching TV and video console as a main feature. With a

130

practised ease, Peter Dutch took a position with his back to the bright sunlight coming in through the patio windows.

'Sit down,' he invited. He was smaller than Thane had expected from the TV screens, older too – probably into his fifties. Those fine-boned features were beginning to thicken, there were streaks of natural grey in his dark, curly hair. He smiled at them again. 'I haven't too much time. So whatever this is about, let's get to it.'

They settled in two of the cowhide chairs. All round the room were framed studio photographs showing Dutch in a variety of his programme roles, from beaming quiz show chairman to earnest, microphone-clutching interviewer.

'We need particular help in an on-going investigation,' said Thane carefully. 'It's not television. But I've been told you're on friendly terms with the local fashion world. That you sometimes do freelance work for them.'

'True.' The man's features shaped an easy grin. 'Like tonight, superintendent.'

'Tonight, Mr Dutch?' Thane let one hand rub along the smooth surface of the chair's cowhide. A startling possibility came into his mind. 'What's happening?'

'I'm doing my compere bit at a fashion trade presentation in the City Chambers.' The smile came through again. 'A lot of buyers will be there, a lot of other important people. They're also shooting a promotional video. So – well, it has to be right.' Dutch gave a theatrical gesture with one hand. 'Rehearsals are this morning. There's a taxi on its way to collect me.'

Thane gave a mild nod. There had been no mention of Peter Dutch as compère on the tickets which he had in his inside pocket. 'This won't take long.'

'Maybe we could save you the taxi ride,' suggested Sandra brightly. 'We could give you a lift.'

'No, but thanks.' Dutch shook his head. 'I've somewhere else to go on the way.' He returned to Thane. 'So – what kind of help?'

'We're investigating a major counterfeit clothing team,' said Thane. 'They're big, they can be violent. We're looking for any gossip, any leads of any kind.'

'I've maybe heard a rumour or two, nothing more,' frowned Dutch.

'You're a professional interviewer, Mr Dutch, a good one.' Almost making it up as he went along, Thane added an extra helping of flattery. 'We need someone like you with an inside track on things. If you heard something that might interest us, if you could maybe ask a question or two – '

Thane let it fade there, unfinished. There was a silence in the room while somewhere outside, in another of the suburban gardens, a motor mower rasped its noisy way through someone's grass. All round, the framed studio stills continued to offer their various versions of Dutch's smile.

He had been watching the man's blue eyes. Peter Dutch was a professional who had learned how to control reactions and emotions, to exhibit what was meant to be seen, to mask the rest. But those blue eyes had flickered more than once, a cloaked tension had gradually given way to a faint trace of something close to disbelief.

'What you're really saying is you want me to be your insider, superintendent.' Dutch grimaced. 'I don't like the idea. Some of these people are my friends.'

'Friends you could be helping,' countered Thane. 'And they're likely to suffer if this counterfeiting keeps growing.'

'True.' The man chewed his lip for a moment, then sighed. 'All right, leave it at that. No promises, but if I hear anything I'll let you know.'

Then suddenly it was Dutch who was doing the talking, drifting from the behind-the-scenes problems of conquering a fashion show to a blend of some television gossip mixed with questions delicately probed the edges of the Crime Squad anti-counterfeit operation.

Then, at last, they heard a vehicle draw up outside and a horn give a double beep.

'My taxi.' Peter Dutch's smile increased another notch. 'That's it, I'm afraid, superintendent. You've got my promise. If I hear anything I'll be in touch.'

They found themselves shepherded through the lobby, then out of the front door. Dutch signalled the driver of the idling taxi to wait, said a quick goodbye to his departing visitors, then the house door closed.

'What do you think, sir?' asked Sandra softly as she followed Thane down the path and out to the roadway. The same, unseen lawnmower still rasped somewhere near.

'You were maybe right,' murmured Thane. 'I think we got the treatment.'

132

Something puzzled him. The slabbed runway leading to the closed garage showed signs of regular use, from oil stains onwards. But a small side window showed that the garage itself was empty.

They went back to the Ford, got aboard, then Thane lingered a little over starting it up. At last, he set it moving and they drove past the waiting taxi. When he glanced back again through his rear view mirror he saw Peter Dutch emerge from his house, close the door behind him and walk towards the taxi.

'Sir – ' began Sandra.

'Not now.' Thane gave her a slight grin and drove on.

Once they were round a bend in the road and out of sight of the taxi, Thane turned off at the first side street. He let the Ford coast to a halt, and watched his rear view mirror. A minute passed, then the taxi went past on the main road with Peter Dutch aboard.

'A job for you, Sandra,' said Thane briskly. 'Make noises like you're some kind of researcher. Knock on a few doors, ask about cars. I want to know why Dutch's garage is empty. Yesterday he used borrowed wheels, today it's a taxi.'

'No problem.' She got out of the Ford, paused long enough to take a chocolate bar from her pocket and bite off a chunk, produced her notebook and a pen, then headed off.

Thane watched her walk back to the main road. Then, as she vanished from sight, he settled comfortably against the driving seat and closed his eyes. After fifteen minutes Sandra got back aboard, and collapsed into her seat.

'I was trapped by the lawnmower man,' she said ruefully. 'I said I was doing a survey about car washes, he wanted to talk about gardens – '

'Get on with it,' scowled Thane.

'Peter Dutch drives a Mitsubishi Shogun station wagon – big, and four-wheel drive. But it's off the road for repairs.'

'Since when?'

She shook her head, her red hair like warm gold in the sunlight. 'He thinks a couple of days ago. Dutch doesn't talk much with his neighbours, but the lawnmower man sometimes does gardening things for him and Dutch told him yesterday.'

'See if it checks out.' Thane started the Ford. He saw the unspoken question in her eyes. 'I just want to be sure – nothing more.'

Not yet. It had started as Sandra's hunch. He would leave it that way.

There was never much in the way of parking space around the red-brick City Mortuary, but Thane's luck held for once. He won a head-on dash for a newly vacated slot, beating a well-jewelled woman who mouthed insults at him through the window glass of her Fiat. He chuckled as the woman drove away, then the chuckle died on his lips as he saw the vintage black Daimler limousine, almost a relic from another age, which sat exactly outside the mortuary entrance. It meant that Doc Williams had called for help.

Sandra followed him into the building. They'd been expected. A small, balding attendant who whistled to himself led them down a tiled corridor, then stopped outside a door that said No Admittance.

'The Professor's here, Mr Thane,' he said cheerfully. 'You know how it is with him – the deader they come, the better he likes it.' The man paused, gave Sandra a cautious, measuring glance. 'An' I've a new story for you. A mother-in-law joke.'

'Go on,' said Thane resignedly. It was as much mortuary routine as avoiding drinking their tea, which was truly awful.

'Well.' The attendant beamed. 'Like, there was this punter who knew his mother-in-law was at the door when his Rottweiler hid under the bed.'

He paused for laughter and Thane gave a duty snort.

'I know one,' said Sandra mildly. 'I've a friend who wouldn't say her mother-in-law was ugly, but when she came visiting the mice threw themselves into the traps.'

'Uh?' The attendant's mouth fell open. Then he swallowed quickly, nodded, tapped on the door, opened it, and waved them through.

The brightly lit autopsy room had tiled walls, stainless steel work tops, and a hose-down concrete floor with built-in drains. Its air reeked of disinfectant. A shape occupying one table was covered by a sheet; on the next table, naked and cleaned up, lay the body of Terry Anson. Long, crudely closed incisions showed that the post-mortem examination had finished. Doc Williams, wearing green surgical overalls, stood beside the table listening to an older, taller, skeletally thin figure who wore an old-fashioned

134

white coat and whose expression, as usual, resembled that of a benevolent vulture.

'You're prompt.' Williams greeted their arrival with relief.

'Better timing than your usual, superintendent.' Professor John MacMaster held the Regius Chair of Forensic Medicine at Glasgow University. Once, years back, Doc Williams had been among his students. 'Ah – ' His watery eyes focused on Sandra, a bony forefinger pointed. 'She's new, I believe.'

'Sergeant Craig,' said Thane. 'Sergeant Dunbar has been promoted.'

'Sergeant Craig,' mused MacMaster. 'You've a first name, sergeant?'

'Sandra, Professor.' She met his fierce gaze calmly.

'A young woman with your looks should be able to find a more suitable way to earn a living,' advised MacMaster severely. 'You could easily become a doctor of medicine, sergeant. These days, any damned fool can be a doctor.'

Doc Williams made a frantic throat-clearing noise. 'I asked Professor MacMaster to be in on this because I thought we could use extra expertise.'

'Always happy to help a colleague who has a problem.' MacMaster gave a small, deliberately wicked wink towards Sandra. 'You would do the same for your superintendent, eh, sergeant?'

'I'd always try, sir,' said Sandra demurely.

'Anyway, to our subject.' MacMaster nodded at the naked corpse. 'He's mildly interesting, wouldn't you agree, Williams?'

'Yes, Professor.' Doc Williams fought down whatever he was feeling and kept a face like stone. 'No real change from what you had already, Colin. He was shot through the back of the head at close range – '

'Very close range,' murmured MacMaster.

'Very close range.' The police surgeon swallowed as he took the correction aboard. 'Death would be instantaneous and occurred about eight hours before he was found. There is considerable ante-mortem bruising around face and body, with extravasation of blood into the skin and subcutaneous tissue.'

Meaning Terry Anson had been badly beaten before he was killed. Thane nodded. It was what he'd expected. Anson's captors had wanted to know how much talking he'd done.

'We'll leave the – ah – routine aspects to our official report,' said MacMaster with some impatience. 'The usual delights, including a last meal of lasagne and brown sauce.' He gave a brief, graveyard smile which took in Sandra and settled on Thane. 'But consider the way he was killed. A single shot through the back of the head, a small, punched entry wound, the bullet track through the cerebral hemispheres with laceration of brain tissues. Usual large exit wound with an outward splintering of bone. No bullet. However – '

'However, you're looking for a Smith and Wesson .38 automatic,' said Doc Williams, taking the cue.

'Show them,' preened MacMaster as Thane and Sandra exchanged a puzzled glance. 'It's – ah – fairly unusual. Not unique, but unusual.'

Doc Williams bent over the corpse, used one arm to raise its shoulders, and then brought the back of Terry Anson's head round under the light. The area of dark hair around the bullet hole had been carefully shaved away and there, etched in black on the exposed skin, Thane saw the fine detail outline of a self-loading pistol.

'It looks even better under infra-red,' said MacMaster. He was pleased to explain. 'Of course, we've photographs. When the pistol was fired, it was in almost direct contact with our corpse's head. So close, we're left with at least singed hair, then carbon deposit and powder tattooing.'

Thane drew a long, deep breath, then let it out slowly. 'You said a Smith and Wesson.'

'An apparent Smith and Wesson,' said MacMaster with typical Regius Chair caution. 'That's going by firearms textbooks. Naturally, we've asked Ballistics for their opinion.'

'Naturally,' murmured Sandra.

MacMaster winced a little, then nodded to Doc Williams. The police surgeon lowered the corpse's shoulders, then stood back.

'Now to his somewhat over-ripe friend.' MacMaster touched an edge of the covering sheet. 'If you want to see him – '

'Once was enough,' said Thane quickly.

'Your choice.' MacMaster nodded. 'Again, shot in the back of the head. But in this case, we've recovered the bullet.' He saw Thane's surprise. 'The explanation is simple enough. The bullet smashed through the skull and caused damage that looks like an exit wound, but which is pressure and splintering. Credit where due – Williams realised we were dealing with a ricochet. He located it, lodged at the back of the skull.'

The police surgeon managed a wary grin. 'As bullets go, it was damaged, Colin. But it looked like a .38. We sent it off to Ballistics.'

'So we might be talking about the same gun?'

'We might be, we might not.' MacMaster frowned in disapproval. 'What is certain is that this fellow had an even rougher time before he was killed. Several of his fingers appear to have been deliberately broken, among other things. But in terms of identification we've been able to give the Records people a rather interesting dental chart.'

'We heard something about fingerprints, Professor,' reminded Sandra Craig.

'Fragments, sergeant. Only fragments,' cautioned MacMaster. He turned to Thane. 'From experience, I'd suggest that Dr Williams' estimate of death as six months ago is more likely to be eight months. Say last September.'

Doc Williams didn't comment. The way he glared at MacMaster when the Regius Professor's back was turned was enough.

They mopped up the remaining details. The cord and canvas used to wrap both bodies had been photographed, then removed. Along with the clothing they had been wearing, they had gone to the partly government-funded forensic science laboratory at the Strathclyde police headquarters building.

The formal autopsy reports would take another day or two. Until they came through, there was nothing more likely to come from the two medical men.

Thane and Sandra Craig made suitable noises and left. When they got back to the Ford, it had acquired a parking ticket.

Strathclyde police headquarters building was about ten minutes away, on the other side of the city centre, a building that kept having extensions added and still never seemed to have enough space for the army of civilian workers and police who were housed within its floors.

Thane dumped the Ford in one of the levels in the building's subterranean car-park. From there they took an elevator into the main building and started along a corridor towards the forensic science department.

137

'Hey, Colin,' hailed a voice behind them, and a lanky, balding man wearing a grey suit and with rimless spectacles caught up with them. Steve Chester was nominally number two at Criminal Records. He grinned at them. 'There's an assistant chief wants to see me, then you were to be next call on my list.'

A cluster of uniformed policewomen passed by, having finished their coffee break, still chattering like budgies.

'You've got a name for our body?' asked Thane hopefully.

'What else?' Chester nodded. 'We were pretty certain earlier. It's on the dental chart – forget the fingerprints, we didn't receive enough to be conclusive.' He reached into a pocket and hauled out a notebook. 'Your second gent's name was Pepe Weide, age thirty, Spanish by birth but London-based. No particular dependants. Convictions for cocaine trafficking – mostly as a courier between here and Europe. He just vanished.'

'When?'

Steve Chester shrugged. 'Nobody's certain. There are a couple of warrants out for his arrest in France, one in Dublin, but he hadn't been seen since last summer. Nobody's going into mourning.'

Chester gave a vague salute and wandered off while the two Crime Squad visitors went on down the corridor. Another fifty yards brought them to the forensic laboratory door, where the female dragon who seemed to always be on guard looked at Thane, nodded, and waved them through.

The laboratory area was large and spotlessly clean. Most of the wall space was occupied by a mix of drug company calendars and sports page pin-ups, from football stars to sweat-and-cleavage female athletes. Someone had a transistor radio softly tuned to a horse race commentary. But the white-coated laboratory staff at the work benches, an equal mix of men and women, were too busy at the apparatus and instruments around them to even notice they had visitors.

Thane led the way across to a glass-fronted office, tapped on the glass, and the man on the other side looked up, grinned, and came out to meet them.

'Shopping for miracles again, Colin?' asked Matthew Amos wryly. A slim, bearded civilian who always wore a dazzling line in bow ties, he had come to the job from a top university research team. Amos, an irreverent anarchist at heart, fought guerrilla wars against any kind of authority but also kept winning international forensic awards. Beaming now, hands stuck deep in the pockets of his laboratory coat, he considered Sandra Craig. 'And the new sergeant – I've heard about you. Good luck, girl – with a boss like this one, you'll need it.'

She grinned but said nothing.

'Come into the goldfish bowl.' He gestured them into his room then raised his voice to a near-bellow. 'Anna, it's an invasion. Come and help!'

'On my way.' One of the white-coated figures, petite, slim and raven-haired, left the electronic equipment she'd been tending and followed Amos into his office to join them. She carried a thin cardboard file and what looked like a collection of supermarket till rolls filled with bar-code symbols.

'These?' asked Amos.

She nodded and spread them on his desk.

Thane knew her. Anna Huang was Hong Kong Chinese by birth, raised in Canada, and now in Scotland on a doctorate scholarship. In brains as well as looks, Matt Amos had assigned the Crime Squad work to one of his best people.

'So.' Amos hummed a tune under his breath for a moment while he glanced at the bar-code slips and checked a couple of items in the file. 'Suppose we start with what Ballistics say. Tell them, Anna.'

'Yes, master.' Anna Huang said it drily, in her pronounced Canadian accent. 'You're certainly looking for a Smith and Wesson, superintendent. The muzzle imprint from the autopsy matches up. The bullet out of the second skull isn't too damaged. It's definitely from a .38, jacket markings say it was fired from a Smith and Wesson, but not necessarily the same weapon.'

Also on the report from Ballistics was confirmation that cartridge cases found at Dark Loch had been from a Kalashnikov automatic rifle. All except an item which pointed to at least one other member of the grave-digging group being armed, a single used cartridge case ejected from a 9mm Luger.

Then it was Amos's turn, tweaking at his bow tie, theatrically clearing his throat.

'Right. Bits and pieces, no particular order. We found nothing special about the clothes taken from either of your bodies, Colin. Ordinary multiple store stuff, empty pockets like you'd expect.'

'There was a separate blouson jacket,' reminded Thane.

'Uh-huh.' Amos tapped at one of the bar-code rolls. 'Complete with bloodstains. Anna's done a full DNA blood profiling on that.'

Thane had expected that much. A full Deoxyribonucleic Acid autoradiograph, the Sunday name for a DNA bar-code readout, could be obtained from a sample as small as a speck of blood or a flake of human skin – and there had been so much blood on the shoulder of the blouson jacket found near the loch that the only real surprise would have been if it hadn't happened.

DNA readouts could do wonderful things. They could give a genetic profile several million times more comparison-accurate than blood-typing and many times better than fingerprinting. They could say things about an individual's parents and indicate genetically inherited medical conditions.

But until a second sample existed to be matched against the first it could only lie in waiting. Giving some civil rights activists another thing to campaign against.

'Now it's my turn,' said the forensic scientist, tugging his bow tie again. 'Did old MacMaster feed you a line about experience telling him that body number two died around last September?'

Puzzled, Thane nodded.

'Total garbage,' snorted Amos. 'He found exactly the same as we did. There were traces of vegetation and insects trapped inside number two's canvas wrap-around from when he was being buried. Vegetation and insects each have their life cycles. A child's home botany kit could provide a date that would be accurate to a lot less than a month at any time of year.'

'He's a tricky old devil,' admitted Thane. 'But smooth with it.'

Sandra Craig frowned. 'But what about the way they were wrapped?'

'You were the first to spot the nautical knots, right?' Amos nodded. 'That wins a gold star, sergeant. Definite full rolling hitches on both.'

'Anything more on that?' asked Thane hopefully.

'Yes – and no.' Amos took a single typed report sheet from the file then gave a mild curse. One of his team out at a bench in the main laboratory was looking over and signalling. Giving a grimace, Amos handed the report sheet to Thane. 'Read it. I'll be back.'

The scientist headed off. Leaning back against a filing cabinet, Thane looked at the report. It had been prepared by Anna Huang, who already had a surprising number of qualifications after her name, and had also been signed by Amos as assistant director. The lengths of cord tied round the bodies had come from an apparently common source: they were both of off-white nylon with a blue marker thread.

He glanced at Anna Huang. 'How about possible sources?'

'We tried.' She shook her head. 'It's not for climbing or nautical use, superintendent. It's just a strong, thin, multi-purpose nylon cord, sold in quantity for plenty of uses. The blue marker thread indicates strength, nothing more.'

Thane murmured his thanks and read the rest of the report. The two sections of canvas used to package the bodies had been cut from different weaves of medium-weight rubberised sheeting. They were badly weathered and faded, but both had originally been green in colour. He passed the report sheet to Sandra Craig as Amos returned.

'Sorry, folks.' Amos gave an apologetic shrug. 'That was something else which doesn't do you much good. Scenes of Crime found some traces of tyre tracks up near where the blouson jacket was lying and we'd been trying to do something with them.' He shook his head. 'There's not enough for us to say more than that they were probably made by heavy-duty tyres on a four-wheel drive vehicle – and no way could we say more.'

'Four-wheel drive – like a Mitsubishi station wagon?' suggested Thane softly. He glanced at Sandra. 'We've maybe got one in the frame, Matt.'

'Don't try to nail me down, Colin. That's as far as I'll go.' Amos reached for an earthenware jar marked Poison on his desk and removed the lid. The jar was filled with toffees and he popped one into his mouth before offering the jar around. Sandra Craig helped herself to a couple.

'Four-wheel drive,' said Thane again, but saw Amos wouldn't be drawn. 'All right. Anything still to come?'

'Maybe.' Amos spoke through his toffee. 'We've a few other tests to go, but the kind that take time. Like there are some strange stains on the canvas sheeting, small but maybe enough to identify a source.' He beamed at Anna Huang. 'More night work together, Anna?'

'Why not, master?' she said stonily, then winked at Sandra Craig. 'Don't worry about him, sergeant. He's certified harmless.'

141

They made to leave. Amos grinned and shoved the jar of toffees towards Sandra again. She took an unashamed handful as they went out.

The rendezvous point for the factory raid was at Lanarkshire Business Park, a green field development of warehouses and office units located in open country about fifteen miles east of Glasgow. It was close to the M8 Glasgow–Edinburgh motorway, new enough for some buildings still to be awaiting their first tenants.

Gypsy Adams had scheduled the raid for noon. Thane drove the Crime Squad's Ford into the park with a few minutes in hand, Sandra Craig beside him, Phil Moss and Francey Dunbar sharing the rear seat. Jock Dawson's dog-van was close behind and also had Joe Felix aboard. They followed instructions and parked in the shelter of a delivery yard at the rear of an unoccupied warehouse where a number of other vehicles were already waiting, crews standing around in small groups in the bright sunlight.

'I'll see what's happening,' said Thane. 'Wait here.'

He got out of the Ford, saw Gypsy Adams at the warehouse door, waved, and walked towards him. On the way, he recognised some of the faces around and some of the vehicles. They ranged from Customs officers and Inland Revenue to a couple of Immigration officers, some people from the Trading Standards CATS team, and a squad of local police.

'Good to see you, Thane,' said Gypsy Adams as he arrived. Adams had a small, anxious man in a business suit with him. 'Superintendent Thane, this is Tom Harris. Mr Harris is site manager for the business park. He's being very helpful.'

Harris gave a weak smile as they shook hands, then took a bewildered look around. 'I didn't expect so many people.'

'More people, less trouble,' said Gypsy Adams heavily. 'We'll get it done quicker that way. But that's about everybody now – ' He glanced at Thane.' Right?'

'Nearly.' Another Crime Squad car load should have arrived with them, led by Tina Redder. 'Any minute.'

'Fine.' Adams glanced at the business park manager. 'Let's go up to your viewpoint again, Tom.'

Thane followed them into the empty building. Together, they

climbed a long spiral of concrete stairway, their footsteps echoing. At the top, there was a window. Harris took a moment to recover his breath, then pointed.

'Across there, superintendent. The red roof, Unit Eight East.' He paused for another breath. 'Temple Brown Clothing – they moved in about six months ago, they had bank references and they paid a year in advance.'

'Bank references can be faked,' said Gypsy Adams unemotionally.

They were standing three floors up and looking out across a network of service roads and buildings towards the far side of the business park. Unit Eight East's red roof made it stand out from its neighbours. A modest two-storey building, windows sparkling in the sunlight, the only sign of life it showed as a large van and two cars parked near a service entrance.

'We've never had any problems with them, superintendent.' The site manager was rueful. 'All I know is they claim to make contract clothing – uniforms, that kind of thing. Any time we've had to discuss anything, I've met with one of the partners – usually Mr Temple Brown himself.'

'Friendly?' guessed Thane, looking out again towards the red roof.

'Yes,' said Harris. 'Very.'

'That's how they operate,' said Thane sympathetically.

'I suppose you're right.' Harris nodded sadly. 'I'd like to keep out of this. Can I leave you?'

Gypsy Adams agreed and the site manager thankfully retreated.

'Well?' The fat, unshaven Trading Standards supervisor grinned at Thane. 'You see it all.'

'What do you know about inside the place?' asked Thane.

'I've gone over the interior plans with Harris, I've had one of my lads looking around as a telephone maintenance man.' Adams leaned his elbows on the windowsill. 'We reckon there are around thirty-five people in the unit. They take a lunch-break at twelve ten. We'll go in at twelve fifteen, as they start eating. There's a canteen area where we'll probably scoop up most of them.'

'Fine.' As a plan, it made sense. Thane joined Adams at the windowsill, looking down towards the clustered, hidden vehicles. 'Why are Immigration along?'

Adams grimaced. 'We're always likely to turn up a few illegals

143

on a deal like this. They'll work for sweat-shop wages. Without papers, it's the only work they can get.'

'So they lose out.' Thane nodded a wry understanding, then, although the windowsill was warm in the sunlight, he felt a sudden chill. He'd been looking down at where his Crime Squad team were waiting, with still no sign of Tina Redder. But further back, behind the squad of local police, there was another newly arrived vehicle, a white Range-Rover. The police driver standing beside it wore black combat boots, blue coveralls, and a blue beret. Startled, he stared at Adams. 'What the hell are tactical armed support doing here? What makes you think we'll have shooting?'

'The local divisional commander authorised them as back-up. My Mega Mickey says some of The Cutters could be carrying.' Adams' expression made it clear he didn't totally accept his informant's word. 'Maybe they are, maybe they aren't. Anything wrong with having insurance?'

Thane couldn't argue.

Gypsy Adams' plan was simple enough, an encircling of the Temple Brown unit, a last-minute warning by loudhailer, then a simultaneous invasion through the main front door, the service entrance at the side, and two small rear fire doors. Thane volunteered to take the service entrance and suggested a couple of minor changes to the rest of what Adams had in mind. They then parted, Thane going back down to the Crime Squad group.

'Any word from Tina Redder?' he demanded.

Moss gave a shrug and an off-key belch.

'Ever known a woman who could read a map, sir?' asked Joe Felix. 'She'll have lost her way.'

'Very funny. Now shut up, gather round, and listen,' Thane told them wearily. He used the toe of his shoe to scrape a rough map on the gravel at his feet. 'Here's what we've got to do and how we'll do it. Phil, you'll take Francey and Joe. Sandra, you and Jock and his dogs will be with me.'

He explained the plan. When he'd finished, each had their own small preparations to make and left him alone. Thane was glad. Leaning against the sun-warmed metal of the Ford, he allowed himself the luxury of a sigh. There had to be something wrong about the raid ahead. Somehow it was all too simple. Was a team as efficiently organised as The Cutters really going to be taken out so easily?

144

He doubted it. Every new fact he had gathered seemed against it – and the feeling had only been strengthened in the brief time he'd spent at the Crime Squad base when he returned there from Strathclyde's headquarters.

Now there was a definite lead into some heavyweight drug dealing, and he'd found the Squad's drugs specialists excited at the news that the second body at Dark Loch had been identified as Pepe Weide. They had their own file on the Anglo-Spanish cocaine courier. They knew him as an operator with an almost equal interest in heroin, working between Britain and several countries in Western Europe.

When Weide had vanished those months back, he'd remained an annoying enigma for Interpol. Now, although few people would mourn him, it meant a lot of new questions would have to be addressed.

In other areas, there hadn't been time to add anything that seemed to matter to the file Crime Squad were now running on Emma Raleigh and Peter Dutch. And things weren't much better concerning the Pizzaro Truck Rental company. Burrowing on, Francey Dunbar had discovered that Pizzaro was administered through a chartered accountant's office in Edinburgh. The chartered accountant acted for nominee shareholders and a tax-haven investment bank in Bermuda.

But why go to that kind of trouble for a flea-size truck company unless it had something to hide?

The Crime Squad group were in position behind the shelter of a long, brick-built shed which housed a couple of quietly buzzing electrical transformers. Dawson's dogs were with them, a tail occasionally swishing or a soft, questioning whine showing that they were impatient. From the edge of the shed, the view was directly across to the service entrance. The van and cars were still parked outside, another delivery van was inside the service entrance, backed against a deserted loading bay. Easing back, Thane nodded to his red-haired sergeant and heard her murmuring into a personal radio, advising the county car acting as control that they were ready and standing by.

Seconds crawled. Still nothing showed at the factory unit although they could hear a faint throb of machinery somewhere inside, then a woman's loud laughter.

Suddenly, the harsh rasp of a hand-held loudhailer bellowed over everything, the voice belonging to Gypsy Adams. 'Temple

Brown factory, this is a combined Trading Standards and police operation. Stay exactly where you are.'

Adams appeared in the open, over towards the front entrance to the building. Feet wide apart, a bulky, intimidating menace of a figure, he made to raise the loudhailer to his mouth again. But he was beaten to it.

'Go. Go.' The bark came from the personal radio in Sandra Craig's grasp.

'Now,' yelled Thane. 'Move!'

His group charged forward. He could glimpse other groups doing the same and Adams had begun bellowing with the loudhailer again.

Then suddenly all hell was breaking loose.

It began with screams and shouts inside the building, punctuated by loud crashes as things were knocked over. A window smashed, then another. The screams and shouts grew louder and people began to pour out of the door behind the service bay. Forcing their way through everyone, two men in particular rushed along the bay's loading platform and tried to scramble into the waiting delivery van. One of them was waving a silver-coloured handgun. When he saw the charging group of police he swung the gun towards them.

'Take them, you pair,' ordered Jock Dawson, slipping the leashes from his charges.

As the two men reached the van doors, both dogs sprang forward like hairy thunderbolts. The handgun fired once, the bullet ricocheting off the ground near Thane's feet. Then Rajah's dark, snarling bulk was there, his white fangs clamping on the man's gun-arm above the wrist. They went down together. Rajah snarling and worrying, bodily shaking the terrified thug. The gun fell to the ground and Thane kicked it away. Goldie, different by nature, waited until her separate quarry was hauling himself into the driving seat. The slim yellow Labrador bitch took a single effortless leap, her teeth sank into the man's exposed rear and his scream was high-pitched agony.

Thane ignored them. Vaguely, he saw Joe Felix tackle and bring down another fleeing man, then he had to push his way in through a panicking flood of women in work overalls trying to get out. Somehow he got past them while the shouts and screams continued, then he shoved his way in through the inner doorway with support close behind him.

They had arrived in the main factory area. More people were trying to escape, a window was smashed, and a man dived through the gap as a fresh group of police and CATS officers arrived from the front of the building. The loudhailer had gone silent and the turmoil was subsiding. Scattered, bewildered groups of workers, some sullen, some frightened, stood around the factory floor.

Unit Eight East was no shoe-string operation. The plant around Thane ranged from gleaming modern sewing and embroidering machines to a giant colour photocopier and what looked like a packaging line devoted to wrapping and heat-sealing. Stacked empty cartons waited to be filled. Piles of cheap, bought-in clothing, the raw materials of any counterfeit operation, waited to be put through a surface metamorphosis which would at least quadruple their value.

'Everything damped down outside,' reported Francey Dunbar, reaching him. 'The gun was a Colt .32, nothing like what we're after.' He paused and gave a puzzled glance at the people around. 'Now what do we do about this lot?'

'Round them up, hold them outside.' Thane winced as he saw two women standing together, one grey-haired, the other in her late teens, both Asian, both in tears. 'Francey, do it gently. God knows who we've got here and they're in enough of a panic. Pass the word.'

He left Dunbar to get on with it. Gypsy Adams had appeared at the other end of the factory unit. The big, unshaven CATS supervisor was holding a man pinned against the wall using one massive hand. Signalling, Thane made his way over past more silent machines, and Adams greeted him with a nod and a scowl. The man against the wall was middle-aged, grey-haired, and looked extremely unhappy.

'What's the problem?' asked Thane.

'This is!' Gypsy Adams made it a snarl. His prisoner, dressed in a grey business suit with white shirt, yellow tie, and brown suede shoes, shrank even further back. 'This is – he is! Thane, we've been set up, used! Will I tell you what we've done?' He rammed his captive against the wall again. 'We've taken out a counterfeit factory, yes. But here's the owner – Paddy Mackin, someone I thought was still in a prison cell in Cyprus. He's not The Cutters – he's one of the nearest things they've got to competition!'

'But non-violent, Mr Adams – you know me,' quavered Mackin.

147

He moistened his lips and gave Thane an appealing glance. 'Totally non-violent – ask anyone!'

'Then what about the bampot who took a shot at me at your loading bay?' asked Thane sardonically.

'That was just Sonny Kenton.' Mackin quickly moistened his lips. 'Sonny's job is security. Sometimes he panics. But he wouldn't mean any real harm. You've got to believe it!'

'Right now, we're believing damn all,' rasped Gypsy Adams. He glanced at Thane. 'I'm going to radio back to my office – and I can guess what I'm going to hear about Mega Mickey, who should be waiting there to collect from us.' He released Mackin, and the man remained too terrified to move. 'Do me a favour, Thane. Watch him for me. You could maybe ask where his sister Ruth is hiding – they're in most things together.'

The CATS supervisor hurried purposefully away.

'Mister – ' Mackin eyed Thane anxiously. 'Who are you?'

'Police.' Thane showed his warrant card. 'Now where do we find sister Ruth?'

Mackin nervously chewed his lip for a moment, sighed, then nodded in the direction of a door which said Women. Thane saw Sandra Craig passing, and beckoned.

'Yours, sergeant.' He indicated the door. 'Her name is Ruth.'

Sandra went in. She emerged moments later, bringing out a glum-faced woman in her late forties who was slightly built and had mousy fair hair. She glared at Thane, then went to stand beside her brother.

'Just bad luck, sis,' said Mackin bitterly. 'They thought we were Cutters.'

Ruth Mackin shrugged.

'Seen this, sir?' Sandra Craig brought over an almost-finished sweatshirt from the nearest work table. 'They seem to work at the better end of the market!'

The flimsy sweatshirt had a fake Lacoste crocodile badge on the chest. An equally fake inside label was partly stitched to the neckband.

'We had a good run this time,' said Paddy Mackin sadly. 'More than eight months, and no problems.' He nodded at the sweatshirt. 'This was a new line – the first part of a damned big order from Ireland, with another waiting after it from Belgium.'

'And plenty of others like them,' snapped his sister. She paused,

148

looking past them, seeing Gypsy Adams on his way back. 'Well, I might have known that bastard would be part of this!'

When Adams reached them, his scowl was as deep as ever. He ignored brother and sister and shrugged at Thane.

'He's done a runner,' he reported gloomily.

'Mega Mickey?' Thane almost smiled at the CATS man's gloom over the way his information had backfired.

'The same.' Adams folded his arms and grimaced like a disappointed Buddha. 'We had him waiting at Trading Standards. Except he vanished out of the building about half an hour ago.' He swung on the Mackins. 'I can't prove it yet. But my money says The Cutters set you two up.'

The Mackins exchanged a shrug. Behind them, Thane could see the Customs squad and the Inland Revenue team had already taken over the office area around the main door. The Mackins' work-force – at a rough count, around forty, the way it had been suggested – were outside in the open, some already being questioned.

'Well,' mused Gypsy Adams. 'You'll lose this lot.' He gestured at the equipment around. 'How much money is here, Paddy?'

'Two hundred thousand or so. Win some, lose some.' Mackin wasn't too perturbed. 'We've made enough. At least it won't be another Cyprus prison, thank God. You wouldn't believe the lousy food they serve, out there.'

'You can still get a little of your own back,' suggested Thane softly. 'What do you know about The Cutters?'

'Not a lot, mister.' The answer, with a grimace, came from Ruth Mackin. 'Except they've already warned us off. We've been annoying them, getting in the way, taking some of their trade.'

'Do they have names?'

The Mackins exchanged an unhappy glance. Again Ruth Mackin answered. 'No, and that's for real. We've had phone calls, bricks through windows, Paddy had his car shot at. But we don't know names, and I'm glad. Can you understand why, mister?'

Thane nodded. He did.

But he tried again and so did Gypsy Adams, with no more success from their questions. Finally, giving up, they left the brother and sister partnership in the care of two CATS officers and went out of the building. Outside, the line of detained workers was beginning to thin. Some had already been released, others had been taken away for further questioning. Jock Dawson and his dogs were there, in theory keeping watch on those left. In practice, Rajah was lying on his back and allowing one of the office juniors to tickle his stomach. Goldie was sharing a sandwich with another.

Thane raised an eyebrow at Dawson. 'Any problems?'

'The dogs are fine, sir,' said Dawson with a poker face. 'A wee bit of exercise never does them any harm. I've told Inspector Moss I'll make the usual arrest reports.'

'They did well,' mused Thane.

'Aye.' Dawson's face thawed to a grin. 'And those two they took out won't forget it!'

Thane left him and walked on again with Adams.

Suddenly, Adams stopped and gave a sigh. 'Sorry we wasted your time.'

'You got a result,' reminded Thane. 'Maybe not the result you expected, but don't knock it. And we both learned a few things.'

He stopped at that and Adams was on too much of a low to say more as they began to help with the rest of the mopping up. They had barely started when a Crime Squad transit van arrived, Tina Redder and her people piling out as it halted.

'Welcome,' said Thane drily. 'What happened to you?'

'What happened was a bomb scare at Glasgow Airport,' snapped Tina Redder. 'We were diverted as back-up, we sat in that damned transit for over an hour and weren't needed.'

'Couldn't you have radioed?' asked Thane.

'You were supposed to be told,' she said grimly. 'Then I tried to radio you that we were on our way – and that damned transit's set is dead. On top of which the idiot constable driving us took a wrong turning.'

'Happens to us all,' said Thane woodenly.

'Platitudes I can do without,' she said icily, then looked around. 'Colin, a warning. Tell your new baby sergeant that if I hear just one crack about this then I'll wear her guts for garters!'

'I like the thought,' said Thane. 'Then why not dance on a table top? Maybe we could sell tickets.'

'Don't push your luck – sir.' The words came from her lips like chipped ice. 'I could get you in the frame for sexual harassment or some damned thing.'

He stood where he was, grinning a little, while she walked away. Sandra Craig joined him.

'What happened to our Tina?' asked Sandra with a straight-faced concern. 'Couldn't she get her broomstick to kick-start, sir?'

Thane winced. He liked Tina Redder. She was a highly efficient chief inspector, but there were times when she could act as if she'd be perfectly at home on a broomstick. Probably with a very large black cat perched on her shoulder.

'Stop it right there, Sandra,' he said stonily. 'That's an order.'

Acting Detective Sergeant Sandra Craig read the signs and obeyed.

7

Even using Tina Redder's reinforcements and some additional local assistance, it was another two hours before the real heat had gone out of the Unit Eight East operation.

By then, there were sixteen people, including nine illegal immigrants, in custody on a variety of charges. Four were wanted by other forces on outstanding warrants. At least five thousand completed garments, a mix of fake Lacoste and other design counterfeits, had been seized. Roughly the same number again, partly completed, had also been taken. The Customs team and the Inland Revenue squads were looking unusually happy.

'I'm pulling out,' announced Gypsy Adams, meeting Thane outside the factory's front door. The swarthy, balding CATS supervisor gave a grimace which was hard to read. 'I've got to get back and explain this lot to my bosses. It's maybe worth a couple of faint cheers, but it isn't what anybody expected.'

'You've still a result,' said Thane. Part of his attention was on Phil Moss, several feet away and leaning against one of the cars. Moss was grimacing with pain, with one hand holding his stomach. Even by the scrawny little man's standards, his face was grey.

'And tomorrow's another day, right?' Adams couldn't see Moss, who was behind him. 'And what we've got is a reasonable enough haul.'

Thane nodded. Sandra Craig had appeared from somewhere and was talking to Moss. From Moss's scowling reaction, her attention wasn't being welcomed. With Phil Moss, that was no surprise. But he had a question of his own to ask Adams. 'What happens to the clothing you've seized?'

'In theory, a court will order it to be forfeited and destroyed.' Adams shrugged. 'In practice, it'll end up as a back-door gift to some overseas charity agency. They'll cut out the naughty bits

152

and some poor devils out in Bosnia or somewhere will be wearing what's left a few months from now.'

'So somebody somewhere still wins,' mused Thane.

'Something like that.' Gypsy Adams nodded. 'Anyway, I'm going to take tonight off, have some rest and relaxation. Then I'll be in touch.'

He ambled off, thumbs hitched into his broad leather belt, nodding to Moss on the way. Moss was alone again, and most of the pain seemed to have been ironed from his face. Thane went over.

'You feeling all right?' he asked quietly.

'Plain, ordinary gut-ache,' said Moss defensively. 'Maybe something I ate.' He released a long belch as sour punctuation. 'No worries.'

Thane raised an eyebrow, but didn't press things.

A little later, he pulled his team out and left Tina Redder to cope with what remained. By late afternoon, he was back at Crime Squad headquarters. Half an hour later, he summoned everyone through to his office and they arrived one by one – Francey Dunbar first, then Jock Dawson without dogs, followed by Moss and Joe Felix.

'Where's Sandra?' asked Thane.

'She went out,' said Dunbar vaguely. 'She had to collect something.'

'Something?' That was all anybody knew. Thane sighed. 'All right, let's get on with it.'

He sat at his desk while the others took positions around the room. For a moment Thane considered the few notes in front of him. Two in particular might matter. Liam Riley had telephoned while they were on the raid. The trade union man might have something useful to pass on, but would be out of town until the next morning. He'd be in touch again. And Anna Huang had faxed a message from Strathclyde headquarters. The forensic examination of stains on the canvas shrouds had identified them as road tar.

'For now, we work on what we've got,' he told the others. 'Keep at it, and hope that tomorrow could be a better day – ' He stopped as Sandra arrived, out of breath, hurrying from wherever she'd been.

'Sorry, sir.' She flushed red under the grins from the others.

'That's all right, sergeant,' said Thane stonily. 'Thank you for finding the time to come.' He took a moment to build a slow steeple with his fingertips. 'So, now I won't have to repeat myself, everybody works on at what they've been doing. Francey, you and Joe stay with the Pizzaro Trucks angle – everything and anything about them.'

Francey Dunbar nodded soberly. 'Suppose it looks like we should go up there?'

'Then do it. But I want to know first.' He switched his attention to Sandra Craig and Jock Dawson. 'You two stay on Dutch and the Raleigh woman – background, find out more about why Dutch's car is off the road, any wisp of a drugs link – I don't have to spell it out.' He thumbed at Phil Moss. 'Inspector Moss is in the driving seat.'

'While you're doing what, sir?' asked Dunbar with a bland curiosity.

'Taking some time off.' Thane considered them carefully. 'Or that's how it's going to look. I'm going to a fashion show and my wife is going to be with me. Any comment?'

'Enjoy,' said Dunbar, a look of gradual understanding on his face.

They broke up. Thane made a few phone calls, including one to Anna Huang to thank her for her fax about the road tar stains and another to check that the divisional team out at Dark Loch hadn't come up with anything fresh. Then he called it a day, clearing his desk, and said goodnight to Moss on the way out.

'About this fashion show,' said Moss gravely. 'Maybe Mary deserves an occasional present – she puts up with a lot.'

'And maybe you should mind your own damned business,' said Thane.

They exchanged a grin, and he left.

It was after 6 p.m. when he arrived home, but there was no sign of Mary's car. Tommy and Kate were having another of their full-scale rows while Clyde barked from the half-way landing on the stairs.

'Where's your mother?' he asked as soon as some semblance of glowering order had been restored between the two teenagers.

'Out,' said Tommy.

'She won't be long,' said Kate.

It was communication, if nothing else, and Mary had left a

frozen meal for the pair beside the microwave. Kate had it ready to serve by the time Thane had poured himself a whisky. He watched a TV news bulletin and sipped while they ate, then Mary arrived. She was carrying a long package over one arm.

'I could use a drink,' she declared. 'I've had that kind of a day.'

Thane poured her a glass of dry white wine, and she took a grateful gulp.

'Shouldn't you be getting ready?' asked Kate.

'Yes.' She beckoned as Thane topped up his own glass. 'Both of us.'

When they went up to their bedroom, Thane found his dinner jacket already laid out. Mary left the package over a chair and showered. It was Thane's turn when she came out. When he emerged, his wife scooped up the package from the chair and disappeared into the bathroom. He had almost finished changing when she appeared again.

Thane stared.

'Like it?' she teased.

He nodded, momentarily lost for words, the package explained. The simple black silk dress his wife was wearing was dateless in style, total in effect, emphasising a figure which made a nonsense of the existence of the two teenagers below.

'You look good,' he said quietly.

'I think so.' She grinned and twirled in front of a mirror. 'I got lucky. Don't ask, I'll explain later.'

He raised an eyebrow but nodded. The telephone rang. It was answered downstairs, then Kate shouted up that the call was for him. Thane took the call on the bedroom extension.

'Sorry to chase you.' Francey Dunbar's voice didn't hold any particular regret. 'But you wanted to be told if anything started shaping. It might be that way, sir.'

'Go on.' Thane cradled the phone between chin and shoulder and grimaced at his wife.

'It's Pizzaro Trucks. They've something moving.' Dunbar was confident. 'Thank my Federation contact up at Crieff. Pizzaro's manager had backed out of a local business dinner he was invited to attend tonight. He made noises about unexpected work, that they were a driver short, and that he'd need to handle one of two trucks going on a run south tonight.'

'Good. Better than good.' Thane bared his teeth at the telephone mouthpiece. Suddenly there was an even stronger reason for the

155

way the CATS team had been steered towards the modest counterfeit operation in Lanarkshire. If The Cutters had an important
delivery run scheduled but were worried about the way things
had been stirred up, it had been the perfect way to distract
attention. 'Where's Phil Moss?'

'Gone out to Dark Loch again. The local cops are making
worried noises about something they've found.'

Thane winced. 'Are we talking another body?'

'It's vague, but it doesn't sound that way, sir.'

'Then let's hope it can wait.' The Pizzaro developments could
matter much more. 'Give Pizzaro priority. We need to know when
these trucks leave and where they're heading. If necessary, make
it a special search request, all forces – sightings to be reported, but
they're not to be stopped. Keep Pizzaro up front.'

'For how long?' asked Dunbar warily.

'As long as it takes,' Thane told him.

'Understood,' said Dunbar sadly.

'Something wrong?' queried Thane.

'It's not a something, it's a someone,' said Dunbar gloomily,
'and the second time in a row I've had to call off.' He sighed. 'I'll
survive. Enjoy your own evening – sir.'

Thane said goodnight and hung up. Then another small war
was breaking out downstairs and he was yelling for it to stop.

At last, when Mary was ready to leave, they went down
together. Kate stared open-mouthed at her mother, who was
wearing a fine antique lace shawl across her shoulders. Tommy
whistled. They went out to the car and Thane opened the passenger door for Mary.

'Right.' She settled the lace shawl around her once she was
aboard, then winked. 'Into battle.'

Thane got behind the wheel, started the Ford, and looked at his
wife again.

He already had his winner.

Parking space around the City Chambers was usually reserved for
elected council members. But it had been thrown in for the night
with the fashion show hire. Thane left the Crime Squad Ford
beside an exotic line-up of other guest vehicles from Rolls Royces
to Jaguars, then he and Mary walked through the dusk to the
main entrance to the building. Uniformed commissionaires

checked entry tickets, then they joined the steady trickle of arrivals heading up the broad marble stairway which led to the banqueting hall.

'Try and look happy, Colin,' muttered Mary Thane, elbowing him. 'This was all your idea.'

He grinned and they went in. The banqueting hall, a place of rich wood panelling, marble pillars and crystal chandeliers, had an eight-piece band playing in one corner. It was background to the hubbub of conversation of two or three hundred guests. A temporary catwalk ran down the centre of the hall, with drapes and lighting.

'There's your Peter Dutch,' said Mary softly with a slight nod towards the catwalk. The corners of her mouth crinkled. 'I thought they were just showing him as TV repeats these days.'

'He's alive,' said Thane soberly. The television presenter, resplendent in a white tuxedo and scarlet bow tie, was kneeling on the edge of the catwalk and talking to a large woman with a sparkle of diamonds who had to be one of the organisers. 'Alive, and maybe worth watching.'

Waiters were offering trays of drinks and savouries. They sipped champagne, nibbled, and Thane looked around for any sign of a familiar face. He was found first.

'So you made it! Good!' Stewart Rae eased his way through the other guests around. He had a beam on his rugged face, an attractive, dark-haired woman in tow. The sportswear agent dragged her closer. 'Thane, this is Sophie – '

'The wife,' completed Sophie Rae. She was wearing a green silk two-piece suit, and gave a friendly smile towards Mary as they completed the introductions. 'I should say thank you. Your husband is the reason that Stewart decided we'd better come tonight.'

'Hell, I just thought you could maybe use a guide or something.' Rae gave Mary an admiring glance. 'You're a bonus. I wasn't sure what a cop's wife would be like.'

'Now you know,' said Sophie Rae cheerfully. She took Mary's arm. 'Come on – they'll be safe enough on their own.'

She swept Mary off into the general bustle. Stewart Rae collected a glass of champagne from another passing tray, then eyed Thane shrewdly.

'You've seen Dutch?'

Thane nodded.

157

'There's a rumour going around about a raid on a Lacoste counterfeit factory,' murmured Rae. 'True?'

'True,' agreed Thane.

Rae shrugged. 'Well, I'll introduce you to people as a friend, no police label. You take it from there, right?' He stroked his small, dark moustache with a thoughtful air. 'Your wife has damned good dress taste, Thane – and if you make it, spend it, that's my motto!' Then he looked past Thane and his expression changed. 'And here's someone you should meet!'

Thane found himself shaking hands with a small, plump man wearing a chunky gold bracelet on one wrist. His name was Sandros, he ran a string of out-of-town fashion stores, and he had a companion, a smoothly tailored Belgian who was something vague in marketing designer underwear.

They talked, then Thane drifted with Stewart Rae again, meeting more of the same, including two women who were queen bee buyers for department stores. Each time he left it to Stewart Rae to steer their small-talk round to gossip about counterfeiting, using the Lacoste raid as a starting point. Each time, he ended up with little that registered as mattering.

The Belgian who marketed designer underwear had heard a whisper that items from one of the new-season collections due to be paraded on the catwalk were already being produced in a counterfeit factory. On at least three other occasions a quick, tight smile and a rapid change of topic left Thane sure that he was with someone who probably knew more than they intended to reveal.

Then, suddenly, he found himself being dragged away by Stewart Rae.

'Look over there,' said Rae in surprise. 'That's something I didn't expect!'

Thane looked, then smothered a curse. It took a moment to recognise Gypsy Adams. Usual beard stubble shaved away, hair newly cut, wearing a faultlessly tailored dinner jacket and black tie, the barrel-shaped CATS supervisor was coming straight towards them.

With a smiling Emma Raleigh on his arm.

'What goes on?' asked Stewart Rae, bewildered. 'Thane, I thought – '

'Just don't,' said Thane quickly. 'Play it straight.'

Emma Raleigh greeted them both with a calm, assured nod. The slim blonde boutique owner wore a designer outfit of cream silk trousers and matching blouse, teamed with a dark brown silk embroidered waistcoat. The gold ring set with diamonds was on her wedding finger as before, but now backed by a thin gold chain at her throat with a large solitaire diamond set in a gold pendant.

'I didn't expect you to be here, superintendent.' She frowned.

'That makes two of us,' said a startled Gypsy Adams. 'You didn't tell me!'

'Did you?' asked Thane drily.

'I – uh – well, I kind of gave you a hint, Thane,' said Adams with an embarrassed grin. 'I called Emma last night. My idea was we could go out for a meal somewhere – '

'But I had to be at the show, so we're here.' Emma Raleigh left it there and glanced at Rae. 'Stewart, didn't I see your wife back there, with some woman in a black dress?'

'My wife,' said Thane.

'Is she?' Emma Raleigh looked surprised and gave Stewart Rae an odd glance. 'Nice dress. She looks good in it.'

'Nice party,' said Gypsy Adams briskly. He helped himself to a fresh glass from another passing tray of drinks and beamed. 'God bless whoever is picking up the tab.'

'Not necessary,' said Emma Raleigh sardonically. 'It's tax deductible.'

Thane shook his head when the tray of drinks reached him. Strathclyde's traffic department gave no quarter when it came to drivers and breath tests. He'd already had enough. Then his attention was drawn back to the catwalk area as its lighting brightened, other lights dimmed, and the background music grew in volume. A first trickle of guests headed for the tables around the edges.

It was cabaret time. A red-nosed comedian came out and launched into a red-nosed routine. As he did, Peter Dutch appeared in the background, down from the catwalk but standing where it disappeared behind curtains which cloaked the backstage area. This time the TV presenter was talking to a stranger who wore a dinner jacket which looked one size too small for him.

'There's something I've got to do,' Thane told the others. 'I'll be back.'

Leaving them, he made his way across the dimly lit hall. Peter Dutch was still talking to the stranger, who was heavily built with short, dark hair and who looked in his late thirties. The stranger reached out to dump an emptied glass on a passing waiter's tray.

Even in the dimmed light Thane had a brief glimpse of the edge of a tattoo mark on the other man's wrist, then a gossiping, laughing quartet of people screened him from view.

When they had passed, the man had gone. But Thane managed to reach Dutch as he also made to leave. Seeing him, the TV presenter's eyes hardened for a moment, then the professional smile was back in place.

'Superintendent!' The smile became surprise. 'I didn't expect you to be here!'

'I got two late tickets through a friend,' lied Thane easily.

'Then you're not here to check up on me?' Dutch switched to an almost boyish grin, then took a step nearer, dropping his voice. 'Like I promised, I'm watching and listening. Nothing yet – but don't worry, I'm still trying!'

'I appreciate it, Mr Dutch. You're one of our best hopes,' said Thane earnestly. Up on the catwalk, the red-nosed comedian was laughing loudly at one of his own limp jokes.

'He's nearly finished,' promised Dutch. 'They get him cheap.' He grinned. 'But then it's fashion time. My turn to earn my corn. See you again, superintendent.' Turning, he took a quick single step up on to the catwalk and disappeared behind the curtains.

The comedian was leaving to lukewarm applause as Thane made his slow way back to where he'd left the others. Emma Raleigh and Gypsy had gone, but Mary and Sophie Rae were back and Stewart Rae was there, talking to the large woman with the diamonds. They left it to Rae and his wife to dispose of the fat woman, then suddenly the lighting around the catwalk had changed again, the band had switched to a new blend of mood music, and Peter Dutch made his formal entrance carrying a microphone and being greeted with applause.

'Hello, and welcome everybody!' Dutch waved an all-round greeting, presented his warmest smile in turn to the two video cameras which had begun operating, then went into his warm-up routine.

'Showtime,' said Stewart Rae. He led his party towards the tables beside the catwalk, which were filling fast. As they settled at one, Thane saw that Gypsy Adams and Emma Raleigh were already seated at another, further along.

Then the first group of models were on the catwalk, someone's collection of autumn outfits, and Dutch's commentary was being punctuated by steady applause.

160

'What happens if I see something I like?' murmured Mary.

He winced. 'We leave.'

'That's the man I love!' Mary winked at Sophie Rae, who had been eavesdropping. 'So far, you're safe.'

Then, at last, it was interval time. Some of the main lights came back up and a folk singer with a guitar took over on the cat-walk. Thane looked around, then frowned. There were two empty chairs where Gypsy and Emma Raleigh had been sitting. A couple of sausages on sticks and a cautious sip of champagne later he looked again and this time Gypsy Adams was back. But there was no sign of the blonde boutique owner. Thane got up and went over.

'Hi.' Adams greeted him with a wry nod.

'Where's the lady?' asked Thane.

'Headache.' Adams scowled. 'My usual luck. Anyway, I put her in a taxi and she went off home on her own. She wanted it that way.'

Thane gestured towards his own table. 'Want to join us?'

'Thanks, I will.' Adams sighed and gave a wry grimace. 'I've learned one thing so far, Thane. There are plenty of chancers around here. Balloons.'

'Meaning?'

'Faking it with counterfeit Rolex watches. As phoney as this one.' Adams pulled back his cuff and showed his own wrist-watch. 'I've spotted at least ten for sure – gold-coloured watch case, gold-coloured bracelet, but back-street Hong Kong phoneys. Cheap garbage but they look good for show.' His broad face creased in a slightly shame-faced grin. 'Hell, that's why I borrowed this one.'

Thane smiled, but said nothing.

The CATS supervisor was more in a mood for talking than listening. There was a glass in front of him and he emptied it at a gulp. 'Like to know about fake watches, Thane? Want to know how to spot a fake?'

'Why not?' Thane saw he was going to be told anyway.

'Right. Always check the second hand.' Adams leaned on his elbows and looked up earnestly. 'On any genuine quality watch the second hand moves in a smooth sweep around the dial. But on an El Cheapo the second hand quivers from second to second. Quivers? Hell, it jerks! What's driving it is Toy Town electronics.'

'I'll remember,' promised Thane drily.

'Even so, that's almost out of date.' Adams lumbered to his feet. 'The faker brigades are getting better. The word is there's a new Mark Two coming out of Singapore which is smoother than real!'

They went to the other table at the same time as Peter Dutch returned and the fashion show got under way again.

It was the recipe as before – the brightly lit catwalk with the video operators at work again, the same long-legged models with yet another designer range, this time mostly wool, most of the rest of the banqueting hall dimmed to near-darkness and once again Peter Dutch soon had the fashion gathering captivated with his blend of sales pitch and chatter. Model followed model, applause followed applause, then it was time for another interval, the folk singer was back, new supplies of drinks and tiny sandwiches were being circulated.

The main hall lights came back up. The time was just after 10 p.m. and the video operators were packing up their gear, getting ready to leave. The remainder of the fashion show would go unrecorded – and in the background behind them Thane saw Peter Dutch slip quietly down from the catwalk and make his way towards one of the exit doors. But Dutch wasn't alone. The burly, dark-haired stranger was close behind him.

'I've a phone call to make,' apologised Thane, rising. 'Time I checked in with my people.'

Then he was making his own way out through the tables, heading after Dutch and the stranger as they disappeared out through the exit door. Thane followed and reached the top of the marble staircase in time to see the two men arrive at the bottom. This time they were heading straight across the broad lobby towards the street door.

The staircase was thronged with guests out for an illicit smoking break. Thane weaved down through them, made the street door, and went out into the warm night air. The outside of the City Chambers was floodlit as usual and Dutch and his companion were a stone's throw ahead. They paused, and Thane ducked back into the shelter of the arched doorway as the dark-haired man took a brief glance back.

Counting seconds, Thane looked out again. There was no sign of the men in the floodlit area. He walked in the direction he'd last seen them heading, into the quiet length of Cochrane Street, where there were only ordinary street lights – and they were ahead. Thane followed, staying at a distance, balancing the risk of being spotted against an instinct which told him he should keep on.

They reached the deserted length of Ingram Street. Suddenly, a car parked ahead switched on its lights. Dutch and the stranger hurried towards it and Thane hugged another doorway.

The car was Emma Raleigh's white Mazda coupé, this time with the hood up. The two men got aboard, the Mazda started up, and in another moment it drove past Thane's doorway, paused at the next street corner, then snarled away.

Emma Raleigh was behind the wheel.

It had been no casual rendezvous. Another part of the overall pattern seemed to be coming together. Slowly, thoughtfully, Thane walked back towards the floodlit entrance to the City Chambers building and as he reached it another figure strode out to meet him.

'What's going on?' asked Gypsy Adams, frowning. 'You took off like a scalded cat when you left. There's something happening, isn't there?'

'There's something,' said Thane almost reluctantly. 'I'll tell you. But you won't like it.'

Taking the burly CATS supervisor by the elbow, he drew him to one side, away from the doorway. He told Adams what he'd just seen, and how it followed on from what had gone before involving Emma Raleigh and Peter Dutch. After a silence, Adams gave a bitter growl.

'Why didn't you tell me?' he demanded bitterly.

'On what we had right up till now?' Thane shook his head.

'Hell. I thought you looked pretty startled when we showed up.' Adams grimaced. 'Now I know! I thought my luck was in when I wasn't turned down, when she suggested we come here.' He was silent for another moment, thinking. 'I should have known better – and she was certainly keen enough to know what kind of progress we were making.'

'Against The Cutters?'

Adams nodded wryly. 'Don't worry, she didn't get much. I'm tight-mouthed enough when it comes to work.' He shrugged. 'Win some, lose some – damn her.'

They went back inside. When they returned to their table the fashion show was under way again with a woman in a cornflower blue suit commentating. When Stewart Rae raised a questioning eyebrow, Thane shook his head and it was left that way.

Shortly before eleven the fashion show was obviously coming to an end. A slow drift of guests were starting to leave, others were clearly going to hang on to talk business.

'Like to come back to our place for a nightcap?' asked Stewart Rae across the table.

Thane shook his head. 'I've an early start.' He glanced at Mary, and they both rose while Gypsy Adams made a noise that he'd be in touch.

Saying goodnight, they left and Mary draped the lace shawl across her shoulders again before they went out into the night. Thane wasn't quite sure how it happened, but by the time they reached their parked car they were holding hands.

'Was it worth it?' asked Mary as he began driving.

'Not the way I expected.' Thane told her what he'd seen.

'Maybe Gypsy had a lucky escape.' A faint twinkle showed in her eyes. 'I only spoke to the woman briefly. Her kind would mug old ladies on pension days.'

'That part we've still to find out.' Thane gave a warning flash of the Ford's headlights and prevented a rogue taxi cutting across their front. 'I want to know about your dress.'

'You like it?' she asked mildly.

'Never mind me.' He gave her a sideways glance. 'You were scoring points every other minute back there. It was getting serious money attention from professionals. Why?'

She grinned. 'They knew it was a Chanel.'

Thane swallowed. Even he knew the name.

'A Chanel.' She chuckled in the darkness. 'For real. There's a story.'

'Go on,' said Thane warily.

'You landed me in tonight, I warned you I'd nothing to wear, right?' She didn't wait for an answer. 'Though you forget it most of the time, I have a job of my own, right? So when I panicked, I began phoning around – and Maggie Fyffe came to the rescue.'

'Maggie?' Thane blinked at the Squad commander's secretary coming into it. 'How?'

'She told me about a place in the West End. No shop window, no advertising – just a woman who runs a business from her spare room. She sells nearly new designer label dresses.'

'Top People discards?'

'Don't be a peasant, Colin.' She laughed at him. 'If this has been worn more than a couple of times before, I'd be surprised. New, it could cost bars of gold. I got it for less than a month's pay. I've also got a good idea who had it before me.'

'How?' Thane wasn't happy.

'You'll see.' She wouldn't say more.

It was around midnight when they got home. Tommy and Kate were asleep, Clyde was snoring in his basket. Thane poured malt whisky into two kitchen glasses, they sipped for a moment, then they took their drinks up to their room.

'It fits pretty well,' mused Mary, displaying the black dress in front of a mirror. 'Except she's maybe broader in the beam than me.'

'Who is?' asked Thane, puzzled.

'Wait.' She took a larger gulp from her glass, then very carefully unzipped the dress, stepped out of it, and spread it on a chair.

There was a slim band of black silk lining inside the neck. Thane saw a Chanel label. But the other thing there made him stare.

Even a cop knew an embroidered royal crest in fine gold threat. Beside it was an ornate gold S.

'Waste not, want not,' murmured Mary.

She finished her drink. But that wasn't what she meant.

A lot later, when the telephone began ringing, Thane dragged himself out of a deep, dark sleep. He heard Mary mumbling protest noises beside him as he switched on the bedside light, lifted the bedside receiver, and automatically glanced at the clock. It was almost 3.30 a.m.

'Thane,' he said muzzily.

He listened to the voice at the other end, and suddenly all sleep had gone, his stomach had tightened.

'Say again,' he said harshly.

The Crime Squad duty officer repeated it.

'I'm on my way in,' Thane told him. 'You know who else to call.'

'What's happened?' asked Mary sleepily, propping herself up on one elbow.

'Francey Dunbar and Joe Felix were in a car crash,' he told her, already out of bed and reaching for his clothes. 'It's bad.'

165

She stared. 'How bad?'

'Joe's dead, Francey's critical,' said Thane bleakly.

The Crime Squad building was a blaze of light in the night darkness when Colin Thane arrived after a hard, fast drive across the deserted streets of the city. It was just after 4 a.m. when he left his Ford with the other vehicles already in the parking area. More cars were arriving as he hurried into the building.

It was busy with people, day shift and night shift. Telephones were ringing, there was a real sense of shock in the mood all around. He saw the scrawny, unshaven figure of Phil Moss hurrying to meet him. But Jack Hart got there first.

'Colin.' The Crime Squad commander beckoned and led the way into his private office. A man in uniform had been using a telephone but put it down as they entered. John Mitchell, a uniformed inspector, was night shift supervisor. He nodded to Thane as Jack Hart closed the office door, cutting off the outside noise.

'You made good time, Colin,' said Hart bleakly. 'Everybody did.'

Including Hart himself, somehow bandbox neat as usual despite the hour.

'There's no doubt?' asked Thane.

'None. Felix was killed outright. Francey Dunbar is in Carlisle Infirmary – possible fractured skull, broken shoulder, chest injuries.' Hart's lined face shaped a grimace. 'Condition stable, but not fit enough to talk.'

Thane drew a deep breath. 'So what the hell happened?'

Hart nodded the question on to Mitchell.

'They crashed on the northbound carriageway of the M6 motorway, about eight miles south of Carlisle, sir.' Mitchell referred briefly to a clipboard. 'That was around 02.50. Cumbria police attended, then contacted us at 03.25. Both our people had to be cut out of the wreckage.'

Tight-lipped, puzzled, Thane nodded. The English force hadn't wasted any time. For the crash to have occurred more than a hundred miles away was one thing. The M6 was the main west coast route south from Scotland to the English Midlands and London. But the northbound carriageway meant that the Crime Squad car had been heading north again –

166

'Cumbria say that road conditions were bad, sir.' Mitchell's manner was frankly sceptical. 'The way their traffic people put it together, DC Felix was driving and had his foot down. Our car was overtaking a milk tanker when the tanker suddenly swung out to pass something else ahead.' The night supervisor shook his head. 'They didn't have a chance. Their car hit the rear of the truck and almost vanished underneath it. The road was blocked for northbound traffic for almost an hour.'

'There's more,' said Jack Hart softly. 'Approximately ten minutes before the crash, Francey Dunbar telephoned – '

'Here?'

Hart nodded. 'They were at Southwaite Services on the M6, continuing observations on two Pizzaro vehicles which were heading north again. Then something cryptic about a change of containers.' He shrugged and glanced at his watch. 'That can wait. I'm sending you down to Carlisle. Formal identification of DC Felix, then check on Dunbar's condition. You'll get a lift by helicopter from here to Glasgow Airport. Take Sandra Craig along.'

'But – ' began Thane.

'Just do it,' snapped Hart. 'Joe Felix has a wife, remember? No children, thank God! But nobody's going near her until we're sure that it was Felix who died. Dunbar's next of kin deserve the same kind of treatment. Don't they?'

Thane nodded.

'You've a couple of minutes to see your people. The Cumbria cops know to expect you.' Hart dismissed him with a nod.

Thane left. He found Phil Moss in the main duty room with Sandra and Jock Dawson beside him. Somehow, he wasn't surprised to see Tina Redder there, talking quietly to Sandra.

'You're going down?' asked Moss.

He nodded. 'Sandra too.' Out of the corner of his eye he saw the redhead bite her lip. 'Phil, how much do you know about what they were doing?'

'Not a lot.' Moss scratched a thumbnail across his patchy stubble. 'Francey logged what they had.' He held out a single sheet of paper. 'For once, he did it by the book.'

Thane took the typed sheet and scanned it quickly. At 22.40 hours word had come from Crieff that two Pizzaro traction units without trailers had left their depot, heading south. The next sighting had been an hour later when they had appeared again, both now towing containers and on the A74 heading towards the M6 south. The rest of Francey Dunbar's report was a single, laconic sentence. 'As instructed earlier, we will intercept and follow.' The report was timed at 00.10 hours.

Less than three hours laters, Joe Felix was dead and Francey Dunbar was in an ambulance.

They'd been doing exactly as ordered. Thane returned the sheet.

'Whatever it takes, Phil. Do it.'

Moss nodded. 'There's Southwaite.'

'I know.' The crumpled diesel fuel receipt found in Terry Anson's lock-up at Blenheim Rise, something that now seemed years back, had been issued at Southwaite Services. 'Any problems – '

'There won't be,' said Moss simply.

They could both hear it: a moment later the helicopter was coming in overhead, landing lights blazing. When Thane looked round, Sandra Craig was pulling on her coat.

The helicopter, a Bell-Sikorski borrowed from Strathclyde force, swept them across the city and over the river to Glasgow Airport in a matter of minutes. It landed near to where a small turbo-prop Beechcraft with Royal Air Force insignia was already warming up, and they were hustled from one machine to the other. The moment they were aboard the Beechcraft the throttles opened and it took off.

They climbed fast over the lights of the city with the Clyde a mere ribbon of silky grey water through the middle. Then they were into cloud and the outside world ceased to exist until the Beechcraft had climbed through into the upper moonlight. A crewman offered them coffee from a flask. Almost by the time they'd finished the coffee the Beechcraft was beginning to descend again and that new glow of lights ahead was England and the border town of Carlisle.

When they landed at Carlisle Airport, a Cumbria police car swept in to stop beside them. The sergeant driver saluted Thane, helped them aboard, then they were moving. The airport was a few miles out of Carlisle, but less than an hour after leaving the Crime Squad building they drew up at Carlisle Infirmary. A uniformed Cumbria superintendent was at the hospital doors, waiting to greet them.

'Harry Swan, chief constable's office,' he greeted Thane, then shook hands with them both. 'Hell of a way to meet people.' He paused and shrugged. 'But it goes with the job, right? If you want anything, ask. That's why I'm here. So – were they both known to you?'

Thane nodded.

'Then you can make the formal identification of DC Felix?'

'I'll do it.' Thane indicated Sandra. 'Can my sergeant check on DI Dunbar?'

Swan raised a hand, snapped his fingers, and a uniformed constable led Sandra away.

'Right.' Swan hesitated. 'Your man Felix – it isn't pretty. He was damned nearly decapitated.'

Thane nodded his understanding. Together they set off along one of the long corridors. The hospital mortuary was down a flight of stairs towards the rear of the building. Once again, the way had been prepared. A male attendant in green overalls was waiting and silently lifted the top edge of the hospital sheet that covered the shape lying on a metal table.

Most of the top of Joe Felix's head had simply gone. There were gashes, there were cuts. His upper chest had been crushed. But there was no doubt. It was Felix's plump face. Death or injuries had given the dead detective constable's mouth a vaguely amused twist not too far away from the expression Thane had known so well in life.

'Thane?' The Cumbria superintendent cleared his throat gently. 'Enough?'

Thane nodded. As the attendant replaced the sheet the two policemen silently left the room. Neither spoke until they were back in the main corridor again.

'Who is next of kin?' asked Swan.

'His wife.' Thane had only met her a very few times. Joe Felix had kept his home life private. Her name was Maureen, a comfortably plump easy-going woman.

'You'll – well, warn her what to expect?'

'Yes.' It wasn't easy for either of them. Scotland or England, it made no difference. 'Thank you.'

They went along more hospital corridors and up a stairway to Francey Dunbar's room, located in the intensive care area. Dunbar's mop of jet-black hair against the white of his pillow and the way he lay so still added to the obscenity of the tubes and wires which connected his body to a collection of monitors and other equipment. A pale-faced Sandra Craig stood near the bed with a balding, grey-haired doctor who wore thick metal-framed spectacles. His name was Jarrold Erskine: he was the consultant in charge of accident and emergency admissions.

'However he may look, your officer was very lucky,' said Erskine gravely. 'He should have been killed, like his colleague. As it is, my money would be on a complete recovery.'

Given time. But for the moment Francey Dunbar was under heavy sedation. When brought in, he had obviously suffered severe concussion.

'His other injuries are serious enough.' Erskine frowned behind his thick-lensed spectacles. 'But I think we can discount the fractured skull – we'll need more tests, but it's most likely a hairline crack.' He anticipated Thane's question. 'I'm going to keep him sedated for at least a couple of days, superintendent. You can't talk to him any earlier – and don't expect much when you do.'

Thane went over to the bed, laid a hand for a moment on Dunbar's heavily bandaged shoulder, then thanked the consultant. He pretended not to notice the tears forming in Sandra Craig's eyes as they left the room.

'Finished here?' asked Swan patiently.

Thane nodded. The English officer piloted them through more corridors and they arrived at the hospital' main door again, the same police car waiting outside.

'There's a flask of coffee in the car, sergeant,' said Swan pointedly. As Sandra took the hint and left them, he shaped an unhappy frown. 'Thane, exactly what the hell is going on? We didn't know these two were police until we found their warrant cards. We didn't know you were operating on our side of the border. Your duty man in Glasgow gave me a story so vague it hardly made sense.' He snorted. 'And I've a chief constable who can be very, very sensitive.'

'I'm sorry.' Thane knew exactly how the man felt. 'Any fault is ours. Things happened in ways we didn't expect. We've been targeting a major counterfeit clothing ring. Plus a drugs link. Plus a couple of murders.' Looking out at the night, still sick in his stomach at what he'd seen, he told the outline in a few brief sentences.

'Problems.' The Cumbria superintendent shaped a silent whistle

170

of sympathy, then rubbed a hand thoughtfully across his chin. 'Well, the crash was a pure accident – a rain squall, a tanker driver who didn't check his mirror before he pulled out. The man's in a genuine state of shock.' For a moment he paused, sucking his lips. 'I checked your people's notebooks – I'll give you them. But they don't help. This message from them said a switch-over of trailers at Southwaite?'

'And we think they've used Southwaite before.' Thane nodded.

'Plenty of legitimate outfits use motorway service locations that way,' shrugged Swan. 'There's always a tunnel link under the road so that drivers can swap loads, then head back the way they've come. Doing the swap only takes a few minutes.'

'But with some kind of a meeting?'

'Maybe yes, maybe no.' Swan was cautious. 'Leave a trailer, pick up another one that's lying. Who knows? These damned service areas are like mini-cities on the move, twenty-four hours a day.'

But a motorway patrol unit would run a check on Southwaite, for what it might be worth.

It was 6 a.m. They were offered breakfast in the Carlisle station canteen, but that could wait. Thane telephoned Glasgow, spoke to Jack Hart, told the Crime Squad commander how things stood, then was ready. Swan gave them a small package containing the two police notebooks, shook hands again with Thane and Sandra Craig, then that was it.

The same car took them back to Carlisle Airport. The same Beechcraft turbo-prop flew them back through the grey of early dawn to Glasgow. It was sunrise when they landed, and a car was waiting at the tarmac's edge to collect them. The time was 7 a.m.; it was the end of a bitter three-hour round-trip mission.

At Crime Squad headquarters there was bright morning sunlight and the birds were singing. An orderly was waiting at the main door to usher Thane straight through to Jack Hart's office. As he settled in a chair on the other side of Hart's desk, Maggie Fyffe brought in coffee and a pile of toast for them both, then left them.

'It's a lousy job,' said Hart unemotionally. 'But it's done.' He gestured at the tray. 'Help yourself.'

As Thane did, more hungry than he'd realised, Hart added, 'I'm arranging for Francey Dunbar's parents to be flown down to Carlisle. They've been told, they want to be with him.'

171

Thane nodded. Francey Dunbar's parents ran a small farm over in the east of Scotland. He'd met them, he liked them: they were devoted to their policeman son. 'What about Joe Felix's wife?'

'Telling her is my job.' Hart glared down Thane's immediate protest. 'I'm Squad commander, Joe was one of my people. I claim the right, Colin. Understand? Your turn can come later.'

'Sir.' Thane took a deep breath, then nodded. 'But – '

'But nothing,' snarled Hart. 'I thought I'd let her have her night's sleep first. I'll take Maggie Fyffe with me.'

It was the compassionate way. Maggie Fyffe was a cop's widow, Maggie Fyffe knew what it was about.

'So – ' Hart chewed on a slice of toast, then took a swallow of coffee. 'You've got your own job, and I don't need to spell it out. Do I?'

'No.' Thane shook his head.

'Find the bastards, nail the bastards,' said Jack Hart grimly. 'Any help you need, just ask. Whatever you need, HMCI says you get. So do a lot of other people.' He watched Thane eat for a moment. 'You have their notebooks. Any help from them?'

'No.' Thane produced the Cumbria supplied envelope from his pocket. Both police notebooks inside were bloodstained, many of their pages stuck together. 'It's the way they reported. They tailed two Pizzaro artic outfits down to Southwaite services. The Pizzaro vehicles unhitched their own trailers and picked up two already parked.'

'No welcoming committee?'

'None they could see.' Thane had tried to make sense out of the sparse blood stained scribbles on the Beechcraft flight north from Carlisle. 'There were two people aboard both Pizzaro vehicles, but it was raining hard. They were just people in waterproofs.'

Hart grunted. 'Cumbria say they've checked out Southwaite. There was another team waiting somewhere. Both trailers have gone.' He slammed a hand on his desk with enough violence to slop coffee from his cup. 'And that's that until Francey tells us more – but we can't wait.'

'Then I'd better get to it,' said Thane woodenly. He collected another slice of toast as he rose. 'I asked Phil Moss to keep working on a couple of angles.'

'I rather think he has,' said Hart drily and a brief, wintry smile touched thin lips. 'But I'll let him tell you. And if he's been playing dirty along the way, I don't want to know.'

172

Along the corridor, the main duty room was a buzz of talk which died away as Thane entered. When he glanced towards Joe Felix's desk, its surface had already been cleared of its normal accumulated junk. Someone had laid a small posy of pink carnations in its middle. He felt every eye following him as he went into Moss's tiny corner office, nodded to the waiting occupant, then closed the door on the others.

'I spoke with Sandra.' Moss cleared a chair for him by the expedient of dumping a pile of papers on the floor. 'So it was rough?'

'Very rough.' Thane dropped into the cleared chair. Moss had perched himself on the edge of the scarred relic of a desk he'd found. 'These trucks are back in Scotland again, Phil. Somewhere.'

'But not back at the Pizzaro garage. It's being watched.'

'Better than last time?' asked Thane sardonically. 'What the hell happened last night?'

Moss shrugged. 'A local car watched them leave and tried to follow. But they got jammed in traffic going through Crieff. When they won through, the trucks had vanished. It was just ordinary bad luck.' He gave a low-key belch and a grimace. 'But we've maybe scored another way. They've a manager and a mechanic, right? The manager's name is Brian Masson, the mechanic's name is Seumas Hall – Seumas spelled the old Gaelic way. No form for either of them that we know about.'

'So?' Thane made it a grunt.

'We know Masson was on one of the trucks. But not Hall – he's on the sick list with a heavily bandaged arm. The apparent story is he hurt it at work.' Moss showed his teeth. 'Except at least two people he drinks with remember him with a grey blouson jacket!'

Maybe it was beginning to happen. Too late for Joe Felix, but at least it might help avenge his death. Then Thane saw the faint smile on Moss's lips and knew there was more.

'We know where Emma Raleigh is – at home. She has a cottage out Eaglesham way, I've a car keeping an eye on it. Peter Dutch we don't know about – he's vanished. But – ah – ' Moss made a brief show of examining a new stain of what looked like jam on his tie. 'We know where his car is.'

Thane swallowed and stared. 'Where?'

'We got lucky last night. You know, while – '

'While I was at that damned fashion circus.' Thane moistened his lips. 'Go on.'

'We had a list of Mitsubishi dealers within a thirty-mile radius of the city. A string of local beat cops made checks on the most likely – gossiping with night security men, that kind of thing.' Moss's grin widened. 'Dutch's vehicle is lying in a repair yard only a couple of miles from here. Gypsy Adams at CATS says contact him when we want to go in. Trading Standards don't need a warrant for that kind of search. They just tell a small lie or two.'

'Then get him,' said Thane fervently, with a silent prayer of thanks to the ordinary, ubiquitous beat officers who lurked behind so many successes.

'I've got them on standby,' said Moss. He came down from the desk top. 'What about the Raleigh woman?'

'Maybe later.' Meaning when they had any kind of real evidence against her. He suddenly remembered something that Francey Dunbar had mentioned in his telephone call. 'You were out at Dark Loch again. Why?'

'They found another body,' said Moss. He paused for a moment, watching Thane's reaction. 'The only thing is, Doc Williams reckons it's at least two hundred years old. Like time-barred.'

There was one more development, then Thane was up to date.

Criminal Records and Strathclyde's Drug Squad had got together on the matter of the late, unlamented Pepe Weide, brought in from his shallow grave at Dark Loch and now resting in a mortuary drawer. Between them they had assembled a few names of known associates. Two of them, Mickey Wood and Tam Black, were established Glasgow hard men.

Tam Black had convictions for razor assaults. The word was out. They were to be located.

Altman Motors in Buckler Street, Govan, opened its workshop for the day at 8 a.m. Staff arrived at the long, low, steel-framed building, then had their routine rudely disrupted. A group of unsmiling men and women came in through the front door as it opened. In the lead, waving his Trading Standards warrant card like a banner, Gypsy Adams located the workshop manager, threatened dire penalties for anyone who didn't co-operate, and announced they were running a routine check.

Within minutes the Altman workshop force of twenty mechanics and body shop technicians were taking an enforced break in the sunlight outside. Some of them began a game of football, someone produced a pack of cards.

And inside the workshop their visitors made a brief show of looking at other vehicles but concentrated on the light blue Mitsubishi Shogun station wagon – big, with four-wheel drive and with obvious accident damage to its front and along the passenger side.

'What happened to this one?' Thane asked the workshop manager, who was thin, bald, and anything but happy.

'No idea,' shrugged the man. 'Peter Dutch, the TV man, owns her, he said he ran out of road somewhere.' He shaped a knowing wink. 'Probably drunk. Not my business.'

'No,' Thane admitted. He caught the eye of the large, hairy detective constable waiting nearby. The Animal and his usual partner, a petite china doll blonde, were two of the officers temporarily added to his strength. He thumbed at the blue Shogun. 'Try this one. And the two at the far end.'

The Animal nodded and walked away, leaving Thane wishing he could remember the man's real name. As a twosome, the blonde and The Animal were known as Beauty and the Beast. The blonde was an honours sociology graduate. Put together, her brain and The Animal's muscle were an awesome combination.

'Uh – exactly what are you looking for?' asked the workshop manager cautiously. 'You see, if I knew – '

'El Cheapo brake hoses,' lied Thane. 'Counterfeit spares.'

'Here?' The man relaxed. 'Not our style.'

Something about the Shogun's interior caught Thane's eye and he took a half-step nearer. The vehicle's entire rear seat was missing. 'What happened in there?'

The workshop manager shrugged. 'He took it out so he had more load space. Then rats or something got at the thing so he dumped it. We've ordered a new one.'

'When does he expect the car back?'

'Middle of next week – and that's pretty good going.' The workshop manager hesitated. 'Do we have to tell anyone you've been here?'

'Not if you're clean.' Thane shook his head.

Boomerang and The Pawnbroker were already ambling over. The two Scenes of Crime men weren't likely to miss anything on this one. The Pawnbroker had been a guest at Joe Felix's wedding.

It took about an hour. Gypsy Adams took the workshop manager away and pretended to inspect invoices and paperwork. Others made an equal pretence of examining the two other selected vehicles. But the real focus was the blue Shogun. The tall, thin Boomerang and the small, fat Pawnbroker crawled over and under it from end to end. They produced their own lights and a tiny battery-powered vacuum cleaner. They brushed, they sampled, they took photographs.

At last they finished and came over, ready to leave.

'Home and dry on this one, superintendent,' said The Pawnbroker. 'All you're likely to want. Same style of tyre patterns we found at Dark Loch, even if there's not enough for a positive match. But we've taken plenty of mud samples from the vehicle's underside.'

'Want an easy bet?' asked Boomerang. 'I'd put money on the laboratory saying some of that mud came from Dark Loch. There's the same texture.' His eyes glinted. 'We've better. There are dried specks and drops of blood around some of the trim edges in the rear passenger area, as if someone tried hard to clean it – but not hard enough. That has to be why the rear seat was dumped, the way it was blood-stained. They just gave up on it!'

'Hallelujah,' agreed The Pawnbroker in an unusual display of enthusiasm. 'The blood has to belong to the character your farmer wounded. The one they ferried away.'

Thane moistened his lips. 'You're sure it's blood?'

The two Scenes of Crime men exchanged a glance and a nod.

'We've seen, we've taken samples,' said The Pawnbroker flatly. 'The laboratory white-coats should be able to confirm human blood within the hour, basic precipitin testing.'

'All right.' Thane knew they had enough years of experience to back that kind of judgement, with not too much of a gamble involved. But he needed something more. 'How long for a DNA match?'

'Like with the blood on that blouson jacket from the loch?' Boomerang elected to answer and nodded their understanding. 'I'd double check with Matt Amos at Forensic. But it'll take around fourteen hours for a full profile result.'

'That long?' Thane took a couple of steps nearer to the Mitsubishi and laid his hands flat on the cool metal of its roof. 'No short-cuts?'

'Ask Matt Amos, superintendent.' Boomerang's attention wandered as the hairy, broad-shouldered figure of The Animal ambled past them, heading towards another car. 'Now I haven't seen that big fellow for a while. Been keeping him in a cage?'

Thane kept his answer to a shrug, other things on his mind.

'I knew a Crusher built that way when I was in the navy,' mused the Scenes of Crime man. His thin face shaped a reminiscent grin. 'I remember being terrified every time he even looked my way.'

It took a moment before what he'd said connected. Then Thane swung round, grabbing him by the arm.

'Say that again – what Crusher?'

'Uh?' The Scenes of Crime man blinked, startled by Thane's reaction. 'I knew this big devil of a Crusher, that's all. I was five years in the navy, as a telegraphist. I was on a destroyer, and this Crusher – '

Suddenly seeing the light, Thane cut him short. 'What the hell is a Crusher?'

'Navy slang. Ship's master at arms – sort of ship's police sergeant, a petty officer.' Boomerang was still puzzled. 'That one was built like a brick privy and as hard as they come.'

It fitted. Thane drew a deep breath. 'We've got a Crusher. He enforces for The Cutters. Try navy slang on Duff.'

'Duff? D like in – ?'

'Dog, Delta, anything you want,' urged Thane.

'Duff – could mean useless, could mean a kind of pudding.' Boomerang stopped and snapped a triumphant finger and thumb together. 'Not Duff, superintendent. But make it Buff, short for Buffer – that's a three badger chief bos'un's mate.' He gave a soft, appreciative whistle to himself. 'Put them together and they'd make a hell of a pair.'

Thane drew a deep breath and nodded. He was on a run of luck. Any cop knew about runs of luck. They didn't happen too often but when they did you went along with them as far and as fast as you could.

He looked around, saw Phil Moss, and beckoned him over. 'We're finished here. Pull everybody out.'

'Right.' Moss refused to show surprise. 'Where next?'

'Back to the ranch. Then we'll work on it.' Thane turned to the

Scenes of Crime men. 'See Matt Amos. Tell him I need that blood sample as total priority, then anything else he gets.'

'If it's for Joe Felix, you've got it,' promised Boomerang. A strange twist of a smile touched his thin lips. 'We'll get back to you, superintendent.'

'Leave it with us,' agreed The Pawbroker softly. 'For Joe.'

Thane knew they meant it.

8

The procession of Crime Squad cars arrived back at headquarters at 10 a.m., after driving through heavy rain. They found Her Majesty's Chief Inspector was visiting. This time, it was no surprise.

The usual bank of security monitor screens were flickering at the reception desk when he entered. Maggie Fyffe was there, ending whatever she'd been saying to a young uniformed constable, then coming towards him.

'Commander Hart wants you. Straight away.'

He nodded, noting the slightly strained look on her face, remembering that she'd gone out with Hart to Joe Felix's unsuspecting widow.

'How was it, Maggie?' he asked.

'Bad.' She shook her head. 'He did his best, she did her best.' The way Maggie said it, too many old memories had been brought back.

At Hart's office she knocked, opened the door, gestured Thane straight in, then closed the door again behind him as he entered.

Jack Hart was behind his desk and greeted Thane with a small grimace of a smile. Patrick Ronaldson sat in a chair near the window and the HMCI's face was a thin, impassive mask.

'Sit down, Colin.' Hart thumbed towards a vacant chair and watched him settle. 'You first. It went well?'

Thane told them; he heard his two-man audience give occasional satisfied noises along the way then saw them exchange an approving glance as he finished.

'We don't lose them all,' said Ronaldson softly.

'What's the latest on Francey?' asked Thane.

'Some improvement.' Hart glanced at his desk clock. 'His parents should be with him by now.'

Ronaldson nodded. 'For the moment, the only information

going out to the media from Cumbria is there was a car crash, one dead, one injured – but no names until relatives are contacted. No mention of police officers being involved.'

'Cumbria can keep it that way for maybe twenty-four hours,' mused Hart. A frown crossed his leathery face. 'That's how long you've got, Colin. When The Cutters learn the truth, they could get very twitchy.'

It was an understatement. Thane sucked his teeth. 'No word from anywhere on the Pizzaro trucks?'

Hart shook his head. 'It's like they vanished. I tried Cumbria on the two trailers that were switched over and probably went south.' He gave a scowl and a shrug. 'They stayed polite, but did I have any idea how many container trucks go down the M6 every hour?'

'So we're back to what you've got, Thane.' Ronaldson stated the obvious with a cynical relish. 'Fourteen hours until your DNA result?'

'Around midnight,' agreed Thane sadly.

'And much of what you've got is thin, unsubstantiated, based on possibilities.' Her Majesty's Chief Inspector of Constabulary folded his arms and rocked gently on his chair for a moment. 'A well-known TV face teamed with a prominent, apparently respected businesswoman – she's even a Chamber of Commerce member.' He sighed. 'Whatever you have, double check it. Then take another look around – at everyone. What about the CATS people – can we rely on them?'

Thane nodded. 'I believe we can.'

'It's your case.' Ronaldson looked at Thane, then at Jack Hart over his fingertips. 'I can't stay. I'm flying up to Inverness, a snap inspection at Northern Constabulary. But keep me posted.' He got to his feet. 'Watch your paperwork on this one, Thane. Every step of the way, understand? No foul-ups like last time.'

'No, sir,' said Thane stonily, also on his feet. Hart was already on his way to open the door.

'Good.' Ronaldson gave a thin smile of thanks as Hart held the door open. 'I know the way, commander. You've things to do.' He glanced back at Thane, his voice suddenly harsh. 'If it helps, Thane, I think you're right. Now prove it – and get them.'

Then he had gone. After a moment, Jack Hart slowly closed the door and turned to face Thane.

'You heard the man,' he said wryly. 'Did you bring your magic wand?'

The Squad commander thumbed Thane back into the chair, grimaced to himself, then went to a filing cabinet and opened a drawer. Reaching in, he brought out a bottle of Oban malt whisky, always his favourite, then produced two tumblers, uncorked the bottle, and half-filled each tumbler.

'We've earned this.' He handed one tumbler to Thane, then raised the other in a grim toast. 'Joe Felix.'

'Joe.' Thane took a swallow of the faintly peat-flavoured liquor. Oban was a fourteen-year-old single malt, never to be vandalised by water or a mixer. When Jack Hart poured Oban, things were for real.

'So – ' Hart sipped his own drink and stood near the window, looking out. 'Maggie told you we'd seen Maureen Felix?'

Thane nodded.

'It's not easy, telling a woman she's a widow.' Hart scowled at his reflection in the window glass. 'She doesn't want to see him. She wants to remember him as he was.' He paused. 'She thanks you for what you did.'

Hart was watching the window again. He gave a quiet grunt as they had a brief glimpse of Ronaldson's white Jaguar leaving. Crossing over to his desk, he lifted his internal phone, tapped a button, and waited.

'Maggie, have you still that friend up in Northern Constabulary?' Hart paused long enough to hear a confirming noise. 'Give her a buzz. Let her know that the enemy is on his way. HMCI is flying up.' Satisfied, he hung up and grimaced at Thane. 'I owe them one. Now, we'll quietly finish this whisky with the respect it deserves. Then you can get out of here and get on with things.'

When Thane left Hart's office, he went straight to the duty room. He found Moss and most of the raid team already there. But once again there was one absence.

'Where's Sandra?' he asked.

'Gone out. She needed ten minutes.' Moss made an embarrassed noise. 'Something I know about.'

It was time for an update. He went with Moss into Moss's cupboard-sized office, which now had somehow acquired a computer terminal of its own. Other signs that Moss knew how to play the system included a set of brand new filing cabinets.

One by one, the two men ticked off items from their list.

Peter Dutch still hadn't returned to his West End home. Conversely, Emma Raleigh showed no signs of leaving her place, a cottage at Eaglesham village, on the fringe of the city. Dutch had told friends in advance that he was taking a few days off to research a programme idea up north. Emma Raleigh's office only knew that she wouldn't be in for a couple of days. She'd kept both dates clear in her diary for some time.

Then they were on to another set of updates. The morning report on the state of the razor-slashed Liz Hill in the Royal Infirmary described her as 'comfortable' – in hospital-speak that usually meant anything on the right side of outright agony. The search for Tam Black and Mickey Wood, the razor thugs linked to the ripely dead Pepe Weide, was still under way.

Climbing up the ladder from there, the two Pizzaro container trucks were still missing. The watchers at the Pizzaro garage at Crieff still reported that only the regular Pizzaro mechanic, the bandaged Seumas Hall, was being seen.

'So think about what else we've got, Phil.' Thane leaned against a filing cabinet and nursed one of the mugs of coffee brought into them by Jock Dawson. 'Think Crusher and Buffer. 'Masson, the Pizzaro manager, was the man with Peter Dutch at the fashion circus. He could fit as Crusher, the enforcer. His mechanic pal Hall is The Buffer and could have been shot by our farmer out at Dark Loch.' He shrugged. 'We need the DNA test result, Phil – it ties a lot together. But if we try naval records on these two – '

'Being done now,' grunted Moss. 'The same for Peter Dutch – you know, maybe three yo-ho-ho pals together at some time.'

There were other checks under way, scattered around the extra Crime Squad officers drafted in by Jack Hart, including Tina Redder's team. Leaving them to it, Thane went through to his own office. The door closed, he settled behind his desk and placed a call to the scientific branch at Strathclyde headquarters. He got through almost immediately to Matt Amos, and the laboratory's deputy director was brutally business-like when he came on the line.

'I know the score, Colin. But you were told fourteen hours for a DNA result, and fourteen hours it is. We're running the test through the semi-automatic scanner rig, and nothing will do it faster,' said Amos bluntly. Then he relented. 'Look, if it helps, the stains from the Shogun reacted positive to the basic main-line precipitin checks. They're human blood. Anna Huang ran a blood grouping test and they're Group O Negative – same as the blood on the Dark Loch jacket. And same as half the population – it stops there.'

'Thank God for that much,' said Thane fervently. The laboratory team had carried him a major step forward. He remembered one other prospect.

'Anna faxed us a report that she'd identified road tar stains on the canvas lengths from the bodies – '

'When you mean shrouds, say shrouds,' said Amos laconically. 'I'll ask her. I think she came up with more.' There was a pause, a murmur of background voices, then Amos was back on the line. 'Mainly road tar, the way she told you. But she also isolated traces of coarse salt, the kind used in snow clearing.'

'So they could be chunks of old cut-up vehicle tarpaulins?'

'Likely,' agreed Amos. 'Sourced from a truck operator. Which could also be where the nylon cord originated.'

They ended with a promise from Amos that he'd fax a note confirming the laboratory's additional findings. Thane hung up – but before he could even sit back the instrument was ringing again.

'Me,' said Mary Thane's voice when he answered. 'What's the latest on Francey's condition, Colin?'

'Improving. His folks are with him.'

'Gloria Hart called me. We're going over to see Maureen Felix this afternoon. Maggie Fyffe thought it might be a good idea,' said Mary. 'Just to – well, you know.'

'Fine.' He meant it. The visit sounded a good idea. Mary and Jack Hart's wife Gloria got on well together. They could equally be relied on to help Joe Felix's widow in her trauma. 'And if there's anything she needs – '

'We'll find out,' promised Mary.

She said goodbye and the call ended. This time he sat for a few minutes while he went through his own mental checklist, trying to ensure he'd forgotten nothing that might conceivably matter. Only when he was finished did he lift the telephone again and dial the number he needed. When he got through to the GMB Union switchboard he was told that Liam Riley was on a call. But after another couple of minutes the union official came on the line.

'You were looking for me,' said Thane.

'Yesterday.' Riley paused. 'I might have something for you.'

'I'll come over,' suggested Thane.

'Not here,' said Riley sharply. 'It would knock hell out of my image. Make it Lobey's statue, in twenty minutes. On your own.'

'I'll be there,' promised Thane.

He hung up, then went back through to the duty room to tell Moss. When he got there, Moss already had company. Sandra Craig had shown up and they were in an earnest, low-voiced discussion. That ended abruptly when they saw Thane approaching and Moss hastily shoved a small package into a jacket pocket.

'Something happening?' Thane raised an eyebrow.

'Just a personal thing, sir,' said Sandra warily.

'Nothing fresh yet,' said Moss.

'And you're going to be here for a spell, sergeant?' said Thane with mild sarcasm. 'I usually like to know.'

'Sir.' The redhead flushed. 'I'm sorry.'

He told Moss he was going out and why. It would take about an hour, and he was to be contacted if anything anywhere altered in a major way.

'Sir – ' began Sandra Craig.

'No, sergeant,' he said drily. 'You're not invited.'

Colin Thane made the meeting place exactly on time. Woodlands Road was on the edge of the city's business heart and he parked the Ford, then walked from there, a slight smile on his lips as he neared the rendezvous.

Liam Riley had made a sardonic choice. Glasgow was the only city in the world where it seemed perfectly natural to have erected a full-sized bronze statue to a comical cartoon-strip Western sheriff named Lobey Dosser mounted on his two-legged horse El Fideldo. The cost of the statue had been raised by public subscription through a newspaper column, and Lobey Dosser, sheriff of Calton Creek, Arizona, had several hundred card-carrying honorary deputy sheriffs as a result. Thane was one of them.

Liam Riley was already standing beside the two-legged horse. The broken-nosed General, Municipal and Boilermakers official greeted Thane with a nod.

'We've something to sort out first,' he said without preliminaries. 'We had an agreement that you weren't interested in any of my members.'

'True,' agreed Thane.

'You raided the Temple Brown factory yesterday. Two of the

people arrested are GMB members. Foolish, but members.' He reached into an inside pocket of his jacket and produced a slip of paper. 'You'll do something about it?'

Thane nodded, took the slip of paper and tucked it in his own pocket.

'Good.' The union man looked happier. 'Then I've maybe got what you want. It's a place called Ellanwood. It used to be a big dairy farm, this side of Stirling. There's a counterfeit factory operating in what used to be the cattle sheds – has been for months. Maybe fifty of a work-force – they've been recruiting more lately. We've three members there, maybe more – I've spoken to another who was offered a job but knew better.' He reached into his pocket again and took out another slip of paper. 'Names – and how to get there.'

'Go on.' Thane took the new slip of paper and put it beside the first. Stirling was less than an hour's drive out from the city, and half-way to the Pizzaro Trucks garage at Crieff.

Riley shrugged. 'Usual story. When you're long-term out of work and someone offers you a job, maybe you don't ask too many questions. There's a local bus service passes the end of the farm road. If you haven't anywhere to live, they'll find you something.'

'It fits,' said Thane softly. 'Anything on who runs it?'

'Not a lot.' The union official frowned, and removed a flattened beer can someone had jammed between El Fideldo's crossed legs. 'Damned vandals, some people.' He tossed the can aside. 'Who runs it? There's a weasel of a manager and a couple of hard-case foremen, sometimes one or two others. But the real bosses aren't always around. There is a blonde woman and she's often with a dark-haired minder who can put the frighteners on anyone. He has a nickname – '

'Crusher?' suggested Thane.

'If you know, why ask?' growled Riley. He slapped a hand on the rump of Sheriff Lobey Dosser's metal horse. 'This is still the only kind of lawman I'd really trust.' But he twisted a grin at Thane before he turned on his heel and walked away.

'Thanks you two,' Thane told the bronze monument to sheriff and horse. Then he walked back to where he'd left the Ford. When he got aboard, the car's low-band radio was murmuring his call sign. He answered, and in another moment he was talking to Phil Moss.

185

'You're in demand,' reported Moss, his voice a rasp over the car speaker. 'Emma Raleigh phoned from Eaglesham and wants to see you. Says it is urgent.'

Thane frowned and nursed the radio handset he was holding. 'Did she say why?'

'Does she talk to the lower ranks?' asked Moss sarcastically. 'No. She's still at home – she wants you to go there. I said I'd call back.'

Thane glanced at his watch. Eaglesham was about ten miles out. After what he'd learned from Liam Riley there were other things to be done. Except this was the unexpected.

'Say I'm on my way,' he told Moss.

'Will do.' Moss paused and he heard a faint murmur of voices at that end. Then Moss was back with him. 'Sandra asks if you want her to meet you.'

'I'll try to manage on my own,' said Thane drily. 'Tell her I want a check on a farm named Ellanwood near Stirling. But quietly – very quietly.'

He obtained the Eaglesham address from Moss, signed off, and set the car moving out into the traffic.

The journey out gave him time to think about Emma Raleigh and remember that Eaglesham, a fashionable eighteenth-century conservation village on the edge of the Fenwick Moor, was only a few miles away from the Dark Loch.

Every way he looked, time and distance were becoming important.

When he reached Eaglesham, it was easy enough to find Emma Raleigh's cottage. On the outskirts of the village, it was a single-storey stone building, painted white and with a tiled roof. The windows were small, a porch at the front door was covered in budding climbing roses, and the white Mazda coupé was parked on the concrete runway which covered most of the front garden area.

There was enough room for him to park the Ford behind the white coupé. By the time he had left the car and had walked to the front door it was already opening.

'I appreciate this, superintendent,' said Emma Raleigh, looking out. 'I just hope it will be worth while.'

She was wearing old denims and a man's shirt, her hair caught back in a braid of dark leather. Her feet were bare. If this was the informal Emma Raleigh, she still managed to create a cool, blatantly sexual magnetism. Her hand lightly on Thane's sleeve, she ushered him in.

'This way.' She led him through a narrow, cool hallway and into the cottage kitchen. 'Do you mind if we talk in here?'

'This will be fine,' he agreed.

'Sit down, then. I made coffee.' She waited until he settled on one of the wooden stools at the narrow spotless kitchen table. Then she lifted a bubbling coffee pot from the stove. She had two mugs waiting. 'Milk, sugar, superintendent?'

'Black on it's own.' Thane looked around. The kitchen was expensively equipped, but showroom-spotless. It had the air of being owned rather than used. 'How long have you lived here?'

'A couple of years.' She brought one of the coffee mugs over to him and somehow contrived to brush her shirt front against him as she laid the mug on the table. Her eyes stayed innocent. 'Like it?'

'What I've seen,' he said woodenly. If Emma Raleigh was trying to soften him down, he had one grim antidote to whatever she tried – the antidote he'd seen at that hospital in Carlisle. 'You said this was urgent, Ms Raleigh.'

'You told me anything to do with the counterfeiters was urgent.' As she spoke, she went over to the stove, returned with her own coffee mug and sat at a stool on the other side of the narrow table. 'You meant it?'

Thane sipped his coffee and nodded.

'I left last night's fashion showings early, superintendent. Did you wonder why?' Her eyes were cool and unreadable.

'I heard you weren't feeling too good.' He waited.

'That was an excuse.' She shook her head and considered him earnestly across the table. 'Can I ask you something? Have you ever thought that a few things lately did not go the way you expected?'

'Maybe.'

'When I went with Gypsy Adams to last night's fashion showing, it was the first time I'd been out with him. I met two people there, two people I trust. Both told me separately they'd heard a rumour about Adams. That he worked both sides of the fence.'

Thane frowned and sucked his teeth. 'That's why you left?'

'Counterfeit pirates badly hurt me once, superintendent.' Emma Raleigh laid her hands flat on the kitchen table, looking down at them. 'I despise them. I couldn't have stayed. I went home, I stayed there, I had to think. I waited until this morning, then called you.'

She did it well, but she was lying. He had seen her collect Dutch and the man who was probably Crusher outside the City Chambers. Now he had to play her along.

'I'm glad you told me,' he said soberly. 'Now I need to know who told you.'

'Sorry.' She shook her head. 'What will you do, superintendent?'

'Try to check it out. Maybe bring Adams in for an interview.' Something touched his ankle and he looked down. One of the blonde's bare feet had strayed under the table to make contact. Then it was his turn to lie. 'What you've told me could matter a lot more. We'll be working on it, believe me.'

He rose to leave, and Emma Raleigh escorted him back through the cottage to the front door.

'You'll tell me what happens?' she asked.

'You'll hear,' he promised, and left her. He drove away, knowing that somewhere nearby a Crime Squad surveillance team had logged his arrival and now would have listed his departure.

Time was slipping past. It was almost noon before Thane reached the Crime Squad building. He met Moss for the briefest of updates, then they were summoned into a meeting with Jack Hart in the Squad commander's office. Hart nodded them into seats across from his side of the desk as Maggie Fyffe came in, to lay a note in front of him. She left as he read it.

'Still no real change in Francey Dunbar's condition.' Hart screwed up the note and tossed it towards a bucket. 'And that legal vulture Hilson was in again, making noises about Gonzo Patrick. We threw him out.' He leaned his elbows on the desk. 'All right, Colin. You've two separate areas I want to hear more about. There's what you're now getting from your trade union pal, but Moss said you'd gone out to see the boutique woman. What happened?'

Thane told them, keeping both stories as short as he could. He raised a few surprised grunts from Hart and an incredulous bellow from the same source when Gypsy Adams came into it. Phil Moss gave only one small, almost polite belch along the way.

'So now we decide what we do.' Hart sank back on his chair. 'Better bring him up to date, Moss.'

188

'Sir.' Moss reached out for an envelope already lying on Hart's desk, then turned to Thane. 'Courtesy of a Royal Navy computer. You were right, they've even wired us ID photographs. Masson and his mechanic Seumas Hall were both navy, both served on the same destroyer. Masson was the ship's master at arms, Hall was chief bo'sun's mate. They were court-martialled together about two years ago for a fraud involving ship's stores and were dismissed their ship – the navy couldn't pin enough on them to jail them.'

'So we've got Crusher and The Buffer,' mused Hart. 'Show him, Moss.'

Phil Moss delved into the envelope then laid two passport-style photographs on the desk. Thane looked and nodded. Of the two men one was a stranger, gaunt-faced with thinning hair and sunken eyes. But the other man was dark-haired, with a broad, arrogant face. Brian Masson, nickname Crusher, was the man who had been with Peter Dutch at the fashion night and afterwards.

He glanced up. 'What about Dutch?'

Moss shook his head. 'Never in the navy. Not according to the computer.'

Thane shrugged. It would have been too easy as a link. He wasn't sure it particularly mattered. Then he saw Moss had taken two more photographs from the envelope and was laying them down.

'From Strathclyde's records,' said Moss laconically. 'The late Pepe Weide's associates, Tam Black and Mickey Wood. Records as long as your arm – Wood is the twin-blade artist. They've vanished from the scene along with a couple of others.'

Both men were from the same hired muscle mould. Mickey Wood had probably been handsome once but now his photograph showed a mass of scar tissue from collecting second prize in too many battles. Every police force had others like him on file.

'Which leaves this place Ellanwood Farm.' Taking over again, Jack Hart showed his teeth in a totally humourless smile. 'Colin, it looks like your friend could be right. It would take us out of Strathclyde territory into Central Scotland's patch – which some-times helps. I phoned there when I heard, I had a word with their chief constable.'

When a commander telephoned a chief constable direct, things usually happened. They'd also played golf together a few times.

A team of Central Scotland officers had made discreet inquiries at other farms around Ellanwood and now had it under observation.

Ellanwood Farm had a chequered history, from once being large and prosperous to being finally seized by creditors when the last owner had gone bankrupt. Its milk herd of Jersey cattle had been sold off. Neighbouring farms had bought its land to incorporate into their own fields. A displenishing sale had taken away the rest except for its big, modern, suddenly empty buildings.

'Then about nine months ago the creditors had an offer. Prospective tenants wanted to rent the buildings.' Hart carefully knitted his fingers together and cracked his knuckles, smiling drily. 'Good money, so they took it. The deal was done through an Edinburgh chartered accountant, the same chartered accountant who set up the Pizzaro truck rental firm – surprised, Colin?'

Thane shook his head.

'Anyway, the creditors didn't worry too much about their new tenants. They were told they were dealing with a charitable trust which wanted to set up a job creation scheme for the unemployed.' The Squad commander snorted. 'It worked with them, it worked with anyone else who might be interested – like magic! Everyone loves a do-good cause!'

And that was how it stood. The Central Scotland team were waiting, ready to help. But they would do nothing more until asked.

'So.' Hart suddenly got to his feet and prowled his office for a moment. 'That's how things stand. You're still half a day away from the DNA test results you need. But we've got options. Maybe beginning with what we should do about Gypsy Adams.'

He looked at Thane – who spent a long moment saying nothing, then suddenly surprised them with a chuckle.

'Suppose we pick him up, drag him in.' Thane saw their faces. 'Make it look for real as far as he's concerned.'

Hart stared at him. 'Are you serious?'

'Look at it this way,' suggested Thane. 'We make like we've taken in a senior Trading Standards supervisor for questioning. If Emma Raleigh has any kind of contact there she's going to hear about it. What's that going to tell her?'

Moss gave a soft, understanding chuckle. 'That we've no real leads about The Cutters, that we'll grab at anything. It's nasty, it's rough on Adams – I like it!'

Jack Hart frowned in thought. 'She'll tell The Cutters, The Cutters lower their guard, and we – ?'

Thane nodded. 'We go in.'

Gradually, Hart's leathery face shaped a widening smile. 'But who's going to explain it all to Gypsy Adams after we've hauled him in?' He saw Thane and Moss look at him, saying nothing, and sighed. 'Dear God, why do I get all the dirty jobs to do? All right, but get on with it!'

They left the Squad commander before he could change his mind and went back through to the main duty room. Minutes later, The Animal and his small blonde partner had been despatched to bring Gypsy Adams in for questioning. They weren't told why.

Sandra Craig surfaced from making yet another round of telephone check calls.

'How do two damned great container trucks just vanish?' she demanded. 'Call it four, if you count the two that probably went down the motorway south after the swap-over at Southwaite. How?'

Thane shrugged. In his mind again were the words of the Cumbria superintendent at Carlisle. A motorway like the M6 counted its traffic in tens of thousands of vehicles per day. The Cumbria man had declared that if they could stop and search every vehicle along its length on just one day the number of criminals arrested and the amount of bent or stolen property recovered would put the courts into overtime mode for several months.

As his sergeant finished, Maggie Fyffe came in and gave him a handwritten note from Jack Hart. She left again as Thane read it. Wordlessly, he handed it to Moss. Hart was authorising firearms for the Cutter operation. He was also asking Central Scotland for an armed response team.

Thane glanced at Sandra Craig as Moss passed the note on to her. His sergeant was firearms-trained; she held instructor rating. More and more Scottish cops, from beat officers upwards, were now firearms-trained. More and more of the younger officers wanted to end the traditional unarmed image and to hell with going in waving a wooden baton against an armed criminal.

A telephone beside them rang, and Sandra answered it. She grabbed paper and a pen, scribbled furiously for a moment, then thanked the caller and hung up.

191

'Sir.' She placed her scribble in front of Thane.

There had been sudden activity at the Pizzaro Truck Rentals garage. The Crieff police team on stake-out had seen a small unmarked blue van drive up and sound its horn. Seumas Hall had emerged from the building, locking the door behind him. He had been carrying a large toolkit which he loaded into the back of the van. He climbed into the van's passenger seat and the van had driven off again. The driver had not been identified, it was believed the garage had been left empty.

'It fits.' Thane could guess what had happened. 'We know Hall is the Buffer, and also their mechanic. Suppose the trucks are hidden over at Ellanwood Farm, suppose they're being prepared for another run south – and he needs a lift over there because that wounded shoulder means he can't drive.'

'I'll go along with that.' Moss nodded.

'Right.' Thane glanced at his watch. 'Then we wait. Central Scotland will tell us when he arrives at Ellanwood, you and I take a lunch break while we can – then Sandra has her turn.'

'She'll call it starvation,' said Moss drily, then nodded. 'But give me a moment first.'

He rose, crossed the room, and went inside his little office. Thane waited a couple of moments, then impulsive curiosity made him follow. He found Moss in the act of taking a small tin box out of a desk drawer . . . Moss flushed, shoved the box into his pocket, and slammed the drawer shut.

'What goes on?' asked Thane softly.

'Nothing much.' Moss scowled, then gave an almost sheepish shrug. 'I suppose you'd better know.'

He produced the small box again and opened its lid. A small length of black covered electrical flex was coiled inside, the ribber cut open along its length, exposing the wiring. An inner layer of white insulating powder had spilled out.

'Go on,' said Moss resignedly. 'Try it.'

Thane rubbed a forefinger into the powder, then touched his tongue. The taste was sharp, strangely familiar, yet hard to place.

'Sandra,' said Moss resignedly. 'Her grandfather was an electrician who had gut troubles like mine. He swore by this stuff – mineral-insulated fire-resistant cable.' He shrugged. 'You get a chunk, cut it open, use the powder – it seems to work as good as most things.'

192

'What the hell is it?'

'I ran it past Matt Amos. That's industrial-strength magnesium oxide. It'll stun any ulcer going, but you've got to know the make of cable to use. Some makes use other powders.'

'What happened to grandfather?'

'He died.' Moss helped himself to a large pinch of the magnesium oxide, and grinned. 'Dropped dead with a heart attack at ninety.'

'And this is why she's been disappearing?'

Moss nodded. 'Finding some. There's not a lot of it around.'

'Just don't blame me if you blow a fuse,' said Thane sardonically. He had learned another side to the redhead. 'Now can we eat?'

They did, in the basement canteen. They were finishing when they heard that Gypsy Adams had just been brought in and was in Jack Hart's office. When they went back up, there was a message in from the Central Scotland team. A small blue van had just driven into Ellanwood Farm with two men aboard it.

Thane told Sandra to take a lunch-break. As she went out, the door of the duty room burst open and the angry, bear-like figure of Gypsy Adams stormed in. The puzzled, equally bear-like figure of The Animal was close at his heels.

'Clever bastard, aren't you?' snarled Adams, coming straight towards Thane. 'Big deal way of stirring things up, right?' He glared. 'Your boss has explained, so I'm supposed to just laugh it off?' Swinging round, he pointed an indignant fist at The Animal. 'Do you know what this character did? Clapped me in handcuffs, took me from a meeting with our deputy director, dragged me out past half of Trading Standards' staff!'

Thane considered The Animal. 'Why the handcuffs?'

'Because he wasn't co-operating, sir.' The Animal scowled defensively. 'And nobody told me this was a set-up.'

'True.' Thane held down a grin, sent The Animal on his way, then faced Adams again. 'We needed to do it, Gypsy. It had to look good. You'll get all the apologies you want.'

'You're damned right I will,' growled the CATS supervisor. He nodded at the telephone beside Thane. 'Can I use that?'

'No. No calls, no messages out.'

Adams swore long and pungently. 'You people can't be for real.' Then he sat down hard in a chair and shook his head. 'It just damned well better work.'

'Amen,' said Thane.

They gave Adams coffee and sandwiches, saw his eyes widen when they offered him a large-size bullet-proof waistcoat, and left him scowling his way through some newspapers while they made more of their own preparations.

Then, after another hour, another telephone rang. Moss answered it, listened, then gave a happy, reverberating belch that silenced everything else going on.

'We're in business.' He bared his teeth in a grin. 'Emma Raleigh has left home. She dumped an overnight case in the back of the car and she's heading north.' He looked across at Thane. 'Do they tail her?'

'Far back. Very far back,' said Thane. 'We know where she's going.' He straightened and glanced at the faces around. 'Our turn. Let's do it.' As the others began moving out, he saw Gypsy Adams gazing hopefully at him. 'You've got a reserved seat if you want it.'

'Try and stop me,' said Adams happily. 'Just try.'

Crieff, a quiet little tourist town on the edge of the Perthshire Highlands, is just under fifty miles from Glasgow. One half of the six-car convoy of Crime Squad vehicles split off before Stirling, the other half made Crieff through thinning then almost non-existent traffic in just under an hour. They were met by a local patrol car, and followed it through Crieff, then on a side road for a couple of miles while hills and heather began to close in.

At last they halted where a patch of rhododendron bushes gave cover. The Crieff observation team were waiting there; the compact Pizzaro garage buildings were a long stone's throw down the same road.

'Still empty?' asked Thane.

The local sergeant who had been running the observation nodded.

They went on.

First, there was the small just-in-case matter of cutting telephone wires. Then, as the cars stopped outside the garage and the officers aboard piled out, the main door yielded to a single heave by The Animal using a large, sharp-clawed jemmy.

They poured in, Thane in the lead with Moss, Gypsy Adams and the small flood of others close behind. Another couple of locked inner doors had to be jemmied; Sandra and Gypsy Adams headed for the office area, and Thane led another group deeper into the garage complex.

Feet echoing loud on the concrete floor, they checked two large and empty vans and a smaller truck which had its engine partly dismantled. An old Volkswagen was on an inspection hoist beside a servicing bay, with signs that work on it had been interrupted.

They kept looking. A sudden shout from Moss brought Thane across the concrete to a grimy stores area. When he arrived, Moss was already struggling to drag out a large roll of old blue plastic truck tarpaulin. Two of the local officers helped spread it out on the oil-stained concrete. Several large sections had been cut from its edges, one very similar in size and shape to the makeshift shroud used before Terry Anson had been dumped at Dark Loch.

When they kept looking, they found the hacked remains of another, even older blue tarpaulin. The same storeroom next yielded several rolls of white cord with the distinctive blue marker thread, then Thane left them and went in search of Gypsy Adams. He found him with Sandra in an upstairs office area, where the CATS supervisor was rummaging his way through the opened drawers of a desk.

'Take a look at this, sir,' said Sandra in an unemotional voice. She was standing with a framed photograph in her hands. 'I think it is what you wanted.'

Thane looked and pursed his lips. Three people in naval uniform grinned at the camera from a handful of years back in time. Two were master of arms Brian Masson and chief bo'sun's mate Seumas Hall. The third was Emma Raleigh in a female petty officer's uniform. Across the bottom of the photograph was written, 'Me, Brian, and his sister Emma. Party Time!'

'I should have checked her name before she married, sir,' said Sandra bleakly.

'That makes two of us,' said Thane. Another gap had been bridged. He turned to Gypsy Adams. 'Anything useful?'

'Enough for now,' said Adams. 'Then there's a safe to be opened.' He gestured around the scattered papers. 'But this is a good start – some hints, some names, some pointers.'

'The Cutters for real?' asked Thane.

'For real,' agreed Adams. 'Enough to make it worth being handcuffed. So what about Ellanwood?'

'They're next,' said Thane.

Leaving the local officers to guard Pizzaro, they drove back to Crieff and from there headed south for Stirling under almost unbroken blue sky. Then as the great medieval bulk of Stirling Castle loomed ahead with the old royal town spread beneath it, a police car with Central Scotland badges moved out from a side road and took over as the new guide for the small procession of vehicles.

A few miles on, they left the main highway and started travelling through a maze of narrow local roads which wound a way through tree-lined farming country rich in both cattle and crops. At last, the lead car signalled its charges to slow and they followed it at a near crawl down an almost hidden track among more trees, pulling in to halt at a clearing beside an old, derelict cottage and a roofless barn.

Other cars were already parked in the cover around. They had joined up with the half of the Crime Squad convoy which had been given the task of covering the approach to Ellanwood Farm.

Thane let his Ford lurch and bump to a halt under the broad shade of a gnarled oak tree. When he got out, he saw several Central Scotland cars parked alongside the other Crime Squad vehicles, the two sets of officers talking and watching him. Some were from the Central Scotland armed response team.

Tina Redder came towards him over the rough grass. The detective chief inspector greeted him with a smiling nod and even allowed her good humour to extend to Sandra Craig.

'No problems at Pizzaro?' she asked.

'None,' confirmed Thane. He could see Jock Dawson's dusty grey Land-Rover dog-van parked further back, but as usual there was no sign of the dog-handler. 'How about here?'

'Emma Raleigh arrived at the farm about an hour ago. Your two containers are there, parked in the courtyard.' She glanced at her wrist-watch. 'No one else has come or gone since we got here. What's next?'

'For now, we keep everyone under cover.'

'Like the way they've been since we got here, Colin?' Tina Redder allowed herself a small, justified sarcasm.

'Like that way, Tina.' Thane made it a mild apology. From somewhere nearby, a cross between a grunt and a muffled belch told him Phil Moss had arrived on the scene. 'Have we got a guide?'

'Yes.' Tina Redder turned and signalled. One of a group of men lounging beside a patrol car came trotting over. 'He's the local man who works this patch. Named McColl – Harry McColl.'

McColl arrived, a tall, thin man wearing mud-stained grey overalls on top of his police uniform and carrying a heavy blackthorn stick.

'I need a guided tour,' said Thane. 'Any problem with that?'

'None, sir.' McColl gave a smile. 'Anyone coming with you?'

'No.' Thane glanced round at Sandra and Moss. 'They'll find things to do. Let's go.'

McColl led him further into the trees, where fallen twigs cracked underfoot and mushrooms grew in profusion. A rabbit made a startled dash and disappeared down a burrow, unseen birds sang their alarm calls overhead. They topped a slight rise, the trees thinned, and McColl touched his arm in warning.

'Beyond the trees, sir. Straight ahead.' The local constable chuckled. 'And your dog-handler is on his way back.'

Thane took a couple of quick steps forward, saw the line of farm buildings only a few hundred yards ahead, then swore in near-disbelief. Over there, Jock Dawson was ambling along a narrow ribbon of road which ran beside the farm buildings. Dawson was in his usual overalls and rubber boots, and the Labrador bitch Goldie was frisking beside him.

'He said the dog needed some exercise,' declared McColl, grinning. 'And what's more natural out in the country than to see a man walking wi' a dog?'

'Dear God.' Thane made it a prayer it would be that way. 'All right, do you know the hours they usually work over at Ellanwood?'

'Never varies, sir. 7 a.m. till four in the afternoon, six days a week – they don't work Sundays. When they finish, they leave for home along the road you used coming in.'

McColl produced a small pair of binoculars and passed them over. Thane adjusted them so that Ellanwood came into fine, sharp focus. Built round what seemed to be a central courtyard, it had a

197

grey stone farmhouse as one leg, then a scatter of outbuildings linked across to Ellanwood's other outstanding features. A large, brick-built cattle shed, large enough to have housed a considerable herd under its blue metal roof, it had power lines feeding in and he could see upper-storey windows and a hayloft door. A tall silage tower, also painted blue, was located at one end of the long cattle shed.

Beside it, like a squat pillbox by comparison, was a large circular slurry tank. Maybe twice the height of a man and painted cream, the slurry tank was rusting at the edges and was topped by an even rustier blue 'chinaman hat' roof.

Thane studied the scene again. From his angle, almost all he could see of the inside of the farm courtyard were the tops of the two container trucks. There was no sign of movement anywhere – except when he switched to the farm road where Jock Dawson was still ambling along, now throwing a stick to amuse the Labrador.

He handed the binoculars back to McColl and they returned to the clearing. A little later, Jock Dawson was back.

'So tell me something.' Thane scowled at the lanky dog-handler. 'What the hell do you think you were playing at out there?'

'It seemed sensible enough, sir.' Dawson gave one of his hurt looks of mild innocence and glanced sideways towards Tina Redder as if seeking support. 'You weren't here, nobody stopped me.'

'Nobody.' Thane gave up. 'All right, what did you see?'

'They're working on one o' the truck engines, like it had a problem.' Dawson shrugged. 'They've a few cars parked around the place, and there are machinery noises coming from inside the main shed.'

He had seen only a few people inside the courtyard. His only other impression that mattered was that although the outhouses seemed to be in use the old farmhouse was not. Windows and front door were boarded up.

A little later, Thane called a meeting under one of the trees while an unseen tractor rumbled its way back and forward across some nearby field. He looked round the little group. Tina Redder was there with Moss. So was a Central Scotland chief inspector named Simpson. Sandra Craig was also there, at his elbow.

'It's a case of what we've got to do and when we do it,' Thane told them.

'A timetable.' Tina Redder nodded. 'Starting with what?'

'The work-force.' Thane did a quick mental count. To the twenty Crime Squad officers who had come out with him he could add just short of that number of Central Scotland people including the armed response team. 'They're due to stop for the day in just under an hour. Suppose we wait until they leave – ' he glanced at the Central Scotland man.

Simpson understood. 'No problem. We let them start off for home, then pick them up about half a mile down the road. We can also close the road at both ends – fair?'

Thane nodded. 'Fair. Then we go in for the farm fifteen minutes later.'

'That's maybe too tight.' Moss frowned and brushed an insect away from his face. 'Suppose we made it half an hour after the work-force leave? That way, we might have a chance to see what the real team are doing.'

'Half an hour,' agreed Thane.

But that was his limit.

It all went smoothly at first. Which should have been its own warning.

Exactly on four o'clock the first people began leaving Ellanwood and heading down the road that led homeward. They left in old cars and packed into vans, a few were on motor cycles, a few walked. One was a woman pushing a pram.

The watchers in the trees let them pass. The road block was in position that half-mile on, now reinforced by two coaches brought in by Central Scotland to ferry the Cutters work-force back to Stirling for processing. A radio message from the road block confirmed when that stage was completed.

The rest of the agreed half-hour passed, with no apparent change at the farm.

Standing at the edge of the trees, very aware of the Colt automatic pistol now holstered at his waist, Thane glanced around and took a deep breath.

'Go!'

The main group of police began moving forward. A few fanned out, aiming for the boarded-up farmhouse. Some moved down the farm road, the rest began closing in on the long bulk of the blue-roofed cattle shed. Unexpectedly, they heard an engine start up inside the courtyard. Barely a moment later a van drove slowly out on to the farm road, one which matched the description of the vehicle seen earlier visiting the Pizzaro garage.

Another moment passed, just long enough for the van's driver to sight the line of police coming down the road towards him. The van's brakes squealed; it spun round in a tight turn, engine roaring.

As the van started to retreat, a Central Scotland sergeant made a determined effort to stop it. The vehicle swerved, hit the sergeant, and sent him sprawling. In less than a minute it had raced back inside the Ellanwood courtyard, while the sergeant shakily picked himself up from the roadway, bruised but unhurt.

Everywhere, groups of police who had hesitated began going forward again. The first of the police cars began moving out of cover, any hope of a total surprise now gone.

Waving down the nearest car, Thane took the loudhailer its driver handed out to him. Switching on, he raised it to his lips.

'Everyone in the farm, this is the police.' His voice rasped loudly and some startled birds rose from the trees. 'Armed police. You're surrounded.' He paused. 'You've two minutes to come out. We're counting.'

He lowered the loudhailer. He could see that the group detailed to occupy the deserted farmhouse had reached it, had forced the boarded-up front door, and were going in.

'Any bets about what's going on in the main shed?' asked Moss drily, appearing at his side. 'It won't be a happy time.'

The police radio murmured. The farmhouse had been secured. All round, other police were easing into their assigned positions and cars were beginning to line up, engines purring, while the sun shone down on the tall blue disused silage tower and glinted on the hat-like dome of the silage tank.

A window smashed over at the main shed. Something moved behind it, then an automatic rifle rasped a wild, hosing burst of fire which made anyone near drop down for cover.

The firing stopped and police began worming their way forward again. But something new was happening at the farm. It began with the throb of a heavy diesel engine starting up, then loud, angry shouts were followed by two quick shots. The diesel note rose to a full-bore bellow – then one of the big container trucks was thundering out in a dark cloud of exhaust smoke, charging at the first of the police cars blocking its escape.

'For God's sake move, man,' pleaded Moss hoarsely, staring. The massive truck would steam-roller its way through the patrol car. 'Move that damned car, or get out!'

A figure in blue overalls, blue beret and black boots suddenly stepped out of cover close to Thane. A marksman from the armed response vehicle calmly raised a Savage twelve-gauge pump-action shotgun. It barked four times, and four times at close range a solid shot slammed like a thunderbolt into the truck engine.

It was a twelve-gauge load developed to destory any vehicle engine. While the noise still echoed the giant truck first slewed wildly, then halted like a stranded whale a short distance away from the patrol car and its white-faced occupants. The truck cab doors flew open. Hands raised in surrender, two frightened figures tumbled out.

They had been handcuffed by Tina Redder by the time Thane got there. One of them, trembling like a leaf, was Peter Dutch. The man with him, equally frightened, was a stranger.

'Thane, you've got to believe me – ' Dutch made it a desperate plea. 'I just wanted out! They – they've gone crazy in there.'

'If you don't run the show, who does?' demanded Thane while a uniformed man quickly frisked both prisoners.

'Don't you know?' Dutch moistened his lips. 'It's Emma – always was Emma!'

'You expect us to believe that?' Tina Redder was derisive.

'He's telling it straight,' said their other prisoner unhappily. 'She's the boss.'

'Emma and her damned brother.' Dutch looked past them anxiously. 'We can't stand out here. I don't want to be shot, man!'

A new burst of fire came from the automatic rifle, aimed somewhere else, but Dutch quivered and looked ready to faint.

'Move them,' ordered Thane.

The two prisoners were bundled away. Thane needed a moment before Peter Dutch's claim sank in. It made sense. But it still made no difference to anything for the moment. He looked round and saw Phil Moss beside another of the cars. Moss had brought out his magic box of stomach ulcer powder and was scooping some of the white magnesium oxide out with his fingertips.

'Ready, Phil?' he asked.

'Ready.' Moss licked the powder from his fingers, closed the box, and put it away.

Thane crossed to the leading police car, its exhaust burbling impatiently, and squeezed into an empty rear seat. Leaning forward, he tapped the driver on the shoulder.

The driver nodded. The car snarled forward, scraping round the side of the stranded container truck, racing for the courtyard entrance. A pistol began firing from somewhere inside, then stopped just as suddenly as the armed response team outside began giving covering fire, the Savage shotgun's blasting being joined by the vicious calico-ripping sound of a Heckler and Koch automatic rifle's full twenty-shot magazine.

It was enough to keep any opposition heads down while a whole procession of police cars raced into the courtyard, crews jumping out as each skidded to a halt.

Thane had his Colt drawn as he tumbled out of the lead car like the rest of its occupants. He chose the nearest of the outhouse buildings but the first door he tried was locked. The second swung open, then he was in with Moss, Sandra, and two of the Central Scotland men at his heels.

New shots rang out somewhere ahead as they raced on through a series of interconnected but empty buildings. Then yet another door suddenly brought them into the vast sweep of the one-time milking shed that had originally sheltered an entire Jersey herd.

Remains of stalls and feeding troughs were still dumped like garbage to one side. Open drainage channels still ran like dry rivers down the whole length of the concrete floor. But overhead lights now blazed down on the long rows of sewing machines and embroidery machines alongside glinting cutting and pressing equipment. Most were draped with half-completed garments just as they'd been left at the end of the day's shift.

Except that these garments were not designer sports clothes. Ellanwood was making copies of high fashion skirts and jackets, dresses and trousers in fine wools, velvets and silks. The Cutters had said they would raid the fashion collections and it had been almost about to happen.

A yell from nearby meant they'd been seen, then a figure sprang out, waving a knife. The overhead lights glinted on bright steel as the knife arced towards Sandra. She ducked clear, then Thane swung the heavey Colt in a fierce backhanded curve which slammed the length of the weapon's barrel hard under their attacker's jaw.

The man made a gasping noise, then went down. The knife, two thin blades lashed together for brutal effectiveness, dropped from his grip as he collapsed limp on the concrete. They had taken out Mickey Wood, and the man would have a new scar to add to his collection. The Colt's front sight had torn, a long, bloodied gouge along his face.

They left Wood lying and sprinted on, heading towards where other struggles were going on. Jock Dawson's dogs were in and had someone down. A short distance away, the bandaged Buffer was battling desperately with two Central Scotland men. But Tina Redder was further along, starting to climb a ladder which led up to the loft above them.

She was more than half-way up when a short burst of automatic rifle fire came from inside the loft. Bullets chipped wood from the rungs above her head. Shaken, she lost her grip, then fell from the ladder, landing hard on the concrete with a cry of pain. The rifle stopped.

They reached the Crime Squad woman. Trying to sit up, she bit her lip hard.

'I've broken my damned ankle.' She glared at Sandra. 'Any new joke about a broomstick, sergeant, and I'll personally kill you.' She turned to Thane and gestured. 'They're up there. Both of them, Emma and her brother – '

A loud creaking noise came from overhead, as if a sticking door had been opened. Thane dived for the ladder, scrambled up, then, at the top, left it in a crouch which took him through the hatch and on to the wooden floor of the loft.

Next moment a short burst of automatic rifle fire spat over his head as he rolled clear. One of the hayloft windows in the shed's roof had been opened. Emma Raleigh was there, wearing the same denim jeans and shirt, clutching the automatic rifle, ready to jump. Her brother crouched beside her.

'Take him, Brian,' she screamed. 'It's Thane – I'm out of ammunition.'

Wild-eyed, Masson swung the automatic in his hand and brought the muzzle up. Knowing he was already beaten, Thane made a desperate, hopeless try to aim with his Colt.

Two crisp, carefully spaced shots came from the loft hatch. Both bullets took Masson in the shoulder, spinning him round. One wild shot triggered from his weapon as he let it drop. Then, the revolver in her grasp still smoking, Sandra Craig sprang up through the loft hatch like a jack-in-the-box – and at the same instant Emma Raleigh jumped from the open window.

203

A moment after she vanished there was the sound of rippng metal and a splash. Emma Raleigh screamed, then screamed again in a mixture of horror and despair.

'Sweet Jesus,' said her brother hoarsely. 'Sweet Jesus, no!'

Ignoring the weapons trained on him, Masson dived at the open window and stared down. His face drained of colour. In another second Thane was beside him there – and couldn't move.

They were looking down at the farm's old slurry tank. Emma Raleigh had jumped for its hat-like roof, but the rusty, paper-thin metal hadn't taken her weight. A whole section had torn and collapsed and she had splashed down into the brimming, forgotten liquid the tank still contained.

Emma Raleigh screamed again, thrashing and clawing to stay afloat in the dirt-brown liquid while a dense cloud of ammoniac fumes rose and left the others gagging. Then, suddenly, she wasn't there. A motionless shape was gradually sinking deeper into that foul-smelling soup. Brian Masson was down on his knees, weeping, as Thane took an instinctive half-step forward.

'Don't even think about it,' came a snarl in Thane's ear. Phil Moss's thin, surprisingly strong hands hauled him back. 'She's already dead. Leave it.'

Sandra Craig was there too, equally white-faced, looking ready to vomit. She looked at him and shook her head.

Thane turned away.

It was almost midnight before word arrived that the Strathclyde laboratory had an indisputable DNA match between the blood found on the blouson jacket and the blood traces in Peter Dutch's car. It didn't matter so much any more.

For Colin Thane the week that followed the raid at Ellanwood Farm swept along.

There had been the immediate aftermath of charges and statements, of follow-up arrests and inquiries. A warehouse crammed with counterfeit clothing had been discovered backing on to Emma Raleigh's boutique in Sauchiehall Street. Two satellite Cutters factories had been raided and closed down. A web of counterfeit suppliers and wholesalers was being unravelled from documents.

There were links with other counterfeit teams reaching throughout Europe, some including known off-shoots of drugs cartels. There were fat numbered bank accounts in half a dozen countries. Altogether they had enough to keep several law enforcement agencies busy for some time.

Still shaken by the way his sister had died, Brian Masson was ready to talk about most things. Pepe Weide had died because he had been caught diverting drugs money intended for a new Cutters production line. Terry Anson had died for the very simple reason that he was no longer trusted.

Which left a lot more.

Who had been the real brains behind The Cutters?

'Sis,' had said Brian Masson simply. 'She had the idea, she had the brains. She'd been ripped off herself by another counterfeit squad, she realised how easy it could be – and then me an' The Buffer were what you could call available.'

Then how did he rate Peter Dutch, locked up in a remand cell, in tears most of the time, refusing to talk about anything to anyone?

'A prat,' was Masson's scornful verdict. 'A prat, but a good front man. He used us, but not as much as Sis used him – so what the hell!'

Three days after the Ellanwood raid there had been the sadness of Joe Felix's funeral in Glasgow. It had been family and private, because his widow wanted it that way. But Thane and a handful of the Crime Squad people closest to him had been there – including Francey Dunbar, newly released from hospital and closely escorted by a tall Viking princess of a nurse from Carlisle now somehow assigned to look after him while he convalesced at his parents' home.

Francey would be back. The other casualties from Ellanwood included Tina Redder with an ankle in plaster, a Crime Squad detective constable with a knife wound that had required stitches, and two Central Scotland officers with minor injuries.

That full week on, Colin Thane even felt he was beginning to get on top of sorting out everything from the current Crown Office demands for statement extracts to a howl from Jack Hart about an update on overtime sheets.

The weather was back to normal. It was grey and raining outside as he went through from his office to the duty room, then into Phil Moss's cubbyhole. Moss was out, but he leafed through some of the papers in his in-tray in search of the overtime returns.

He heard Sandra Craig's voice outside. She was talking with two replacements to the Squad, fresh arrived from their home forces. His sergeant was putting them through it.

'You've seen the commander,' she said grimly. 'He's shaken your hand. But don't worry about him, about superintendents, about inspectors. Just worry about me. You call me sergeant, unless we're off duty. When I say jump, you leap. You keep your reports up to date, whatever. You keep your noses clean. Understood?'

Thane heard the two newcomers make a suitable murmuring response. Then he heard a throat-clearing noise at the office door and looked up. Maggie Fyffe was there, a twinkle in her eyes.

'Superintendent, you've a visitor,' she said drily. 'Spare a moment?'

He straightened and nodded. 'Why not?'

Maggie Fyffe stood back from the doorway and beckoned. A wary face looked in past her.

'Hello, Mr Thane.' Smartly dressed, attractive, with a special kind of glow about her, the young brunette in the doorway smiled awkwardly. 'I heard you'd been looking for me.'

Thane stared and swallowed. 'Where the hell have you been?'

'Getting married, Mr Thane.' Hazel Wells, the receptionist from the Dumfries motel, his missing witness for the security van hijack trial, proudly showed the glinting gold ring on her wedding finger. 'It had to be kept secret – from everyone. Our families would have killed us!'

'Married – ' Thane drew a deep breath. 'We've turned the place upside down for you! We checked airports, everywhere!'

'It was all done that way, because of the families,' said the brunette. She dimpled. 'Passport, travel bookings, everything. I'm Mrs Mitchell now – we just got back yesterday. We had our honeymoon in Spain.'

'Congratulations.' Thane said it with an effort. 'And your husband – '

'John.' She dimpled again. 'He works in a bank.' Hazel Wells that was, now Mitchell, placed a slip of paper in front of him. 'I've got to go. He's waiting outside. But that's my new address. See you again, superintendent!'

Then she had gone, being escorted out by Maggie Fyffe.

Thane sat on the edge of the empty desk beside him for a long moment, recovering.

Outside in the main duty room, Sergeant Sandra Craig was still at it.

'On this team, we do it right,' she told her two newcomers. 'Get something wrong once, and you'll regret it. Get it wrong again, and you'll be like the man who swallowed a tin of varnish. He had a sticky end and a terrible finish!'

Colin Thane grinned as Sandra's joke registered. In about two hours' time Martin Hilson was coming in by appointment. Gonzo Patrick's lawyer was having another try at getting the charges against his client dropped because of a missing witness and lack of evidence.

'Have a large varnish, Mr Hilson.' said Thane softly.

Suddenly it was a meeting he was going to enjoy.

SCOTTISH CRIME SQUAD

QUIEN·SABE

The unofficial tie worn by members of the real-life Scottish Crime Squad has a crest featuring a wild goose, a red herring and a crystal ball. I am glad to have been trusted to wear one.

The motto beneath, '*Quién Sabe*', is not always translated literally.